TOO CLOSE TO HOME

BY THE SAME AUTHOR

NOVELS

All in the Telling
The Art of Illusion
Escaping Freedom

SHORT STORIES

The Man Who Loved Books
Mixed Fortunes

TOO CLOSE TO HOME

BRIAN SMITH

Too Close to Home
Brian Smith

Published by JoJo Publishing
First published 2012
'Yarra's Edge'
2203/80 Lorimer Street
Docklands VIC 3008 Australia
Email: jo-media@bigpond.net.au or visit
www.jojopublishing.com

JoJo Publishing
Designer / typesetter: Chameleon Print Design
Edited by Ormé Harris
Printed in Singapore by KHL Printing

National Library of Australia Cataloguing-in-Publication entry

Author:	Smith, Brian (Brian William), 1938-
Title:	Too close to home / Brian Smith.
ISBN:	9780987281357 (pbk.)
Subjects:	Murder--Investigation--Victoria--Carlton--Fiction.
Dewey Number:	A823.4

For Sarah, Rosie and Ella

1

The wind swirled up Lygon Street, tugging at the coats and pinching the faces of the people waiting for the cable tram to the city. There were five of them: a lecturer from the University bound for an afternoon with friends at the Exford Hotel, a young mother taking her two girls to a matinee of *No, No Nanette* at the Princess, and a man who hoped the tram would not come too soon. He was slightly built, with sharp features, pale eyes that were never still and a persistent sniff that made his nose twitch, suggesting why he was known as Ferret Roberts. He wore a brown cloth cap over his straggly, grey hair and a loosely fitting tweed overcoat with pockets large enough to hold his tools of trade.

One night back in May, Ferret stood across the street from the Lemon Tree Hotel, ready to go about his business, when a police constable, who had not stuck to his regular beat, turned up unexpectedly and demanded that he turn out those pockets. It wasn't the month in Pentridge for 'loitering with intent' that irked him; over the years he had done enough time there to cope with that. No, it was the loss of the tools: favourites, they were. That and the sly grins when the news leaked out, with some of them clicking their tongues and telling him he was getting past it and should give it away. But he knew he still had the knack and preferred to take it as a reminder you could never rely on anyone to do what they were supposed to — even the coppers. Besides, what else would he do?

Today his pockets were empty and he was a picture of innocence, apparently awaiting the tram. While the others scanned the road, searching for the tram to swing around the Elgin Street corner, Ferret's attention was fixed on the shop across the street, next to the bank. The sign above the green iron verandah spelled out in bold lettering, '**GOLDSTEIN KOSHER BUTCHER**', but the door was closed, the shop in darkness and no meat displayed in the window, despite the pavement being crowded with shoppers. It was a Saturday and, unlike many of the other Jewish shopkeepers in the street, Pinchas Goldstein was a strict observer of the Sabbath.

Ferret remained watching the door until eventually it swung open and Goldstein, who had that bulky build befitting his trade, shepherded his family onto the street. First, his aged mother and father came with faltering steps. Then his three children skipped past, blown like leaves in the wind and pursued by his plump wife, whose task it was to see that they did not escape too far ahead. Goldstein, wearing a long, dark coat and black homburg, turned to lock the door. Ferret didn't mind how secure he made that door.

The synagogue, known as Stone's Schul by those who never went there, was some distance away in Pitt Street, and Ferret was sure there would be no chance of their returning in the time he needed. They called it Stone's Schul after Joe Stone who, they said, was so pious he made a habit, when walking to the Sabbath services, of spitting in the doorways of the Jewish shops that were still open. If he had a mind to follow this example, Goldstein was kept too busy encouraging his parents and keeping his family together to notice which of the doors they passed were closed and which were not.

Ferret sauntered across the street and entered the lane that ran along the back of the shops. On one side of the lane were tall paling fences and, on the other, small, dilapidated cottages huddled together as if needing one another's support. He walked down the lane with the measured gait of a law-abiding man and did not hesitate when he reached the gate to the Goldsteins' yard, opening it and walking past the outhouse to the back door, on which he gave a confident rap. The lock was formidable and recently fitted: he would need a different entry point. He stepped back as if expecting that the door would soon be opened, giving himself a chance to scrutinise the rear wall of the building. There was a window at a convenient height that should pose no great difficulty for him. He knocked again and, when there was no response, strolled to the window and looked in. Through the muslin curtain he could see a table, still carrying the white damask cloth from the previous evening's meal and, on a shelf behind it, the two silver candlesticks beside a plated Kiddush cup. They said that Goldstein never tired of telling the story of the gruelling journey he and his parents made from Poland, forced to sleep in the open, short of food, harassed by bandits, lucky to escape with their lives, but always clinging to the hope of a better life and holding on to the silver candlesticks that had been in the Goldstein family for generations. It never pays to boast. Mickey Ryan heard the story and tipped Ferret off, saying that he reckoned he knew someone he could fence them to. They weren't worth a fortune but would do nicely. As Ferret continually reminded himself, the main traps in his profession were to be too greedy or too confident. Again, he felt the sting that came to him whenever he thought of his arrest last May. Turning his attention to the window-lock, he saw that it would be child's play. For an instant he regretted not bringing his tools and doing the job at once, but turned away; the night would be safer. He returned to Lygon Street at the same steady pace, well satisfied.

Even the weather pleased him. The wind had moderated, but now rain had begun to fall. If it continued like this tonight, people would want to stay indoors and there would be fewer of them on the streets. Perhaps his luck had changed. Encouraged by this thought, he did not return directly to his digs but strolled to a double-storey, brick building that once housed the fashionable Albion Hotel and now stood bedraggled in the rain. It was still the Albion, although its upstairs rooms, which at their peak were sought after by the well-heeled visiting Melbourne, these days provided a lodging house for those too poor to do any better. The downstairs dining room, that used to boast an elite clientele, had been converted to a 'Ladies'

Lounge', in which the few ladies who frequented it were usually taking a break from working the streets. Only the bar was well supported.

Two men were in the street outside. The hulking one, with huge hands, a shaven head and crooked nose, leaned against the wall of the hotel, protected from the rain by the overhang of the entrance. He looked as though he had gone to sleep standing up like a draught-horse. Basher O'Shea seldom showed much animation, but when he did, look out! He had once been a regular at the Stadium and now scraped a living, hiring himself out as a heavy. His companion, a small man in a broad-brimmed hat and thick coat, stood with a cigarette drooping from his lips and his collar turned up against the rain. He slowly swivelled his head to scan the street in each direction, like a spectator at a very slow tennis match. Ferret nodded to them both and went inside.

The room was densely packed, a cloud of tobacco smoke above and around the men standing at the bar or sitting at the small, circular tables. Ferret edged his way through the crowd until he caught the eye of the barmaid, a tall woman in her fifties, straight and skinny with a pale face and dark hair in a plait that wound around her head like a coarsely knitted cap. 'The usual, thanks, Maureen,' he said. She wore a black blouse with long sleeves and a high, ruffled neck, and reminded Ferret of his teacher in the second grade — one of those spinsters he later came to see as having been disappointed in love and other things as well.

When Maureen first came to the Albion, Ferret wondered how she had scored the job. Perhaps she was related to the publican — his wife's sister or something like that. But Ferret came to appreciate her particular talents, one of which was to remember all the regulars and what they drank without having to be prompted. Now, he leaned forward to watch with pleasure another of her skills. As always, she held the glass at exactly the right angle, pulled on the tap labelled Melbourne Bitter with an easy grace and cut off the flow at the precise moment required to deliver a glass filled to the brim with a perfect head and not a drop wasted. The other pert and blowsy women never remembered what he wanted and were likely to slop the beer onto the counter, leave it with no head or, worst of all, underfill the glass.

'Early for you, Ferret,' she said sternly as she handed him his beer. Her manner at the bar did not endear her to many, but Ferret was impressed by her formidable presence, her commanding voice and the steely quality of her grey eyes, able to quell the rowdiest of drinkers. Ferret took a pull on his beer and said, 'I'm lookin' for Jockey.'

'Not you, too! You're all mad. Betting on the Grand National is a mug's game.' She appeared to speak from experience. 'The gee gees are risky enough on the flat. But over the jumps … And this one's a steeplechase.'

'I've 'ad a tip.'

'You all have. Why do you think Jockey looks so prosperous?'

Following her eyes, Ferret could see the man they

called Jockey, sitting in the corner, writing with a pencil in a book and issuing slips of paper to the men who approached him with their money, which he dropped into a Gladstone bag on the table in front of him. He might have been a jockey once, he was short enough. But now his girth flowed out of his trousers and spilled onto the table. He had a round face topped by tight curls of red hair and a cheerful smile for each of his customers. When Ferret reached him, he said, 'Come to take me money have you, Ferret?'

'Ya seem to be worried someone will. I see you've got Basher standin' guard outside with your cockatoo.'

The smile left Jockey's face and he sighed. 'Yeah. I don't mind keepin' the cops sweet. That's always been the way. But the cheap hoods who think they ought to get a share these days — protection they call it — I can't abide them. So I have to shell out for the likes of Basher to give me protection.' He shrugged and the smile returned. 'Enough of that. What can I do for you?'

'Five bob on Palibi to win the National.'

'Five bob! Come into money have you, me boy? Rich uncle died?'

'Just write out the slip. I'm feelin' lucky.'

'In that case, fancy some two-up? There's a game in the lane shortly.'

'Just write out the slip.'

By the time Ferret left his room around nine that night, he was far less content. For a start, Dundalk had won the National by six lengths, backed into favouritism in a late plunge. Someone knew more than the bloke who told him Palibi couldn't be beaten. But it wasn't the loss of his bet that bothered him most. Nifty Naughton, the man in the room next to his, was still at home. Nifty was a flashy cove, who never stayed in on a Saturday night; if he wasn't chasing skirt at one of the dance-halls he would be at the pictures. But not tonight. Earlier, Ferret had heard a girl in Nifty's room, as there often was, and they seemed to be having an argument. Leastways, Nifty was the one doing most of the talking and he didn't sound happy. After that it went quiet and maybe the girl slipped away, but Nifty was still there; every now and again Ferret could hear his smoker's cough. Had he got wise to the job Ferret had planned and would he be waiting for him when he returned? He left it as long as he could, hoping Nifty would go out, but the light in his room was still on when Ferret made his way to the back of the yard. Glancing over his shoulder, he took some comfort from seeing that Nifty's blinds were down and he could slip into the darkness beside the lavatory. He eased several bricks out from the base, revealing the entrance to his secret cache. He removed a small sack, which contained his tools and, after putting them in the deep pockets of his coat and again checking Nifty's window for any sign of movement, took a couple of split logs from the stack of firewood beside the back door. He fitted them into his sack so that they protruded from the top. It wouldn't fool anyone who knew him well but gave the sack an apparently respectable purpose.

Tonight, in addition to his cap and coat, he wore a woollen scarf which partly covered his face. As he came out the front door, he sensed a movement down the street to his left and caught sight of Basher O'Shea slipping into the shadows of the trees. Was Basher waiting for him as well? For the time being he was safe but he would have to be extra careful on his return. Ferret strolled along the main streets, staying out of the alleyways, until he entered the lane he had walked down earlier in the day. To add to his bleak mood, the rain had cleared and the moon shone fitfully through the clouds, so he needed to stay within the shadows of the fences. He could not be seen from that side and anyone peering out of the gloom of the cottages would be unlikely to report a man with a sack; they had their own reasons for not wanting the coppers poking around. This time, when he entered the yard, he did not walk to the back door but settled into the darkness beside the outhouse, from which he could see a light in any of the windows. The lower ones were already dark — as he had expected, the Goldstein family retired early. Or perhaps not. While he waited, becoming increasingly anxious, a single light continued to burn in an upper window. The muffled sounds of the Lygon Street traffic came to him over the roofs: the clang of the bell and the rumble of the tram as the gripman tightened the jaws on the cable, the throb of a car, the occasional toot of a horn as a pedestrian ran the gauntlet, and the clop and jingle of horse-drawn carts. All of them faded as the night lengthened and his vigil continued until, at last, the final light was doused. His practice was to wait at least an hour after all signs of life had disappeared. It took time to plan a job as carefully as he did and time to wait until everything was square. Nowadays the young coots in their gangs just bash their way in and shoot up the place; there is no art in it anymore. And that Squizzy Taylor had become the darling of the papers, writing letters to them when he was on the run and posing for photographs in his fancy clothes. The six months he was given last year seemed to have slowed him down a bit. But for how long?

Ferret dozed for a time but then roused himself and checked his tools. He moved to the window and, using his glass cutter and rubber plunger, silently created an opening to release the window lock. With the disc of glass safely on the ground, he reached in and twisted the catch, which turned easily. The window itself was more of a problem, stiff in its frame and not easy to raise without the risk of some noise. Eventually he had an opening of sufficient size, and paused to listen. Some of the sleepers, probably the old folk, were heavy in their snoring, but otherwise the house remained quiet. When he was inside he paused again, but only the sounds of sleep came down to him from the bedrooms above. It took only a few moments to gather the candlesticks, wrap them in the cloth he had brought to deaden the sound as he bore them away in his sack, and clamber back over the windowsill. The first and most difficult part of the job was over, but he was not home yet.

This time he went in the opposite direction down the alley, again keeping within the shadow of the fences. He could not take the direct route; that would be past the Police Station in Drummond Street. Better to avoid the main streets as well; the beat men gave the laneways a miss at this time of night, and with good reason, though the alleys had their problems for people like Ferret as well. Since Snowy Cutmore put together his Safe Prosecution Gang, you had to be careful they didn't nick your proceeds on the way home. Honour among thieves? They'd never heard of the idea and were just a bunch of hooligans who spent more of their time brawling with rival gangs and fighting amongst themselves. When Long Harry Slater set up in opposition to Squizzy Taylor and Harry Stokes, it went on for two years before he was seen off in a gun fight. It would probably be the same if Snowy Cutmore ever came back from Sydney.

Snowy Cutmore! He sounded like one of the villains in those penny dreadfuls you could get from the paper stalls. But Snowy was all too real. Ferret thought it was a clever move for him to take a room in Ma Cutmore's house: surely they wouldn't pick on one of his mum's boarders. Now Nifty had taken the other room and, to hear him talk, you'd think he was going to set up a new gang and knock off Squizzy. Fat chance! He'd soon learn that he needed to do more than wear sharp clothes and carry a gun, although he did boast that he'd already killed someone and got away with it.

Ferret had planned to drop his take at Mickey Ryan's

place on the way back, but it was too late now, all the fault of whoever at Goldsteins' kept the light burning, and Mick would be tucked up with his latest, refusing to open his door, even to an old cobber.

He would have to use that hidey-hole he had made at Ma's place when no one was looking.

After waiting for a couple of cars and a Clydesdale pulling a dray from the brewery to pass, he scuttled across Lygon Street. It was a funny time of night for a delivery, probably a sly grog run the bosses knew nothing about. Or perhaps they did. Back in the lanes, the cobbles were oily black and he had to be careful not to step on a broken bottle, a rusty can or worse. At Drummond Street, well south of the Police Station, the sight of a copper on his beat forced him back into the darkness of the lane. Waiting for the coast to clear, Ferret recalled Drummond Street as it was when he first started. Back then, the toffs lived in the big houses along the street, pickings were easy and there was enough for everyone. Now look at it; the toffs had long gone and in their place those Jews had overrun Carlton, and the grand buildings had been broken down and carved up as cheap lodging houses. He could think of tonight's job as a bit of payback.

He thought of circling through Carlton Gardens. There wouldn't be many couples out on a cold night like this, but you could never be sure who else might be hanging around. Instead he hurried down the back of Barkly Street, past the corner shop and into The Narrows. Only a bit over fifty yards to go, but he was not safe yet. Best to go in the back way, even though this meant walking for fifty yards along one of the lanes that formed The Narrows, where rival gangs often brawled with one another. Tonight it was eerily quiet — a reason for greater caution — and moonlight gave the bluestones of the lane a ghostly sheen. There was a bundle in the lane, directly in his path. As he came closer, the bundle formed itself into a distinct shape — a body. Someone too shickered to make it home? The moonlight fell on the face of a woman lying on her back. Her eyes were open and fixed in an eerie stare. He leaned forward to touch her cheek and felt the chill stillness of death. Wait a bit! Wasn't she the girl he had seen with Nifty?

It was a couple of weeks ago, when he was leaving the house. He heard the musical laugh as he approached the front door, and opened it to find a pretty bit of fluff on the doorstep. She had more class than Nifty's other girls, so he stood to one side and held the door for her to come inside. 'Thank you, sir,' she said, giving him a smile that stayed with him.

'Quite the gentleman,' sneered Nifty, close behind her. It was only when he spoke that Ferret noticed him. He hadn't seen her again, but on one or two occasions he thought he heard that laugh coming from Nifty's room. She wasn't laughing now and wouldn't again. Was she the one that had been with Nifty earlier? There had been some laughter before the argument, if that was what it was, and it could have been her. Had she left as he thought, or had she been silenced?

Ferret recoiled from the body and hastily scanned the lane in both directions, but empty silence stared back at him. He had thought Nifty might be waiting in the house to rob him, but now more sinister possibilities loomed. Having killed her, had Nifty waited for Ferret to leave before dumping her in the laneway? Or had one of Nifty's enemies waylaid her? Could it have been Basher?

Grasping his sack, he scrambled through the gate and sank down in the darkness beside the lavatory. He watched and he listened, but all the lights were now out and there was no sign of any movement in the house. He stowed the sack and was about to replace the bricks, when he thought he heard footsteps, and crouched even lower. Nothing followed, so telling himself to get a move on, he pushed the bricks back into place and crept toward the house. The lean-to at the end of the verandah, which served as a kitchen, was empty. He flinched at the squeak of the back door as he tried to ease it open.

Down the passage he could hear Ma Cutmore's heavy breathing from the front room, but she was not the threat. He crept to the door of Nifty's room which, to his surprise, was wide open, and peered in. Everything was silent and still. Emboldened, he entered the room and checked the bed. It had not been slept in. He returned to the passage, carefully opened the door to his own room, ready to flee, but there was no one there either. He sank onto his bed and began to breathe again.

Whoever had murdered that girl — Nifty or someone else — would have done a bunk long ago. But who else might have seen him enter The Narrows and would blab to the flatfoots when they came around? What should he do? It looked like Nifty had gone into smoke, and perhaps he should, too. But where would he go? Should he get in first and cover himself? But going to the coppers? He began preparing to go to bed but could not settle. The face of the girl lying alone in the alley kept returning to haunt him and he could not shake the fear he might have been seen. Finally he told himself, 'Bugger it. You've got to look after yourself as best you can.'

This time Ferret stayed in the main streets, looking in vain for a policeman. Why are the cops never there when you need them? Turning into Drummond Street, he could see the square, red-brick building that was the Police Station, separated from the Salvation Army Citadel by a small cottage surrounded by climbing roses. Where did that come from? He had never noticed it before; probably because he usually gave this part of Carlton a wide berth or was being pushed along by one of the coppers. He reached the Station and hastened inside.

It had been a quiet night for a Saturday and Constable Johnstone was in good humour since his shift had only a few hours to go. 'Ferret Roberts, as I live and breathe. You look upset. Have you been robbed? It's terrible the thieves that get about these days. What have they taken?'

'This is serious.'

'Not robbed? Have you come to turn yourself in then? I'm sorry Fess isn't here. He'll be the one you want to confess to, no doubt. You'll have to wait until he comes in the morning.'

'There's a body in The Narrows. A dead body. A woman.'

'You're sure? Not one of the pros had too much?'

'She's no tom. A proper lady. A young one, though. And she's snuffed it for sure. I reckon someone's done 'er in.'

'Daley!' the constable shouted over his shoulder, triggering the appearance of a tall, young constable who was taking a break from his beat. 'Ferret here says he's found a dead'n in The Narrows. Go with him and check it out. If he's right, you'd better rouse Senior Constable Jordan. He always wants to be told as soon as we have a serious crime. He lives just round the corner. You know his house?'

'No, I don't.'

'A bluestone cottage in Murchison Street. Number Forty-Two. And don't wake up the neighbourhood. Just Fess.' Johnstone scratched his chin. 'I'd better ring Headquarters. You are sure, Ferret? She's not just shickered?'

'I've told you, she's 'ad it. Dead cold.'

'Right then. Off you go, and smart about it.'

Constable Tom Daley did not appear to hurry but he took large steps and Ferret had to hasten to keep up with him. 'Hold on. She ain't goin' anywhere, I can promise you.'

'How did you find her? Did you hear her screams?'

'You're new around here, ain't you?'

'Been in Carlton a few months. It's late to be finding a body. What were you doing in The Narrows?'

'You ask a lot of questions.'

'Don't seem to be getting a lot of answers, though.'

'I thought it was the Plain Clothes blokes who handled the murders.'

'I'm just curious. Do you live nearby?'

Ferret shook his head as if incredulous at the constable's tenacity. 'Look, I live in the house that backs onto the lane where she is. I'd been having a night out with me mates and took a short cut down the lane. Will that do ya?'

'Thanks.'

They continued in silence, Ferret reflecting on how unusual it was for him to be enjoying the security of walking with a policeman. It was a pity there were none of his mates around to see. He was reminded of the possible watchers in The Narrows and was doubly pleased to have the company of Constable Daley; he certainly looked big and strong enough to deal with anyone they might meet. As they crossed into the lane, Ferret was gripped by anxiety that the body might have been spirited away. What would the coppers say then? But he needn't have feared; she remained in exactly the same place, lying straight and stiff, still in her overcoat and her close fitting hat. He hadn't thought about it the first time. She looked so orderly that it was easy to think she was just asleep, but the staring eyes in her swollen face said otherwise. Daley dropped to his knees and touched the woman's neck, confirming her death.

'I'll be on my way then,' Ferret said and began to walk down the lane toward his gate.

'What number is that place?' Daley called.

'Number fifty. I thought all you coppers knew Ma Cutmore's place.'

2

It took only a few minutes for Tom Daley to walk into Murchison Street and find the single-storey, bluestone cottage. He knocked on the door tentatively and waited. He was about to knock again when, from behind the door, he heard the voice of Fess Jordan. 'Who is it?'

'Constable Tom Daley, Senior.'

The door opened to reveal a ruddy-faced man of medium height, with a sandy beard and tousled hair, in a navy dressing-gown. He eyed the constable before giving him a weary smile and saying. 'I s'pose you have a good reason for waking me at this time of the morning. What is it?'

'There's a body in The Narrows. Constable Johnstone sent me to check and asked me to let you know. He said you'd want that.'

'Wait there. Be with you in a minute.'

The door closed, and it seemed very little longer than a minute before it opened again and Senior Constable Jordan emerged in a Donegal tweed overcoat and dark boxer hat, carrying a torch in his hand. Since coming to Carlton, Tom had not had many dealings with Fess Jordan, although he had heard the stories. They said he was called Fess because of his ability to cajole confessions from tight-lipped crims. Some said he had been a Catholic priest before joining the police and earned his name because of his liking for the confessional. A few weeks ago, though, Tom met a couple of blokes who told him they worked with Fess on building sites in Carlton before he joined the Force. They said he was called Fess back then, and he wasn't even a Catholic in those days.

Jordan gestured for Tom to take the lead. 'So who and what do we have?' he asked.

'A young woman, dead, in The Narrows at the back of Fifty Barkly Street.'

'Cutmore's place?'

'That's what he said.'

'That's what who said, Constable?'

'I don't know his proper name, Senior, but Johnstone called him "Ferret".'

'Ferret Roberts. You should know him. He's one of the distinguished thieves of Carlton. Has all the old skills but is getting on now. How did he get into this?'

'He found the body and reported it about half an hour ago.'

The senior man's eyes twinkled for a moment and he ran a finger across his beard. 'Did he now? It's probably the first time he's entered the Station voluntarily.'

'Johnstone said something like that.'

'If Ferret was still up at this time of night, he must have been on a job. I wonder what he's pinched this time.'

'He seemed a bit chary about telling me anything but eventually said he'd been out with his mates and was taking a short cut home when he found the body. He hadn't heard any screams or anything.'

Fess Jordan gave the young constable an appraising glance. 'I'm surprised you got that much out of him. Persistent, were you?'

They entered the lane and Jordan turned on his torch, shining it along the length of the cobbles until the beam met the bundle ahead of them. He quickened his pace and stood over the woman, the torch illuminating her face. After a time he allowed the light to travel down her body until it reached her feet when he switched it off, as though belatedly offering her some degree of privacy. 'Tell me what you see, Constable.'

Daley swallowed hard, surprised to be asked, and began hesitantly. 'A young woman. Early twenties, I'd guess. Fully dressed and, except for her face, not much sign of a struggle. Perhaps she was strangled.' He paused and looked across to his questioner.

'Anything not there?'

'Not there? Oh …' Belatedly the constable caught on. 'A handbag or a purse, perhaps.'

'Maybe an umbrella, too. It's clear now, but there was rain about earlier in the night, and I would expect a girl dressed like this to have an umbrella. What about the clothes?'

'Overcoat fully done up. Hat remains tightly on the head.' Again he paused and looked questioningly at Jordan.

'Pretty good quality. I doubt she's a local. I reckon she was probably chased in here before being attacked. Perhaps she didn't know what a dangerous place she was running into. But let's not get ahead of ourselves. Anything else you notice about the body?'

Daley looked down, searching for something to say. The woman lay stretched out with her arms tucked into her sides and her feet together, the toes of her shoes pointing to the sky. Eventually and apologetically, he offered, 'To look at the way she's lying, you wouldn't think she'd been murdered.'

'You're right. Someone who's been killed doesn't arrange themselves as if laid out for burial. Someone else has done that. I wonder why. Was it her attacker?' Jordan did not wait for an answer. 'Let's have a look around.' He walked down the lane, swinging his torch from side to side, revealing the debris and weeds that cluttered the cobblestones. They reached a spot where the lane linked with two others and a broken-down shed straddled the v-shaped junction.

Jordan trained his torch through a gap in the timber wall and called, 'Are you there, Clarry?' He called again, leaning through the gap and shining the torch around. The dirt floor was partially covered with old newspapers, a tattered blanket lying above the remnants of a straw bale. The only piece of furniture was a battered kerosene tin that carried a few chipped bowls and a beaker. On the floor beside it was a tin dish half-filled with water. 'Strange not to find Clarry here,' he murmured, more to himself than to Tom.

'Someone lives here?' Tom asked, incredulity shaping his voice.

'You should know Clarry Garton, too. There's not much that goes on around The Narrows that Clarry misses. He must have got hold of some dough.' Seeing the puzzled stare of the constable, Fess continued. 'If he's not here at this time of the morning, he's likely been on the grog and passed out somewhere. I reckon it's time you got to know Clarry. Look for a small man, skin and bone really, with grey whiskers, in a threadbare brown overcoat, navy balaclava and old army boots. He'll smell something terrible. Now where will he be?' Jordan paused to consider the options. 'Drifter O'Rourke's place over in David Street is the nearest sly grog and we haven't raided it for a few months, so he's probably back in business. I'd start there.'

'What number's that, Senior?'

'How long have you been stationed at Carlton, Daley?'

'Three months.'

'Three months, and you don't know Ferret Roberts, Clarry Garton or Drifter's place.' Jordan shook his head sorrowfully. 'You're a big, strong lad with more education than I ever had. You've even had the training course they give you recruits these days. But when you're on the beat, you don't just walk around. You watch and you listen and you learn. And one of the things you learn is that Drifter would never let Clarry inside his place. He'll be in one of the lanes nearby. If you don't find him there, speak to anyone who is, have a wider look around and, if you still can't find him in an hour, come back here. I'll wait for the C.I. men to arrive.'

Fess watched Daley walk down the lane leading to

Elgin Street. Although tall and heavily built, with large hands and feet, he moved with the relaxed gait of an athlete. He looked as if he'd make a good ruckman and Carlton needed some new talent. They'd lost again yesterday; St. Kilda was missing a few of their best players but still beat them by four goals. They'd won only three games this year and were third-last on the ladder. The boys still believed in them, though, and had wanted him to take them, but he was working. He'd saved them from a miserable afternoon in the wet and cold watching their team lose again, but they didn't see it that way. Still, he'd promised to have a kick with them this afternoon after ... Struth! It was Carmel's first communion this morning. Bernadette would never forgive him if he missed that. Other times he could plead police duty to get out of going to Mass, but not today; she was so looking forward to this. The white dress had been made specially.

As he continued to search the tangle of lanes, Fess kicked a rusty can against the fence. When Bern heard about this murder she'd be at him even harder than before. It'd been bad enough when that pie man, Pony Dodds, was shot at the United States Hotel a couple of months back. Admittedly, it was only around the corner in Canning Street, but at a pub, not in their backyard like she made it sound, saying that crime in Carlton had become more blatant and more vicious and telling him they had an obligation to the children to get away and go somewhere where it was safe to grow up. She knew he had unfinished business here, but these days that didn't rate with her.

Finding nothing of interest amidst the debris, he returned to stand beside the body. Why had he sent Daley off on a wild goose chase? So that the woman lying in the lane would be spared the further scrutiny of a young man who, in other circumstances, might have been her boyfriend? No, that was just the excuse, and a pretty poor one at that. For a start, she was out of Daley's class: the cloche hat, with its soft felt, upturned brim and fancy stitching, looked to be of high quality. The fur trim on the collar of her woollen coat wouldn't come cheap, nor would the patent leather shoes with their pointed toes and high heels.

No, it wasn't her. Well, not directly anyway. He wanted to absorb this latest blow. How long was it now since he had so unexpectedly come back from Bendigo to take care of his mother? She'd been dead for two years and they would have been here for three years before that. After his mother died, Bern suggested there was no need to remain. 'We don't have your mother to think about now,' she said. 'It'd be good for the kids to grow up in a town like Bendigo, but I don't want us to go back there. I'd like a place where we wouldn't have my mother and my sisters checking on your piety every week, and where you'd be free from your father's past.' He'd been surprised by that last bit. She'd never said anything like that before and he didn't want to leave when there was every chance he might actually surpass his father's achievement. What was wrong with that?

That was before the police strike, before the gangs became so vicious and their crimes so brazen. Now, it wasn't just Bern, but the papers as well, talking of a wave of crime crashing down on the city. The gangs were so much better organised and flush with cash from their rackets in sly grog, gambling, prostitution and drugs. Cocaine had even become the fashion with some of the smart set. He was not going to make any real difference until he rooted out those who funded and ran these rackets. What hope did he have of doing that?

And here he was, standing vigil over a woman murdered on his doorstep. A tragedy for the girl and her family, but with no connection to the gangs and their backers. He looked down on the face of the dead girl. Could this be the face of Carmel in some years' time?

Bern was sure to see it that way. And didn't he hope she might one day be as well-dressed and as elegant as this girl was? He knew you should never get personally involved, but he couldn't shake the feeling that this crime was an attack on him, as well. Silly, really, and arrogant too, but there it was.

Fess was jolted from his reverie by a movement at the head of the lane. He turned to shine his torch in that direction and saw a man in a belted gabardine overcoat and bowler hat shield his eyes from the glare of the torch. 'Senior Detective Thomas, C.I.B.,' he said. 'Can you take that torch out of my eyes?'

'Sorry. Senior Constable Jordan, Carlton Police. The body's down here.'

The C.I.B. man now approached him. 'What's a Senior doing standing here? Your constables scared of the dark?'

The Detective's face was shadowed by the brim of his hat, but his manner suggested a cockiness Fess did not like. He was younger than him with a restless energy that showed itself in the way he rocked forward on the balls of his feet and settled back on his heels, never quite still.

'I sent one of my constables to look for a bloke that usually dosses down in a shed along this lane. He might have seen or heard something.'

'Done a bunk, has he? Could be our man.' For the first time since his arrival the Detective looked down on the body that, in Fess' eyes, was taking on a ghostly quality as the dawn approached. 'She doesn't look like a lane dweller. What's she doing here in The Narrows?'

'I wondered that myself. Perhaps she ran in here off the street, trying to escape.'

'Anyone reported missing?'

'I wasn't at the Station and didn't think to ask when Daley came for me.'

Thomas threw back his head and gave an incredulous laugh.

'What? They got you up so you could come and stand guard over a body? Is that how the Carlton Station works?'

Fess stiffened and then responded as if reciting a formal regulation. 'As the Senior Plain Clothes Constable, I've made it a requirement that I am to be informed without delay about any major crime in our area.'

After a period of silence, with each man standing either side of the corpse, neither one looking at the other, the

Detective said, 'How long's this constable of yours going to be?'

'May be a while yet. Clarry Garton isn't always easy to find. I expected the C.I. would send more than one of you.'

'Yeah, normally, but tonight we're thin on the ground. They had to get me out of my warm bed to come here. There's a wog going through the squad and we've had a busy night already. Someone fired some bullets through a window in Port Melbourne and then blew in the front door with a bomb. You're lucky to get me. Unless we nail this bloke — Garton, did you say his name was? — unless we get him quick-smart, I'm going to need someone to do some leg work for me. Can you let me have one of your constables?'

'C.I. aren't the only ones short-handed. In the winter a lot of the men stationed at Carlton get ill, too.' Fess had been holding himself in against the taunts of the C.I.B. man, and now found a way to release his irritation. 'Do you know the single men have to put overcoats on their beds to keep warm and dry in their barracks because the roof leaks? The neglect of the buildings goes back to my father's time and nothing's changed. The prisoners at Carlton are in better quarters than the constables.'

'Your father?' The puzzlement on the Detective's face cleared. 'Jordan. You're the son of Sergeant David Jordan. We've all heard of him. A hard man, they say, who never let up and was feared by all. What a waste, dying the way he did.' When Fess made no reply, Thomas shrugged and said, 'Your man will be much better helping me than pounding the beat. The crims just watch them going past, regular as clockwork, and then nick round the corner to get on with their crimes.'

'So you agree with Nicholson?'

'Did he say that?' Thomas reached into the pocket of his coat, bringing forth a pipe and tobacco pouch, from which he began to prime the pipe. Like everyone else, Fess began smoking at school and continued for those first few years on the building sites where it seemed unfriendly not to smoke. What else were smokos for? He was happy to give it up when he joined the Force and had never wanted to return to it. His father, also a non-smoker, once told him that men smoked pipes so they had something to do while they tried to think of what to say. Was Thomas one of these?

With the pipe primed, he made no attempt to light it, and said, 'If he did, it's one of the few things the Chief Commissioner and I agree on. We wouldn't have had that strike if he'd got off his backside and done something about our grievances. Super should always have been for everyone and not just the privileged. And what about the spooks? How did you like them snooping about?'

'I didn't mind the idea of having a few special supervisors randomly checking the beat men; some stations were a bit slack. It was a pity he didn't pick better people though.'

'He incites a strike, we have a week of carnage, lose six hundred good men from the Force and then everyone gets their entitlement to super and the spooks go, but the strikers don't get back and, two years later, we're still sorting out the bloody mess. Thank God Nicholson's gone now. When he was appointed, we celebrated having a man who came up through the ranks and not some blow-in, but he's done nothing for us. It happens to so many. They do a good job until they get promoted and then they enjoy the perks so much they forget why they're there and spend their time making sure no one rocks the boat or causes them any trouble. Nicholson was like that after he became Chief Commissioner, toadying up to the Government, but I've seen it happen even to sergeants. Let's hope the new man's better. He couldn't be worse.'

'To hear you I'm surprised you didn't go on strike yourself.'

Again Thomas did not reply immediately, apparently more intent on getting his pipe alight. After that was achieved, he puffed on it several times before taking it from his mouth and saying, 'I went to some of the meetings, and what they said was right. But don't be silly. The strikers were on a hiding to nothing. I'm grateful for what they did but I'm not barmy. Stick your head out and you get it chopped off.'

Fess lifted his chin and stared into the Detective's eyes. 'You like to play it safe?'

'There are causes worth fighting for. I have one or two I'm working on right now. But you're stupid if you put your life or your livelihood at risk. There are always better ways. I said I'd heard about your father. They say he was a police hero, famous for the way he tried to clean up this dump and for the way he died trying to save some derelicts from a fire. What a waste! They said my father was a hero, too. I've got his medals. They said he gave his life for his native land. A load of cobblers. He died in the Boer War protecting the interests of a bunch of crooked, pommy capitalists. He left a wife who had to fend for herself, and a son who had to give up school and get a job in a grocer's shop. Both our fathers are famous, but for the wrong reasons.'

In the growing light of the pre-dawn Fess saw the vapour cloud that issued from each of their mouths, making it look as though they were breathing fire at one another. It was a bit like that. Thomas had a talent for getting under his skin, driving away his normally accommodating style. 'Do you want to be famous?'

'You bet I do. For the right reasons, though. Just like Piggott – a living legend in the C.I., famous for the number of convictions he gets, feared by the crooks and loved by the public, dresses like a toff, with his picture in the papers. Even Squizzy Taylor writes to the papers about him and quotes that jingle,

"*Ashes to ashes, dust to dust,*
If Brophy don't get you,
Well, Piggott must."'

Thomas smiled; the first time Fess had seen him appear lighthearted. 'When they write a jingle about me, I'll know I've made it.'

'It must be good to be so clear about what you want to achieve.' Fess had intended irony, but he often wished he could be more certain of what he really wanted to achieve, and this thought was caught by his tone, so that he ended up sounding as if he were envious.

Thomas eyed him carefully. 'Yeah, I reckon it is.'

What was it about this man? First of all Fess had allowed his annoyance with him to show — something he rarely did. And now he had exposed a private thought — something he never did.

'So do I get some help on this case?' Thomas asked.

'I'll give you a hand. My local knowledge should help and, just like my father, I'm committed to making Carlton a safer place to live. My house is nearby.' He was about to say more but held back.

Thomas' lips curved in a small grin. 'A bit too close to home, eh?' He paused to look carefully at Fess, who made no response. 'You sure you have the time? One of your constables will do.'

'Today was my day off.'

'It's your choice, but let's be very clear.' Thomas again used his pipe to press home his point. 'This is a C.I. case. I'm running it and you're assisting me. Don't ever try to take over.'

'Of course not, Senior Detective. I understand. I'll need to clear it with my sergeant, but that shouldn't be a problem.'

'You come out in the middle of the night to stand guard on a body. When I ask for a constable to assist me, you volunteer yourself. I know plenty of cops who want promotion: I'm one of them. You're the first I've met, who's happy to demote himself. But, if that's the way you want it …' The Detective held out his hand. 'Let's shake on it. I'm Jim Thomas.'

'Fess Jordan.' They stood, shaking hands over the dead body, and were startled to hear footsteps approaching from the interior of The Narrows. Around the bend in the lane came Tom Daley, waving something at them.'

'Did you find him?' Fess called.

'Yeah, but I didn't get much out of him.' Daley came toward them quickly without appearing to exert himself. You were right. I found him dead shickered in a lane off David Street. There was another drunk with him in a bit better shape, who told me Clarry had come into money. I couldn't rouse Clarry, so I picked him up and took him to the Station. You were right again; he's mainly skin and bone and he does smell something awful.' Tom's enthusiastic expression dimmed and he became a little shame-faced. 'He woke up for a moment and threw up over me. I've tried to clean myself up but I wouldn't stand too close.' Daley reached the pair and held out the object in his hand, a long narrow bag with a silk covering and delicate beading. 'I remembered we'd seen no bag or purse, so I went back to Clarry's shed and had a good look round. I found this.'

Thomas took the bag and opened the silver clasp to look inside. He knelt on the cobbles and shook the contents onto the ground. Out tumbled a small purse, a plated powder compact, a lipstick, a comb, a cloisonné pillbox, a folded cotton handkerchief and a door-key. He peered into the bag and extracted an envelope, which had been wedged against the side of the bag, and added it to the pile. He opened the purse. 'No money here.'

Fess picked up the envelope, which was unopened, and read out, 'Miss Mary Worthington, Fifty-Eight Faraday Street, Carlton. Perhaps she is a local after all. That's just back across the road and around the corner.' He looked again at the envelope. 'It comes from the Working Men's College.'

'It's all looking very simple,' Thomas said. 'On her way home she's waylaid by this waster and it gets out of hand. He takes the money and gets himself plastered. Let's go and sort him out.'

Fess spoke quietly but his tone was definite. 'Yes, we should do that. I can tell you, though, you won't get anything useful from him until after lunch; it takes that long for Clarry to sober up. Meanwhile, would you like me to check with the people in Faraday Street that it is Mary Worthington we have here?'

'Yeah, good idea. I'll go back to Russell Street and get them moving on collecting the body. There's a few other things I have to do as well.'

'No sign of an umbrella?' Fess asked Daley.

'No. Not at Clarry's or in the lane. Maybe someone else picked it up.'

Thomas began to walk away, saying over his shoulder, 'I'll meet you at the Station at two o'clock. It's getting light now, so young Sherlock should be right to stay with the body.'

3

As soon as Fess was inside his door, he took off his hat and coat and placed them in their usual positions on the hall-stand. He took the slender bag from his pocket and put it on a shelf of the stand before turning toward the bedroom. Only then did he see Bernadette, standing in the passage. 'What was it this time?' Before he could reply, Carmel appeared in her communion dress with her hair still in the curling rags Bernadette had used last night. 'Just go back and take that dress off, young lady.' Bernadette's voice was stern, but amusement lit her eyes. 'Mass is not until eleven, and I'm not ironing it again. Put on your normal dress and a pinafore.'

'You look very nice,' Fess said to his crestfallen daughter. She had been looking forward to this day for weeks. He never mentioned it to Bern, but Carmel's enthusiasm for the rites of the Church bothered him at times; he hoped she would never be tempted to become a nun. He kissed his wife and said, 'We're all up early this morning.'

'The boys are still dead to the world, but you know I can't sleep when you're called out, and Carmel is just too excited.' Fess entered their bedroom, shrugging off his suit-coat and hanging it in the cupboard. 'You haven't told me. Was it bad?' she asked.

'A dead woman in The Narrows.'

He braced himself for her reaction and was surprised when she said, 'I knew it must be bad. I'm used to you coming home from a call-out, tired or angry or frustrated, or a mixture of all of them, but this morning, when you stopped in the hallway, you looked so sad.' She had come up behind him as she spoke and now put her arms around him, snuggling into his back.

'I think she might be a local girl. We found a bag belonging to a Mary Worthington. The only Worthington I know is George Worthington, the man at King and Godfree, who's been there for years. I don't know where he lives, though.'

'He does live somewhere about here,' Bernadette said. 'I've seen him in the street.'

Fess scratched his chin. 'I hope I'm mistaken but I'll need to call on them and check.'

'Don't forget Carmel's first communion. You must be there.'

'Of course. Of course. But you said Mass isn't until eleven. Plenty of time for me to make myself presentable and call on the Worthingtons.'

'You look like you could do with some breakfast. Sorry.'

A little refreshed but no happier, Fess left his home for the second time that morning and walked into Faraday Street. Across from him stood number fifty-eight, a two-storey brick house that, like all the buildings in the street, was squeezed between its companions on either side. The front wall, which was flush with the street, had been painted blue-grey and the wood of the window frames and door picked out in maroon. He did not cross the street but continued on towards the Station, his head down. Jim Thomas' comments continued to rankle, all the more because he had to admit Thomas might have a point. Perhaps he was becoming obsessed with being involved in every incident and should have more trust in his men. Perhaps he should have given one of them the chance to work with the Detective. Did he feel he should protect them from Jim's cynicism? How long would it take for young Daley to become a cynic? It was a method of survival for many. Perhaps it was a pity he couldn't view his own motives more cynically.

Jim had been dead wrong about his father's bravery, though. Fess had heard the story from his mother countless times. But it was when he spoke with some of the men who had been with David Jordan at the fire that he understood the extent of the sacrifice his father had made. They told him his father had been tipped off that the gang which had shot a bank teller in Kew and made off with a substantial amount of cash was hiding in a house in Dorrit Street. The police ringed the house but were shot at from within, and the stand-off was only broken when a fire erupted at the back of the house, forcing the gang members into the hands of the police. No one knew what caused the fire. Despite the flames having taken hold, his father insisted on entering the house in search of anyone remaining inside. What he found was the wife of one of the gang, abandoned by her husband and huddled in the corner of a room with two of her children. He brought them out safely and, regardless of the warnings from his fellows that the house was now a death-trap, returned to look for a third child but was caught by the fire and perished. Only then was it found that the girl had already escaped. Posthumously, he was awarded the Victoria Police Valour Badge, not for 'trying to save some derelicts from a fire', as Thomas had sneeringly put it, but, as the citation said, 'For pre-eminent valour and bravery displayed in the performance of police duty.' Fess was never going to be able to match that.

It was always assumed he would follow his father and become a policeman. Other possibilities were never mentioned and he grew up knowing it was a noble calling, in which he could play a heroic role — his father did. Even before his death, David Jordan was a legend to many, not just his son. A man with a forbidding presence, he waged an unremitting crusade against crime in Carlton. He was implacable in his hatred and pursuit of criminals and he drove his men hard. He told Fess it was the only way to get the best out of a squad of men. It was also the only way to ensure his son grew into a man worthy of his parents. It was inevitable that Fess would follow his father. But not in Carlton: that was his father's territory.

On joining the Force he was posted to Bendigo, where he settled in quickly and found that policing didn't always require the harsh discipline his father employed so relentlessly. He had first begun to have doubts about his father's ideas when he filled the years between the end of school and becoming eligible to join the Force by working on building sites in Carlton. His experiences there suggested to him that the greatest evil in Carlton was not crime, but poverty, and that much of the crime was rooted in poverty. The wonder was that so few people resorted to crime in their unending battle to look after their families and make ends meet.

His experience in Bendigo confirmed his belief and he developed an approach to crime, less hostile and, to the community, less intimidating than he had been taught would be needed. He didn't say a lot but developed the knack of establishing common ground, quietly asking his questions and listening closely to what he was being told. People responded by sometimes telling him a good deal more than they intended.

After he met and married Bernadette, he looked forward to raising a family and continuing his work in Bendigo. His father was still able to alter the course of his life, though. When he was killed, leaving his widow on her own in Carlton, Fess immediately said she would be better off to come and join them in Bendigo. His mother was unwilling to move and, to his surprise, Bernadette suggested it might be better if he could arrange a transfer to Carlton.

He didn't like the idea, but his mother was adamant, so he put in an application. Gerry Doyle had become the

Sergeant-in-Charge at the Station leaving a vacancy as Senior Constable in the Plain Clothes Section. His mother saw going from wife of the Sergeant to mother of a Senior Constable as a demotion and was incensed that the Force was not more accommodating, but Fess was surprised that his transfer was so easily agreed.

Working under Gerry Doyle had its problems, but he enjoyed the challenge of his new role in Plain Clothes. Prior to his death, David Jordan claimed his methods had succeeded in making Carlton a safer place to live; the crime rate had been slowing after the war and the number of murders had fallen at that time, as well. Nevertheless, Fess stuck to the style of policing that had been successful for him in Bendigo. At first the Plain Clothes men, expecting him to continue in the family tradition, had not known what to make of the change but, once they grew to know him, they responded well and he gained confidence that, despite the doubts of his sergeant, he could continue the improvement his father had achieved. But his father had never mentioned the rise in gang violence, something that must surely have been apparent to him in the year or two prior to his death.

Sometimes he felt that he had never really known his father. The way in which his superior officers spoke of David Jordan made it clear that he had a much more cordial relationship with them than with the men under his command. They referred to unnamed favours he had done for them and assured Fess of their support. When his application for a transfer to Carlton was so readily approved, it was as if his father had reached out from his grave to pull the necessary strings. And at the funeral, several men of influence in Carlton, including a local politician, a businessman and a landlord, approached him to offer their condolences and speak warmly of his father. This was a side of him he had not seen. Even the man who ran the building company that Fess had once worked for sought him out, reminding him of those days. As he came to know more of the world he had wondered how his father had been able to find a job for him, straight out of school, when jobs were so scarce. It seemed he had called in one of the favours he was owed.

Thomas scorned those who put loyalty to a cause ahead of their own safety. Loyalty was a virtue Fess had been taught to prize. Now he had a loyal wife, who could still surprise him. He knew she was anxious about bringing up her children in Carlton and would much prefer they moved to the country. He'd been sure she would fly off the handle when she heard of the murder. But her concern had been for him. Perhaps he should look sad more often. No, that wouldn't work: Bern would see through him straight away and she hated pretence.

He must make that Mass: she would never forgive him if he missed it. It would be tight, though. If he was able to establish beyond doubt that it was Mary Worthington who had been killed, he would need to take a family member to the Morgue to identify the body.

Entering the Station, he greeted the constable at the front desk. 'Morning, Tim. Looks a little brighter this morning, though still nippy. Anything to report?'

The constable rose from his stool and said, 'A quiet start, apart from the dead woman, of course – it is Sunday. We've had a Jew butcher in, wailing and gnashing his teeth. Apparently someone's nicked his precious silver candlesticks. Done a good, clean job of it: got in through a window the butcher swears was locked, without anyone hearing a thing.'

'That sounds like Ferret Robert's work. And he found the girl in the lane. He wouldn't be in any lane late at night unless he'd been up to something.'

Fess stretched his arms into the air and shook his head as though waking. 'No one reported a missing woman?'

'No. Oh, Daley called in before going off shift. He said the people had come to collect the body. And Sergeant Doyle wants a word.'

Before going to Doyle's office, Fess looked into the room that served as the base for the four Plain Clothes men in his group.

'Boss? I thought it was your day off,' Constable Alex McKenzie said, rising to his feet.

'A bit to do on the dead woman, Mac. I agreed to give the C.I. a hand. Meanwhile, I think you should get around to Ma Cutmore's place. That's where Ferret Roberts has a room these days. There's a chance he's the one who lifted the candlesticks I hear are missing. He's probably already fenced his swag but he's had a busy night and that might have delayed him. Have a look round the yard as well as the house. He likes to use hidey-holes.'

'Sergeant Doyle wants to see you.'

'So I hear.'

It was unusual for the Station Sergeant to be in this early on a Sunday. Probably he had heard about the girl. Despite his reluctance to stir from his office, he had the knack of knowing all that was going on in his bailiwick.

'Morning, Sergeant.' Fess spoke with an enthusiasm he did not feel. 'You want to know about the body in The Narrows?'

Gerry Doyle did not look up from reading the document on the desk in front of him immediately. He was not tall but heavily built with a full head of black hair and matching bushy eyebrows. The darkness of his uniform and his colouring, together with his habit of hunching his shoulders and leaning forward to place his elbows on the desk, always put Fess in mind of a spider at the centre of its web. When he did stir, it was to look up at Fess with a humourless smile. 'I know you aren't certain how she died, possibly strangulation, lives in Faraday Street and has been robbed. What I don't know is how you can be stupid enough to think Clarry Garton would have had anything to do with it.'

'He did have the girl's bag so may have seen something. I've arranged for Senior Detective Thomas from the C.I. to interview him this afternoon. Clarry should have sobered up by then.'

'Get him out of here straight afterwards. What's this Thomas like? Must be a fool, if he thinks Clarry could be a murderer.'

'Apparently they're shorthanded in the C.I. at present

and he wants to get some help from those of us who know the local scene. I told him we were shorthanded as well.'

'Judging by the way he started, we'll need to keep an eye on what he's up to and steer him in the right direction. I don't want the papers carrying on about police stupidity in Carlton.'

'You don't want me to do it, though, do you?'

'Why not you? I thought you prided yourself on steering people in the right direction. You can match rank with him, and it would do you good to see how the C.I. operate. They don't pussy-foot around the way you like to. In fact I think we should formalise this, second you to them for this case. You might want to stay there if it goes well.'

'Are you sure about this, Sergeant?'

'The more I think about it the better I like it. I'll tee it up while you go and see the family in Faraday Street.'

'Your call, Boss. But you know I'm not interested in any permanent transfer.'

Walking back to the Worthingtons' house, Fess reflected on the awkwardness of his dealings with the sergeant. From the very first day he had reported for duty, Gerry Doyle had made it clear he did not welcome having Fess on his strength. 'Let's be clear,' he said. 'You may be David Jordan's son, but when it comes to policing in Carlton, I'm his heir. Never forget that.' At the time Fess had not understood what Doyle meant but he came to see that, whilst Doyle lacked the integrity and the steel that earned his father respect, he craved the unchallenged authority David Jordan had enjoyed in Carlton. Perhaps

Jim Thomas was rather similar in his wish to follow his hero, Piggott, at the C.I. All matters had to be referred to Doyle and all decisions taken by him. Fess had learnt how to work around him, just as he had done this morning. It was a game he didn't enjoy but couldn't avoid playing.

The door of number fifty-eight was opened almost immediately after Fess had knocked. In the doorway stood the grey-haired figure of George Worthington, wearing a collarless shirt with sleeves tucked to the elbow and red braces supporting his baggy trousers. When he saw who it was, his face took on that slightly guilty look that comes to many law-abiding people when unexpectedly confronted by a policeman.

'Morning, Mr. Worthington. May I come in?'

George stood to one side of the door and indicated with his right arm that Fess should enter the living room that opened off the passage. As he did so, Mrs. Worthington, a handsome woman in buxom middle-age, came from her kitchen at the other end of the passage. 'Is that you, Mary? Forget your key, you silly …' Halted by the sight of the policeman, she fumbled with her apron, seeking to remove it before following her husband into the room.

'Good morning, Mrs. Worthington,' Fess said politely. 'I don't think we have met before. I'm Senior Constable Jordan from Carlton Police.'

She bobbed her head in acknowledgement. 'What brings you here, Constable? Would you like to sit down?' Mrs. Worthington gestured towards one of the wooden-framed, leather armchairs.

Fess ignored her suggestion and they remained facing one another with George to one side of his wife. 'You have a daughter, Mary, who is not home at present?'

'You heard me starting to go on about her key.' Mrs. Worthington moved her weight from side to side and waved expressive hands as she spoke. 'She's always forgetting it. These young girls have so much going on in their heads, and keys are not important to them. Not that she's a stupid girl. Has a good job with Ball and Welch in the Dress Department and is doing very well.'

'She stayed overnight with a girlfriend,' her husband interjected.

'She and Paula like to go to the pictures on a Saturday night. I don't know what they were going to see last night. Whatever's the latest, I s'pose. Mary stays over with Paula so she doesn't have to come through the streets on her own late at night. Very kind of Mrs. Ryan to let her stay. A very nice woman, Mrs. Ryan.'

'Why do you ask?' Again George Worthington had to stem his wife's flow.

Fess hesitated, not yet ready to commit himself. 'Is this her bag?' he asked, holding it out for inspection but not releasing it as Mrs. Worthington leaned forward to touch it.

'Oh dear. She must have dropped it. I said she could be careless at times. Very kind of someone to hand it in. She loves that bag and will be frantic.'

'How did you know to come here?' George asked, his face sombre.

'In the bag there's a letter from the Working Men's College addressed to her.'

'That letter arrived last Friday.' Mrs Worthington was away again. 'I told her it was here, but she wasn't interested and said it was just confirming her enrolment. She and Paula are training to be secretaries.'

'Doing the typewriting course,' George corrected her.

'And shorthand, too.' Mrs. Worthington nodded her head. 'I mentioned the letter to her again last night, just before she went out, and she got cross with me, like she does sometimes, and stuffed it in her bag. Just as well she did.'

As she spoke, Fess looked past her to the mantelpiece above the fireplace where there were a number of photographs. He walked around the surprised pair and stood examining the pictures. There were four: an oval, sepia print of a bridal couple, just recognisable as the Worthingtons when young, a smaller one of a different and more recent bride and groom, a studio shot of a young man in army uniform who bore a strong resemblance to George and the final one, another studio portrait of an attractive girl with an engaging smile. She wore a simple cotton dress with roses embroidered on the collar; she was altogether less stylish than the woman in the lane, but it was clearly a younger portrait of her.

Fess turned to find the Worthingtons eying him uncertainly. 'That's all our family,' Mrs. Worthington offered.

'I think we should sit down.' Fess walked to one of the chairs, but the couple was slow to follow.

‘What is it?’ George demanded.

‘Please sit.’ When they had done his bidding, Fess continued. ‘I’m afraid I have some very bad news for you. Early this morning we found a dead woman in The Narrows. Your daughter’s bag was found nearby and …’ He gestured towards the mantelpiece. ‘From my examination of that photograph I believe it is Mary who has been killed.’

‘Are you sure?’

‘It couldn’t be. She wouldn’t be in The Narrows.’

The two of them spoke together, both starting forward. George leaned over to take his wife’s hand. ‘Valerie is right. Mary went to meet Paula at her place in Cardigan Street. Even if she decided to come home rather than stay, she would have come from the opposite direction, not through The Narrows.’

‘That is puzzling. But the first thing we must do is put beyond any doubt that it is Mary who has been killed.’ Fess saw the colour start to come back into Valerie Worthington’s face and her eyes lift. ‘I must repeat, though, that I have no doubt myself. Mr. Worthington, would you be willing to accompany me to the Morgue for formal identification?’ Fess used an official tone; it was usually the best in these circumstances. But he stopped short of mentioning the body: that would be too stark.

‘Of course.’ George looked uncertainly at his wife, who had taken a handkerchief from her pocket and was dabbing at her face as she stared vacantly at the photographs on the mantelpiece.

Suddenly her head dropped and she began to weep soft

tears that built in their intensity until they shook her body and took away her breath. George went to her and awkwardly tried to take her in his arms as she turned toward Fess and said through her sobs, 'You must be wrong. She had so much life, so much to live for. It's a terrible mistake you've made.'

'I wish I could give you hope but I can't,' Fess replied and turned to George Worthington. 'Is there a neighbour? Someone to be with your wife while we are away?'

'Best you sit with Elizabeth,' he said to Valerie. 'Our married daughter lives further up the street,' he explained to Fess.

It took some time to organise their departure, Valerie Worthington now silent and withdrawn. When they reached a small cottage with a variegated pattern of brickwork in the front wall, George rapped on the door and was greeted by the woman Fess had seen in the smaller bridal photograph. After she took in the expressions on the faces of her parents her demeanour changed. 'What is it?' she asked anxiously.

'It's Mary. The police think she may have been murdered.' George spoke in a dull voice. 'I'm going with the constable and we'd like your mum to be with you.'

Elizabeth stepped forward to put her arm around her mother and draw her into the house while the two men stood where they were. 'I think we will be gone for an hour or so,' Fess said and turned, keen to be on his way.

The tram took a long while to arrive — there were few trams early on a Sunday morning. Eventually, the two men sat outside on the dummy as the tram ran down Lygon Street toward the city. Since early boyhood, Fess had been fascinated by trams and learnt all the moves the gripmen made to gain traction when getting under way, or braking for cornering, or coming to a stop. He objected when his mother insisted that he sit in the car with the other women and children and much preferred to travel with his father who, rain or shine, chose the dummy.

They travelled without speaking until Fess asked, 'How long have you been at King and Godfree?'

It took a moment for George to stir. 'It will be forty years in December.'

'You must have been very young when you began.'

'Just left school, and got a job as grocer's assistant, doing all the boring jobs and keeping the place clean. We can't employ someone so young now we have our liquor licence.' A note of pride crept into his voice but was soon extinguished. 'A pity, really.'

'You know, I still remember you as the man who could wrap up groceries better than anyone could. Even now I can see you putting a large sheet of paper on the counter, building the week's groceries into a shape, folding the paper around that shape and tying it with string. That was an art.'

George grinned contentedly, the first time Fess had seen him looking a little relaxed. 'Yeah, I was proud of that. Liked to show off, too.'

'And how long have you lived where you are?'

'About six years.'

'I've known you at King and Godfree's but didn't realise you lived so close. I'm around in Murchison Street.'

'You must know a lot of people.'

'I was just telling one of our constables this morning that he should put more time into knowing the people of Carlton and where they live, yet I don't even know people who live close by.'

'Did she suffer?'

It was a common question and signalled to Fess that George Worthington had accepted his daughter was dead. 'The Government Pathologist will tell us how she died.'

George withdrew into himself again and they travelled in silence until the tram swung into Swanston Street.

'Another few months and we'll have to change trams,' Fess announced. George, drawn from his reverie, gave him a puzzled stare. 'They're working on electrifying some of the lines down Swanston Street, and the Carlton trams will have to terminate at Lonsdale Street. I hope we don't lose them altogether. It's no fun being on the dummy when the wind's blowing the rain onto you, but I still like the feel of them.'

George appeared to have no interest in trams. 'Do you come on all these visits to the Morgue?' he asked

'No, not all. I wanted to come with you, though. You live close to me. I have a daughter of my own. I …' Fess paused awkwardly, unsure what to say next.

'What children do you have?'

'Two boys and a girl. They're all still at school. I see you're the other way round — two daughters and a son.'

'John was so keen to join up, he couldn't wait. He got through Gallipoli and was in France just a month or so before the armistice. That's when they first told us he was missing. It's hard to bear the not knowing and the knowing. Now Mary.'

Fess, looked away and was relieved to find the tram rattling past the Cathedral and across Flinders Street. 'Princes Bridge coming up. This is our stop.'

They left the tram and walked down the sloping avenue beside the Yarra. The air was still and a faint mist hung over the river, merging in the distance with the leaden sky. The oars of an eight broke the stillness of the water as the coach rode his bicycle along the bank, shouting instructions.

They reached the tall iron gates that led to the Coroner's Court and the Morgue buildings, their attempt at a Gothic presence drab and forlorn. After entering the Morgue, Fess introduced himself and their purpose to the uniformed officer who sat behind a small desk in the foyer. He glanced impassively at George and took them along the corridor where they were met by an assistant to the Government Pathologist, a young man in a closely buttoned white coat. Mary lay on a marble slab in the white-walled room with a cotton sheet covering her. The room was chilly and the smell of formaldehyde hung in the air. The assistant led George to the side of the body, with Fess a respectful distance behind. George held his hat in front of him, the brim grasped in both hands, as if he were carrying a wreath. The assistant drew back the sheet to reveal Mary's head and neck. Her eyes were still open, but the grimace that had previously distorted her face was gone. So too was her close-fitting hat, revealing the wave in her short, dark hair. Fess could more clearly see the younger girl in the photograph on the Worthingtons' mantelpiece. Only the bruises on her face and neck spoke of violence.

George looked down on her for a long time, saying nothing. Eventually he turned away and nodded, his hand going to his brow. 'Yes, that's her all right,' he murmured.

Fess held out a hand to steady him but thought better of it. The assistant produced a typed sheet, which he explained to George, and asked him to sign. In the passage outside there were several wooden chairs, and Fess went to sit on one, indicating that George should sit beside him. 'If you don't mind waiting here for a minute, I'll just have a word with the Pathologist.' He didn't wait for an answer but rose and made his way down the corridor to an office where a bearded man in a grey suit sat at his desk, writing. Fess entered and said, 'Senior Constable Jordan, Carlton Police. We've just completed a positive identification of Mary Worthington, the deceased woman brought in earlier this morning.' Dr. Ronaldson nodded his acknowledgement. 'Is there anything you can tell me at this stage?' Fess asked.

'Most likely death by asphyxiation, somewhere between eight last night and two this morning. I'll narrow the time after a full examination. Some signs of a struggle prior to death. The C.I.B. will have my full report on Tuesday.'

Fess walked thoughtfully back down the corridor. George stood up as he approached. 'What did he say?'

'I'm afraid it will be a day or so before the Government Pathologist has completed his examination. At this stage, all he was willing to say was that Mary was killed last night after a struggle.'

George turned away and walked out into the street without glancing at the porter. To Fess' surprise, he continued straight across the road to the river bank and stood looking down into the water, which flowed sluggishly, hardly disturbing the flotsam that had gathered along its edge. When Fess joined him he muttered, 'It's my fault, you know. I gave in too easily.'

'You can't blame yourself.'

'She was such an energetic girl, always into new things, always wanting to be older than her age.'

'They grow up so quickly.' Fess thought of Carmel and glanced at his watch. There was time yet. 'Come, let's sit over here for a bit.' He led George to a metal seat on the path beside the river.

George sank down onto the seat and leaned forward with his hands on his knees. 'She changed when we lost John. He liked playing the older brother and was her hero. She was such a sunny girl, always laughing at something and making you laugh, too. After John, she still laughed a lot but was wilder, rushing into things and then giving them up just as quickly. I hoped she would find a reliable man and settle down, like her sister: there were plenty of hopefuls hanging about. But she wasn't interested.'

He paused to flick something from the corner of his eye. 'Although, I think there might be someone new just in the last few weeks. Typical of her not to tell us much these days.'

'Not many young women confide in their parents, do they? She must have been busy, too, with her job and the course at the College,' Fess said.

'I don't know about that. You heard Valerie this morning. Val always wanted our kids to go further and do more than we were able to do. With Elizabeth settled in the same street and John ...' He paused to rub his chin before continuing. 'She pushed Mary to go to evening courses. I don't think Mary was all that keen on the idea, but she did stick at it, I s'pose. She didn't like me meeting the tram when she came from the College at night and made me stop doing it this year. I'm sure that's why she came up with the idea of staying with Paula. I wasn't keen on that, either.' He stared into the water, with Fess silent beside him. Feeling that George had now regained control of himself, Fess was about to suggest they move on, when George put his hand on his brow and gave a cry that was part deep sigh. Tears began to roll down his face. 'But I shouldn't have given in.'

Fess reached out to put his hand on George's shoulder and held it there while George took a handkerchief from his pocket and wiped his face. 'I told them I didn't like the idea of her staying over at Paula's, but she could get her mother to agree to anything. We really don't know what she got up to with Paula Ryan. Mary convinced Val that

Paula's mother was a highly respectable woman and Val was impressed by her connections with society people, but I had my doubts. There's nothing wrong with running a boarding house, I s'pose. There's not a lot of choice for widows. But that end of Carlton …'

'You're speaking of Mrs. Gloria Ryan?'

'I don't know her first name. You've had dealings with her?' George Worthington wore a dark frown, anxious that his fears would be confirmed.

'It seems a well-run establishment, very popular with some of the Italians.' Fess knew a lot about Gloria Ryan and very little of it would be of comfort to George Worthington. 'We really don't know what happened yet.'

'I s'pose you're right. I'd better get back to Val.'

Together the men returned to Princes Bridge and boarded the tram. When they passed the Cathedral, they could see the congregation beginning to enter and Fess checked his watch again. He had very little time to spare.

4

Fess left George Worthington at the door of his daughter's house and hurried along the street towards the church. The rapid drumming of his boots on the pavement attracted the attention of several strollers, who turned to watch him pass. He entered the gates at the back of Carlton Gardens, from where he could see the tower of the Sacred Heart Church and hear the bells calling the congregation to Mass. The grass was still wet from yesterday's rain, but the sun was now breaking through and one lad was wading in the pond, up to his calves in the dark water as he followed the wavering path of his toy yacht. Stately swans cruised close to the boy, hoping he had brought them something to eat.

Fess cut across the gardens to the side gate, willing the bells to continue. As he crossed the road they ceased their tolling and a line of young girls in white dresses came around the corner of the building. Fess crossed the street quickly and stood on the pavement as the procession, now lengthened by the boys in their navy suits and white sashes, linked with the choristers who awaited them at the entrance to the church. The girls passed before him and there, in the middle of the group, was Carmel, her head down but her eyes seeking his and her lips unable to suppress a smile.

As she reached him, the sun glinted on a gold chain she wore around her neck. It was his mother's necklace, bequeathed to Carmel. To his daughter's disappointment, Bern had insisted that she not wear it until she was older and able to take proper care of the delicate heirloom. Today would mark not only Carmel's first communion, but also her first wearing of the necklace. What would Fess' mother have made of that? Neither she, nor her husband, was a devout churchgoer, but Fess had been sent to the Methodist Sunday School for some years, and his mother made no attempt to hide her dismay that he should marry a Catholic. When they came to join her in Carlton there had been some awkward times, the sleeping arrangements in the small cottage and the Sunday morning fast before Mass being some of the most fraught.

The procession had now disappeared within the church, and Fess followed. He scanned the congregation but, at first, could find no sign of Bernadette and the boys. There they were, well forward and close to the side aisle. Fess tried to walk silently down the aisle but was defeated by the squeak of his boots. He slipped into the pew beside Bernadette and whispered, 'I saw Carmel outside. The necklace looks great.'

Bern gave him her look with the raised eyebrow. 'I'm glad you made it.'

Fess was sufficiently familiar with the Mass that he could easily participate whilst thinking of other things. It wasn't only the necklace that had caught his attention. For the first time he was conscious of the small mounds under the bodice of Carmel's dress. Was this the girl who, wearing her shapeless pyjamas, last night had to be restrained from the pillow fight she was waging with her brothers? And what did his boys, in their suits and slicked-down hair, think of the Mass? From the start, he found it difficult to share many of the beliefs that were so important to Bern but, for her sake, was diligent in performing the rites of the Church with an apparent piety. Later, he did so as an example to his children. What sort of example? Hypocrisy was something he deplored in others and detested in himself.

The girls were now going up to the altar and kneeling to receive the host from the parish priest. Had Mary ever done this? He didn't think the Worthingtons were Catholics. How was George getting on now? Valerie Worthington was likely to be a handful, yet, from what he had seen, the other daughter would be a help. What was Mary really like and how did she come to be in that laneway?

Carmel rose from her knees and stood in plain view with her back to the altar before returning to her pew. Almost from birth she had taken after her father. She had his fair hair with the hint of gingery colouring; she had his light skin and his blue eyes. He knew her hair had darkened but now he realised, with the curls Bern had created, she looked much more like her mother. Her eyes were still blue, but her face had lost much of its infant chubbiness and now formed the pale oval that was so central to Bernadette's beauty.

He still carried with him a clear memory of that sunny day in Bendigo when the distraught young woman in a sky blue dress had run toward him, crying out that she had been robbed. The green eyes in her oval face brimmed with her distress as she told him her bag had been snatched by a thief, who had run off toward the Shamrock Hotel. Fortunately Fess was slightly senior to George Mitchell and was able to order him to pursue the offender, while he remained to calm the victim. Despite his conviction that the thief would be well away by now, Fess assured the young woman that the full force of the law would be brought to bear on tracking down the villain and restoring her possessions to her. He also needed to take down relevant details, and these allowed him to learn that Miss Bernadette Mulrooney lived in Vine Street, Bendigo.

The bag was never found, but Fess had learnt enough to suggest there was a chance he might be able to renew his acquaintance with Miss Mulrooney by attending the Saturday night dance at the Sacred Heart Hall. Unsuccessful the first time, his persistence was rewarded by the sight of her the next time he went to the dance. The tight group of young men and women that surrounded her would, in other circumstances, have discouraged him from a direct approach, but Fess was smitten. He was immediately greeted with a warm smile of recognition and an introduction to the group as that very nice policeman she had told them about. His failure to catch the thief or recover her purse was not mentioned.

After a night roster had prevented his attending the dance for a couple of weeks, he was delighted to find he had been missed and, some weeks later, was invited to Sunday afternoon tea at Bernadette's house. She had never asked about his religion, but he was pretty sure she knew he was not a Catholic. It didn't seem to matter. As soon as he saw the crucifix in the hallway, he knew he had a problem, and his anxiety increased when he entered the parlour to find the formidable Mrs. Mulrooney sitting beneath the Sacred Heart portrait of Jesus. Mr. Mulrooney appeared less daunting, as did her elder brother, and her three younger sisters were obviously rather overawed by the presence of a policeman in their house. The story of the theft was retold before Fess was offered tea and cake.

'I don't recall ever seeing you at the Mass,' Mrs. Mulrooney said.

'No, I don't attend the Cathedral,' he replied cautiously.

'Would I be right in thinking you're not of our faith?'

'I'm not closely involved with any church.' Fess thought this might be a more acceptable reply than a bald assertion of his Protestantism, but the immediate chill that descended on the room made him doubt that. Even Jesus looked saddened by his confession.

Bernadette, apparently oblivious to the change in atmosphere, turned to her father and said, 'Fess thinks we would be better off in Bendigo if we had cable trams.'

'What gives him that idea?' Mr. Mulrooney asked, in

a tone that suggested he was genuinely interested in how Fess could have such a mistaken view.

Fess saw the looks exchanged between the other members of the family and wondered why Bernadette had introduced another matter that appeared likely to put him offside with the Mulrooney household. He began tentatively to explain his long-held fascination with cable trams and to express his admiration for the skill of the gripmen who drove them. Mr. Mulrooney greeted his account with surprising warmth and then identified himself as a tram driver with the Electric Supply Company in Bendigo. He acknowledged Fess as one of those rare gentlemen who understood the charm of driving a tram, and pressed him to go with him one day, so that he could demonstrate the superiority of electric traction.

This was the first of many times Fess would appreciate Bern's understanding of what was important to people and her subtle skill in bringing them together. Thanks to her, he gained her father as a friend and supporter, but much more time and effort was required to win the approval of her mother. It was only when she saw how happy he made her daughter and he began the process of joining the Catholic Church that she was willing to contemplate him as a possible son-in-law. What upset his own mother most was that her disapproval held so little sway with him.

When the service was over, the children, now looking much more confident and relieved, proceeded from the church. As Bernadette and Fess watched the group pose for photographs in front of the grotto, she said to him, 'I'm involved with serving the Communion Breakfast to the children in the Parish Hall. Will you take the boys home? I've left a bit of a spread for them and for you.' Fess knew that this was not the way Bern wanted to celebrate her daughter's first communion. Other families would be gathering with grandparents, uncles, aunts and cousins for a slap-up lunch. Bernadette's mother had come to tolerate him as son-in-law, but her sisters had never fully accepted him, and all the family considered he had betrayed Bernadette by dragging her off to the wretched place they believed Carlton to be. There were the occasional visits, but they were rare and awkward.

'I promised them a kick in the park, too. That's going to be difficult now. I have to be back at the Station by two o'clock.'

'But today's your day off.'

'It was until the murder. I have to interview someone we have in the cells.'

'So you've caught the murderer?'

'No. He didn't do it, but he might be able to help us.'

'Isn't this up to the C.I.B.?'

'Yeah. There's a detective from Russell Street leading the investigation, but he's asked me to help with my local knowledge.'

Bern again gave him the raised eyebrow. 'Did he ask or did you insist on being involved?'

'He asked for some help,' Fess replied in an aggrieved tone, telling the truth and masking it in the one sentence.

The boys appeared happy to leave the church as soon as possible, attracted by the promise of the spread at home, but not forgetting the promise of a kick in the park. 'Dad, do you reckon you can show me the drop kick again?' Michael asked. 'Punts are easy, but I can't get the hang of the drop and my stab passes are useless.'

'You're useless you mean,' Kevin scoffed, being older and far more of an athlete than his brother.

'I can remember a time when you always kicked the ground and not the ball with your drop kicks,' Fess said. 'They're not easy and Mick was doing well last time we had a kick.' Fess wondered whether he was going too far in trying to spare his son from the disappointment of failure. His father had been the opposite, continually challenging him with tests of strength or courage, and the sting of failure had made him determined to succeed. When he looked back, he thought it had done him no harm, but it wasn't what he wanted for his children. 'I'm afraid the kick may have to wait. I have to be at the Station this afternoon.'

This time the brothers were in agreement.

'But Dad, you promised.'

'You said.'

'Yeah, I know. But you know I have a duty that sometimes means you have to wait.'

'Duty! That's all you coppers think about,' scoffed Kevin. 'What about us?'

Fess wondered what his boys would swear never to do to

their children. Probably never to put their job before their family. 'Look, I'll make it up to you. Next time I have a Sunday off we'll go on a picnic. We could go to St. Kilda.'

'Not Saint Kilda again. Not in the winter,' Michael complained, unaware that Fess heard the difference in their pronunciation as another gap between them.

'Yeah, it's boring,' Kevin agreed. 'Why can't we ever do something that's fun? Something exciting.'

Fess could not understand why his children didn't share his delight in the seaside. Admittedly his memories were of holidays, the adventure of taking the steam train to Seaford or Edithvale in the summer, when his father managed to get some time off. He loved the clean smell of the sand and the sea, the water on his skin and the sunsets across the bay. He was even content to sit quietly and watch his father demonstrate his prowess as a swimmer or a fisherman. Best of all though, was the building of elaborate sand castles with deep passages inside and thick walls surrounding them. His mother claimed it was his enjoyment of those castles that led him to take up a job as a builder's labourer when he left school. The truth was there really was no choice. 'Well, how about we go out to Kew. There are some good spots on the river. We can light a fire and cook some snags.'

'Yeah, that'd be ace,' Michael said.

Kevin remained surly. 'At least that's better than Saint Kilda.'

When Fess arrived at the Station a little before two, the Constable on Duty met him with an admiring smile. 'You really have the knack, Senior.'

'What are you talking about, Tim?'

'Ferret Roberts. When Constable McKenzie and one of the others went around to Ma Cutmore's, like you suggested, they found his swag in a hole under the dunny floor. Ferret hadn't even put the bricks back properly. I reckon finding that body shook him up good and proper. Either that or he's losing it. You should've heard him when they stuck him in with Clarry Garton.'

'Has Clarry come around yet?'

'Yeah, a while ago. Not that he's ever wide awake.'

'And what about Senior Detective Thomas?'

'Yeah, he's here, all bright-eyed and bushy-tailed.' The reply came, not from the Duty Constable, but from Thomas himself, who had just entered the Station. 'All ready to get our confession.' He removed the gabardine coat and bowler hat he had been wearing earlier to reveal a grey, pinstriped, three-piece suit above a white shirt and paisley tie. The tie was too loosely knotted, allowing the collar stud behind it to show. Were it not for this oversight and the somewhat crumpled appearance of his suit, Thomas would not have been out of place in any of the Sunday afternoon tea parties, soon to take place in the fashionable houses of Kew and Toorak. It was the first time Fess had seen him in a clear light without his hat and coat. He was not tall but strongly built with a round face and deep brown eyes. His dark hair was parted in the centre. The restlessness that Fess had sensed earlier was contained, but barely so, reminding him of a kettle coming to the boil.

'Let's have him in the back room thanks, Constable,' Fess said and walked to the rear of the building where he entered a small room with a stained wooden table, surrounded by four straight-backed chairs. He went immediately to the single window, which he opened as wide as the frame would allow.

'A bit parky in here,' Jim complained as he pulled one of the chairs to the side of the room and deposited his hat and coat. 'You're not one of those fresh air types, are you?'

'Wait and see,' Fess replied, taking a seat on the side of the table furthest from the door and gesturing for Thomas to join him.

Clarry Garton's aroma arrived in the room slightly ahead of him. Fess knew from past experience that it never altered: a stench that reminded him of the chewed remains he had once found beside a creek near Bendigo. Clarry subsided onto the chair, with his arms on the table and his scrawny head down. The grimy stiffness of his brown overcoat surrounded him like the shell of a crab, and his navy balaclava sat awry on his head. Jim pushed his chair back, retreating towards the side wall of the room but making sure he remained the officer in charge of the interview. 'Now, Clarry. That's your name?' He noted the nod from Fess. 'We know you stole this woman's bag. Wouldn't she let go? Was that why you had to strangle her?'

'What woman's that?' Clarry opened his mouth for the first time, showing his rotting gums. 'I seen no woman.'

'The woman you murdered. The woman in the alley.'

'Did ya say a bag?' Clarry put his head back as though searching for a distant memory.

Fess placed the slim bag on the table in front of Clarry.

'There y'are. You've found it already.' Clarry leaned forward with a relieved grin.

'Yeah, in the hovel you doss down in,' Jim said, retreating a little further.

Clarry shook his head, wincing as he did so. 'I seen no body.'

Jim thumped his fist on the table, making Clarry jump. 'Stop this malarkey. We know you did her in.' He rose angrily and stood over Clarry, who had slumped so that his head now lay close to the table top. 'Just admit it. It'll be the worse for you if y'don't.'

Clarry began to cry, huge sobs shaking his body, while the tears made rivulets in the dirt of his face. Jim sneered derisively, shook his head in frustration and sat down again.

Fess, speaking in a soft voice, said, "Try to pull yourself together, Clarry. We need you to tell us what you can remember from last night. Did you hear or see anything from your shack?'

Clarry, still shaking, lifted his head from the table and wiped a filthy sleeve across his eyes, sniffing as he did so. 'That's right. I weren't there long. I'd been down to Flanagan's.' He risked a quick glance at Jim, who regarded him stolidly. 'It's a pub in Brunswick Street. Jerry's an old digger. He gives me a feed some nights.'

'What did you hear?' Jim's tone was still strong, but Fess noticed it didn't have the force of his earlier outburst.

'That's it. I dunno. I just got into The Narrows and I heard it. Some voices. A laugh, a loud one and then some other sounds. P'raps a bloke and a sheila smoochin'. Then some cries, muffled like. Hard t'tell. There it was.'

'What?'

Clarry shrivelled up and whined at Jim, 'I'm trying to tell ya. The bag. Took it to me shack and found a few quid in it. Y'know what they say.' He paused to give a grin that on another face at another time might have been engaging. 'Finders keepers.'

'A likely story.' Jim's attack was now perfunctory. Perhaps he too, now had trouble imagining how this shell of a man could pose any threat to a healthy young woman.

'Boss?' Clarry appealed directly to Fess. 'Y'know I'm no saint, but I gives it straight.'

Fess nodded encouragingly. 'When was this, Clarry?'

'Sorry. It's a bit of a blur. I haven't been well.'

Jim jumped to his feet and shouted. 'He's useless. Take him out, and let's get some clean air in here.' Reacting to the shout, perhaps expecting it, the constable immediately appeared in the doorway, pulled Clarry to his feet and dragged him from the room. 'What a gazob,' Jim said. 'I know I shouldn't have lost it, but those types disgust me. How can a coot let himself get to that state? How can he live like that?'

'He wasn't always like that,' Fess replied. 'When I worked on building sites here, before I joined the Force, Clarry was a carpenter. A good one, too. He left a wife and four kids to join up for the war and, when he came back, they said he had shell shock. He couldn't hold a job and, bit by bit, his family gave up on him. You couldn't blame them. Now he survives on what some of his old army mates can find for him and what he can scrounge. But you said it. How can he go on living like that? I reckon it takes a kind of courage.' When the war began Fess was not one of those who rushed to join up but did feel it was his duty to join the recruitment queue. His sergeant in Bendigo made it clear he needed him to stay in his post, but what decided him was the look in Bern's eyes when he told her of his thoughts. That and the news she was pregnant again. Clarry always made him feel guilty.

Jim took his pipe and a pouch of Maintop tobacco from his pocket and began stuffing the pipe. 'Doesn't change the fact that Garton was a waste of our time.'

'Not entirely. I reckon we can say the murderer wasn't out to rob her. Leastways, not her bag.' Fess fingered his beard. 'We have another bloke in the cells that might be able to help.' Jim paused in his effort to light his pipe and looked questioningly at him. 'He lives just off that lane and reported finding the body. He's a well-known thief, and it seemed to me that he would most likely be in the lane only if he were returning from a job. Some of my men found a swag of two silver candlesticks that had been reported stolen when they searched his place this morning.'

Jim puffed contentedly on his pipe. 'On her way home, she bumps into him with his loot and he panics, drags her into the lane and bumps her off. Then he gets smart and decides to report finding her as a blind. Very neat.'

'It doesn't explain what her bag was doing at the other end of the lane, but maybe he has more to tell us.'

Jim used Clarry's wheedling tone to ask, 'Is he another of your stinking friends, Boss?'

'I've known Ferret Roberts for a fair while. One of the old school of breakers, who seems to be slipping these days. We've picked him up a couple of times lately. I don't see him as a murderer, but he usually knows more than he's willing to say.'

'You mean I'll need to lean on him if we're to get anything from him?'

'That's one way.' Fess thought Thomas had a bit to learn about getting the Ferrets of this world to open up. 'Let's see if he has said anything yet.' Fess went to the door of the room and called, 'Mac, can you spare a minute?'

When Constable McKenzie entered, Fess asked, 'Did Ferret say anything when you brought him in?'

'Just the usual. He'd never seen the candlesticks before and we must have hidden the swag where it was to fit him up.'

'Senior Detective Thomas would like to speak with him. Would you have him brought in, please?'

Entering the room, Ferret sniffed the air, and for a moment Fess thought he was indulging in self-parody, something he had never seen from him before. 'You've had Clarry Garton in here,' Ferret said.

'And now we have you, Ferret.' Jim pointed with his pipe. 'Sit here at the table where I can get a good look at you.' After he was seated, Jim remained standing and Fess pulled his chair away from the table to sit at one side. 'Very smart of you to report that body in the alley.' He paused, but Ferret's only response was to regard his questioner with stealthy interest. 'It won't work, though.' He emphasised his words by stabbing the air with his pipe. 'We know you were caught on your way back from that burglary by the girl you murdered. You were seen.'

'I did no job and I did no murder. You detective types are all the same: ready to fit up the first bloke y'can find. Sure I was in the lane. 'ow else would I've found the poor girl? But she was cold, done in long before I got to 'er. You can parade those flamin' wasters that'll say anythin' for a quid or two, but I've got friends who'll back me.'

Jim's voice rose so that again he began to shout. 'And who are these friends that will perjure themselves for you?'

'D'ya think I'd tell ya? You'd just get at 'em, too. Try puttin' me in Court and see 'ow far it gets ya.'

'We might just do that.'

Fess leaned forward. 'Ferret, you know we've got you cold on the burglary. There might be a way you can help yourself there, though.' Both of the men turned from confronting one another to stare at Fess. 'There's no chance you'll get off, but it's the sentence I'm thinking about. You were in only last May and, as you know, the

Court takes a dim view of repeat offenders. You could be up for quite a stretch. But if I could say how you've helped us in this murder investigation, it might go better for you.' Fess noted the light that had come into Ferret's eyes as he continued to switch his gaze between the two policemen. 'So what else can you tell us? Did you see anyone there?'

'If I was t'tell ya I saw somethin' I'd need more than kind words, Boss: I'd need some guarantees.'

'So what did you see?' Thomas demanded.

Ferret ignored him and continued to look enquiringly at Fess, who said, 'What is it you want?'

'First, you'll speak for me in Court and, second, that Spring'eel Jack over 'ere won't try to stitch me up by throwin' some money around.'

"You know about guarantees. They make promises in big type and take them away in the fine print. I'll listen to what you have to tell us and, depending on the results, will tell the Court how helpful you have been. The more you're able to help us, the more likely Senior Detective Thomas' suspicions may shift. It's the best chance you've got on both scores.'

'Maybe I know somethin'. But fellers can git nasty if they think ya dobbed 'em in.'

'Nobody need know,' Thomas said. 'Not unless we need you as witness, and then you'd be protected.'

Ferret leaned back and looked at the ceiling. Fess had the impression he was weighing his options, calculating the risks. Eventually he said, 'I ain't sayin' 'e did it. All

I'm sayin' is that 'e was lurkin' about when I left t'join me mates.'

'Who was lurking about, Ferret?' Thomas asked.

He hesitated before replying, 'Basher. Basher O'Shea.'

Jim turned to Fess. 'Do you know him?'

Fess nodded. 'Basher was in The Narrows?'

'Nah. I was in Barkly Street. Basher was there, too. That's all I'm sayin'.'

5

After Ferret had been taken back to the cells, Jim looked quizzically at Fess and asked, 'Who's this Basher O'Shea?'

'Much of the time he's an amiable, rather slow-witted cove. Used to be a boxer. Trouble is he can fly off the handle for no reason at all. They said he could have been a champion if he hadn't so often done his block. He'd stop boxing and start throwing a barrage of haymakers. Some of the lesser lights were wiped out by the avalanche, but the top fighters easily stayed out of trouble and then picked him off. It all came to an end one night when the red mist descended over him: he ignored the bell for the end of the round and forgot all about the Marquis of Queensbury rules. He never fought again and neither did his opponent: O'Shea banned for life and the other man unable to walk upright. Basher now works as a bodyguard, but his services often go beyond guarding to intimidating, coercing or actually harming those his clients think might be a threat. He's very familiar with the idea of grievous bodily harm. Many's the time he has been charged with g.b.h. or the like, but it's funny how the witnesses fade away when it comes to Court.

'When the mood takes him, women have more to fear

than his fists and his boots. Once we had him up for bashing and raping a well-known prostitute, but the victim arrived in Court very drunk and too frightened to offer any evidence, so the judge had no choice but to direct the jury to acquit him.' Fess frowned and shook his head. 'I'm sure Basher is well capable of murdering Mary Worthington, but I would expect him to have knocked her around far more than she appeared to have been.'

'You really have some choice types here in Carlton. I was starting to lose heart with that freak show you put on for me but I reckon we're almost home. I can taste it. Let's pick up this Basher monster and grill him.'

'Getting hold of Basher won't be all that easy, either. First, we'll probably have trouble finding him. He doesn't stay in the same lodging for long before falling out with the other lodgers and being chucked out. Secondly, it will need more than you and me to bring him in. He seldom comes quietly.'

'Well, you'd better start looking for him — get hold of a few of your beefy constables. The one you had chasing Clarry Garton last night looked a strong lad. Let me know when you're ready to go.' He began to put on his coat. 'That's about enough for a Sunday afternoon.'

'I'll do all of that. Meanwhile, you don't fancy a stroll in the fresh air?'

'After the air in here, that's just what I need. But there's no fresh air in Carlton. Brighton is the place for fresh air.'

'You have friends in Brighton?'

The note of surprise in Fess' tone made Thomas frown.

'My mother lives in Brighton. In one of the big houses near the beach.' Something gave him pause, and he added, 'She's the live-in cook. She'll have to give it up soon, though. Like your mate Ferret, she's getting past it. Just as well I'm still single.'

Fess thought of his return to Carlton, living with his mother before she died. It hadn't been easy for Bern, but she hadn't complained. It was only after his mother's death that she started her campaign to leave Carlton. 'When I spoke with the Worthingtons, they told me that Mary was going to the pictures last night with her friend, Paula Ryan, and intended to stay at her place. Paula's mother Gloria Ryan runs a boarding house in Cardigan Street and I thought we should speak to them. They might be able to explain how Mary ended up in The Narrows.'

'Do we need that? Get Basher and it's all over.'

'It's on the way back to Russell Street. We shouldn't need long.'

'Well, all right. But look lively. Get your men onto finding Basher and we'll go.'

Fess briefed McKenzie on the need to search for Basher and the two men left the Station. Outside the sun was stronger than in the morning and, despite the chill breeze, a crowd had gathered to listen to the Salvation Army Band. Among the crowd were some of the district's shopkeepers, tradesmen and factory workers, decked out in their Sunday best, together with their families. But the largest group wore the tattered clothes of the poor — old people, the unemployed and street urchins. They too had come for the entertainment, but more important for them was the free afternoon tea in the hall after the performance. Thomas did not hesitate but shouldered his way through the throng, Fess following in his wake. When they were clear Fess said, 'Not keen on brass bands?'

'Don't like being hemmed in by the citizens of Carlton. I've already told you I've had enough of them for one day. I'd heard your father was ferocious in his hatred of crime and criminals. You seem to like the wasters and crooks I've seen you with.'

'I do like the people who live here, even some of the crooks. I've locked up Ferret quite a few times, but he was born to thieving and sees it as his job, which he does to the best of his ability. He's not violent with anyone and, in a way, I see him as an honest man. The people I hate are the cowards that roam in gangs, always looking to hurt people, so long as the odds are stacked in their favour. Worse still, the men in their posh houses who stay in the shadows, raking in the profits from the rackets — the robberies, prostitution and drug deals — but letting others do the dirty work.'

Thomas stretched his arm to pat Fess on the shoulder. 'So calm, cool Senior Constable Jordan does erupt sometimes. Fat chance you have of nailing the silvertails, though. Best to stick to getting the dregs off the street.'

'You think so? Getting rid of one of those rich barons would do more than a hundred arrests of the dregs they use to make their money.'

They reached King and Godfree's grocery store on the

corner and turned to walk past the shops in Lygon Street. The first was a haberdashery and dressmaker's, run by the Misses Fortescue. The shop was shut, but the ladies would be with their Pomeranian dogs in the rooms behind the shop, serving tea in bone china cups to the circle of maiden ladies who gathered there each Sunday afternoon. Fess thought it would have been good to have joined them — show Jim the genteel side of Carlton. Next was a lolly shop, followed by Levy's pharmacy and a bookshop before they reached the butcher's. Fess hadn't checked whether McKenzie had informed Pinchas Goldstein of the retrieval of his candlesticks. If the shop had been open he might have called in, but he didn't want to delay Thomas any more than he had already. They passed the State Savings Bank, Mansons' Bakery and a number of other businesses before reaching the striped poles that supported the verandah of Sam Cohen's barber shop. Not much went on in Carlton that Sam didn't know about, and right now he would be with some of his cronies, probably gossiping about the murder, news of which would have started to spread. There were few people on the footpath and the road traffic was slight, a few cars, more carts and cyclists, and an occasional tram. 'You know this Paula Ryan?' Jim suddenly asked.

'Met her once. I do know her mother, though. I should tell you the story of Gloria Ryan. Now there's a woman.' He laughed, and it was not clear whether the admiration in Fess' voice was real or feigned.

'You may as well. It'll help pass the time on this walk you've forced me into.'

‘Gloria is still quite a handsome woman, but they say she was once a stunner. She came to Carlton when she married Bert Ryan, a timber merchant. The business did very well, but the family did not. They had four or five children, but Paula was the only one to survive early childhood. Perhaps it was a way of dealing with their losses or perhaps they would have done it anyway, but Tom and Gloria became known for their lavish life style. They bought one of the few remaining grand houses in Carlton: most of them had already been converted to boarding and lodging houses.

‘The parties at the house became the talk of the district and even beyond, making the social pages of *The Herald* and *The Sun*. As I’ve told you, Gloria was a looker, but her greatest attraction was that she happily confessed to being ignorant about everything — and feather-brained as well. That’s what she said. People came to think of Gloria as a simple but beautiful woman, not nearly as smart as them, and were charmed by her. Tom’s attraction was entirely different: he could drink anyone under the table. As his talent became well known, many blokes, particularly from the fast set, tried to best him. No one ever did.

‘The Ryans found their way onto the social circuit and started being invited to parties by the toffs. There weren’t many balls or regattas or race meetings where they wouldn’t be found. And people started coming to their parties from across the river. I think they got a thrill out of slumming it. Suddenly, one day, Tom was killed, not by the grog, like people expected, but by a runaway horse.

'Gloria said she didn't have the brains or the know-how to run the timber yard, and put it up for sale. A whole lot of shifty coves moved in, thinking they could put it over her and get a good business for a song. She said she didn't know how to decide and, as she dithered, the price she was offered began to climb. Eventually, she did sell and the codger that won the sale soon found he'd bought a pup. Probably their social life had caused them to neglect the business. Certainly it was in trouble: they'd been living well beyond their means and were broke. The buyer claimed he'd been swindled but, as Gloria had told all and sundry that she knew nothing about the business, he had a job blaming her. She sold the grand house as well, making only enough to pay off the debts and buy part of a broken-down two-storey terrace in Cardigan Street.

'Gloria is not one to stay down for long. She opened a boarding house in the terrace and soon was beginning to prosper, despite her claimed feather-headedness. She was joined by her maiden sister, who was able to provide very good meals, something rare in a boarding house cook, and together they offered a house that was a cut above most of the shoddy dumps in the area. Gloria had Paula serve at table, which pleased the men who made up most of her boarders. As her custom increased, she put on other attractive young women to help out.

'What I've told you so far I learned from others, but now I come to my first meeting with Gloria. She was doing so well she needed to rent rooms in the next-door terrace. She fell out with the owner, who reported her for running a brothel. We couldn't find any evidence; the young women Gloria employed, or at least the ones we were able to interview, were a cut above the women who work the streets in that area. Most of them were shop or factory girls, who earned some pin money with Gloria. She made an offer for the place next door, but the owner didn't want to sell. Again he complained to us, this time that he was being threatened, and feared for his safety. It wasn't Gloria that he feared; it was the man she called her security man, none other than Basher O'Shea. When I heard he was around Gloria's establishment I was more concerned for her girls. I said this to Gloria, but she just batted her innocent blue eyes at me and said, "But what could I do?" She claimed people from the house next-door had made crude advances to her girls and she needed Basher to protect them. She also said that Basher was a gentleman who did a good job. She admitted he could be a scary sight but said the man next-door had nothing to fear as long as his people behaved themselves. She said all this with such an innocent air that I could almost have believed her. As we found no direct evidence of threatening behaviour, we let the matter drop and, soon afterwards, Gloria expanded her ownership to include the place next-door. She then found her girls no longer needed Basher's protection.

'More recently, I've twice been asked to accompany detectives on a raid of her premises. The first was triggered by a report that some of Gloria's boarders were Italian anarchists who were a threat. It's true she has a lot of Italian migrants as boarders and that some of them have come to Australia to escape fascism in Italy. The reason they prefer Gloria's place has nothing to do with anarchism and everything to do with her ability to understand and deliver what Italians want. The pretty girls are part of that, but only part. First of all, she discovered that one of her boarders was a former chef from a top hotel in Milan. She managed, somehow, to edge out her loyal, long-serving sister and install this Italian chef. Apart from his cooking, he showed her how to make coffee in the Italian style and she now has a very well-patronised cafe as part of her house. The detectives found no revolutionaries when we raided. The higher-ups have told me to keep an eye on them, which I do, but they seem pretty harmless to me.

'The second raid involved detectives from the Licensing Branch.

They believed Gloria was selling liquor without a licence. If she was, she had early warning of the raid, because we found nothing except some of her residents drinking wine they had brought to the house for their own consumption — at least that's what they said and we had no evidence otherwise. Gloria was her usual picture of innocence, telling the detectives how deeply disappointed she was that they should suspect her. I haven't been there for a while. A pity, really.'

Thomas gave him a crooked grin. 'As you say, a colourful lady.'

They entered Argyle Square, skirting the bowling club which was deserted, it being a Sunday afternoon, and were heading toward a group of men gathered in the far corner of the square until Fess changed direction and made for the street that ran along the side of the square. 'What are those blokes up to?' Jim asked suspiciously.

'I told you there are a lot of Italians here. They're playing bocce.'

'Boccy?'

'No bocce. It's like bowls except they play it with heavy metal balls. And they don't need a mown strip, just somewhere fairly flat.' There was a shout from within the group and others joined in as several of the players did a celebratory jig. 'They can get pretty excited about it.'

'Italians get excited about anything and everything.'

'Best we leave them to it. They get upset if we poke in where we're not needed.'

They continued beside the square until they reached the corner. 'It's just along here,' Fess said. A few minutes later they stood across from a cream-painted brick building of two storeys, divided into four sections. Wrought iron decorated the upstairs balcony and the iron roof of the verandah at ground level. A central panel rising above the roof line was inscribed with the words 'George's Terrace'. 'Gloria has the three on the left. I s'pose it won't be long until she wants to add the other. I wonder who owns it.'

'Let's get on and interview this lady you're so charmed by.'

Fess knocked on the green wooden door and entered without waiting. The wall between the two front rooms had been removed to form a large open area, filled with an array of tables and chairs, many of which were occupied by men playing cards, drinking coffee or merely chatting as they smoked their cigarettes. Immediately they entered, the buzz of conversation died. A young woman in a simple black dress with a white apron came through one of the doorways at the back of the room. As soon as she saw them, she smiled and walked towards them, the smile acquiring a questioning quality as she came close. Before she could speak, Fess said, 'Good afternoon. Senior Detective Thomas and Senior Constable Jordan to see Mrs. Ryan. Is she in?'

'Just a minute,' the girl replied and went back through the door by which she had entered. As she did so, a group of four men at the far end of the room stood up hurriedly and left through another door. While Fess and Jim stood waiting, the buzz of conversation gradually restarted. Fess noticed a mural had been added to the back wall. It showed a canal scene, probably Venice, he thought. Gracious buildings lined the water and boatmen poled their narrow craft under a stone bridge. Gloria must have gained a homesick artist among her boarders.

Eventually a woman, wearing a calf-length afternoon dress of mauve silk, entered the room. The style of the dress would have placed it in the height of fashion some years ago and Fess wondered whether she always dressed like this on a Sunday afternoon or had put it on to greet them. She was quite short, her body now thickening, but she retained the smooth skin, high cheekbones and full lips that, in her younger days, would have made her the looker he had described. Her straight hair had been blonde but now was silver. She wore it longer than most women did, almost to her shoulders, but it suited her. She smiled at Fess with wide blue eyes, displaying teeth that were so even and white as to cast doubt they were her own.

'Senior Constable Jordan,' she cooed. 'How are you? It's been quite a while since I've seen you, I'm happy to say.' She tilted her head at him and added, 'That doesn't sound very nice, does it? But you know what I mean.'

'Mrs. Ryan, this is Senior Detective Thomas from the C.I.B.'

'Oh dear, what is it this time? At least you've arrived with more politeness than those other ones, rushing in and upsetting my boarders.'

'Is there somewhere we could have a chat? Somewhere less public?' Jim said, glancing around the room.

Gloria gave him an impish smile. 'We're full up right now, and I'm sure you wouldn't be comfortable in my boudoir. Perhaps we could sit in our little garden.' She led the two men along a passage, past the stairs and the kitchen entry to a small door, which she opened. They stepped down onto a covered verandah beside a small area paved with bricks and lined with potted ferns and shrubs. The yard was overshadowed by the surrounding buildings and the air was damp. 'There are some chairs under there,' she said, pointing to a tarpaulin-covered bulk in one corner. Fess removed the cover and found four wooden, slatted chairs, painted in a rusty colour and stacked in pairs, which he disentangled and placed in a rough circle on the bricks. 'Thank you, sir,' she said, nodding courteously, as though following the etiquette of the drawing room, before sinking onto one of the chairs. 'We like to sit here on hot, summer days. It is so refreshing.'

Jim took the chair nearest her and said, 'Let me get straight to the point, Mrs. Ryan. We are enquiring about Miss Mary Worthington and think you and your daughter may be able to help us.'

Gloria frowned and pursed her lips. 'I don't think I can help you, Detective. I don't have a boarder of that name.'

'She's not a boarder. She's a friend of your daughter.'

Gloria continued to look puzzled but suddenly smiled. 'You mean Molly. Silly me, I'm so used to calling her Molly that I didn't think.' Again her face clouded and she asked anxiously, 'Is she in trouble with the police?'

Surprised by her tone, Jim said, 'Is that what you expected?'

'No. It was just…' Gloria paused as if struck by another thought. 'She hasn't been hurt?' This time her tone carried apprehension.

'I'm afraid she was found dead early this morning.'

'Oh, no,' Gloria gasped and sank back onto her chair. She stared at her feet and seemed to be talking to herself. 'I warned her. But not this.'

'What do you mean?' Jim demanded.

Gloria looked at him as if only just recognising he was there. She went to reply but then stopped, reconsidering. 'I tell all my girls to be careful. Carlton can be such a dangerous place after dark. Those lanes. The gangs.' She paused to swing her gaze to Fess and added, 'Despite all the good work you and your men do, Senior Constable Jordan.'

'Mary was one of your girls?' Fess asked.

Gloria gave him the same puzzled stare she had previously given Jim. 'One of my girls?' she repeated. 'She was a friend of Paula's.' Suddenly she struggled to her feet. 'I must go and tell Paula. She'll be distraught.'

'Before you go …' Gloria, oblivious to Jim's words, hurried through the door, back into the house. He turned to Fess and said, 'So what do you make of that so far?'

'We really need to know how Mary fitted in here. Gloria seemed to be holding back on that.'

'Maybe this Paula will be more forthcoming. Although I doubt it. I imagine her mother is wording her up right now.'

Fess leaned back, looking into the foliage of one of the shrubs. 'I got the impression that Gloria thought Mary was in trouble and was not totally surprised we had come. She didn't expect her to be dead, though. I don't think she was talking about the dangers of Carlton's lanes when she warned her, either. There was something else.'

Jim took out his pipe and, after the usual preliminaries, succeeded in lighting it and sat puffing it contemplatively. 'Of course, none of this matters once we pick up this bugger O'Shea and get him to confess.'

Gloria returned with a young woman, clearly recognisable as her daughter. If Gloria had dressed for their meeting, Paula had not. She wore a tight red jumper, the pilling of the wool suggesting it had been washed many times, and a crumpled green skirt that just covered her knees. Her bare legs disappeared into fluffy pink slippers. She also wore a sullen expression that, Fess decided, would never have appeared on her mother's face.

'This is my daughter, Paula,' Gloria announced as she returned to her seat and gestured for Paula to sit beside her.

'Senior Detective Thomas,' Jim responded. 'You may already know Senior Constable Jordan.'

Paula blinked at them but said nothing, her face still gloomy. 'It's been a shock for us both,' Gloria said, although she seemed to have recovered during her time away from them. 'You said you thought Paula and I might be able to help you, but I can't see how. Have you arrested the murderer?'

'We are well advanced with our enquiries,' Jim replied.

'So you don't know who did it?'

Not for the first time, Fess noticed how Gloria could show perceptiveness out of character for a woolly-headed woman. 'We understand Mary was going to the pictures with you last night, Paula,' he said.

Before she could reply, her mother intervened. 'Who told you that?'

'Her parents.'

'Oh, of course.' Gloria appeared to wipe away a tear. 'I must call on them. The poor, poor dears. Do you know when the funeral will be held?'

'Paula?' Jim demanded, stirred into a more aggressive stance by his impatience with Gloria.

'I went to the flicks by myself. I'd rather go dancin' on

a Saturday night but Molly had other things to do. Still I saw a good show.' Paula brightened for the first time. 'I saw *The Arab* at the Capitol. That Raymond Navarro is dishy.'

'What were these "other things"?'

'Molly and Paula were such good friends,' Gloria interjected blithely. They both looked so lovely, going off to a dance. Brought back so many happy memories for me. I loved having her in the house. I told her there was always a bed for her here if she wanted one, no matter what.'

Jim glowered at her. 'I repeat: what was she planning to do last night?'

'She didn't say,' Paula replied dourly, looking at her mother. 'When she didn't come back later, I thought she must have gone home to sleep.'

'But she was here earlier in the day?'

'Yeah. I don't know when she left, though.' Paula frowned at her mother. 'Mum had me flat out servin'.'

Back in the street outside George's Terrace, Jim scowled at Fess.

'Thanks for bringing me here. A good way to waste a Sunday afternoon.'

'I'm sorry you thought so.'

'I wouldn't trust either of those women. It wouldn't surprise me if Paula and Molly had fallen out over something. Despite her mother's protestations, she didn't seem too distraught over her dear friend's death.'

'You may be right,' Fess agreed. 'There was quite a bit they didn't say. I'm sure "Molly" isn't a name she used at home. Perhaps she reserved it for her time down here. The further we go, the less I think Mary's parents really knew about her. It's a warning for all fathers.'

'Not my problem. At least as far as I know.' Jim grinned and turned to face the city. 'I'm going to sign off now. I have to be in Court in the morning but I'll be back by the afternoon. Make sure you get Basher. Until we nab him, there's not much we can do.'

Fess nodded his farewell and began to retrace his steps toward Argyle Square. This time he did not avoid the group of Italians, who were still engrossed in their bocce. When he approached, though, some murmurs went through the group and they turned to scowl at him. Fess never took his eyes from one of them, a man who was taller than most, with a strong frame and curly dark hair that fell untidily around his handsome face, the overall impression being that of a matinee idol. When he was about five paces away, Fess stopped and called out. 'Hey, you. What's your name?' He paused but received no reply. 'Camilleri. That's right. Come over here, Camilleri. I want to talk with you.'

The man shrugged languidly and walked over, his face puzzled. 'What you want?' he asked.

'Come with me.' As the others continued to watch them, Fess led the man away from the group and did not pause until they reached a bushy tree some fifty yards away. He turned so that his back was to the group, gave an apologetic smile and said in a much more kindly voice, 'Sorry about piling on the aggro. I didn't think it would do either of us much good if they saw we were mates.'

'Ah, that is it.'

The frown left Camilleri's face and Fess spoke quickly. 'Don't look too relaxed, Gino. Why did you leave Gloria's place when we arrived?'

'I see you come with Detective after anarchists again. I tell you they are no threat. Only few, and they sit in Matteotic Club, talking big and doing nothing. You know this. I tell you.'

'We weren't after anarchists. But who were those men with you? New, aren't they?'

'They come from my village. They work the terrazzo good. I need more workers.'

'Business going well then?'

Despite Fess' warning, Gino could not keep the smile from his face. 'The banks in the city, even Myer's, they all want my floors. I do very good.'

'That's great. I'm very pleased for you. You haven't moved on from Gloria's and got a place of your own?'

'Maybe one day. Not yet. Food is good. Bed is good. Coffee is good. Why move?'

'And the girls?'

Gino didn't answer immediately, but his tongue peeped from between his lips and he raised an ironic eyebrow. 'You are married, Senior?'

'Gino, do you know a young woman by the name of Molly, who comes to the house?'

'Ah, Molly. We all love Molly.' His expression changed, and he became the stage tragedian. 'Her smile. Her laugh. Molly gives hope to all and heart to none. So sad.'

'So Molly spends quite a bit of time at Gloria's?'

'She used to serve at table two, maybe three times in week. Not so much lately. When she away we miss Molly.'

'And is Molly friendly with Paula?'

'Once, yes. I think not so much now. Paula have boyfriend. He come to the house. Now not so. I think he like all of us. He love Molly. Perhaps why Paula cross with Molly. Gloria she miss Molly, too.'

'What is his name?'

'His name I do not know.'

'Thank you, Gino. You've been very helpful.' Fess turned so that he was facing the group that had largely gone back to their game, although some of them continued to glance in their direction. He looked sternly at Gino and raised his voice. 'If you see any of these men you must immediately report them to me.'

Gino nodded, but then asked, 'Why you ask about Molly?'

'I'm sorry, Gino, but I have very bad news. Molly was murdered last night.' Gino staggered back as though Fess had hit him.

'Terrible. Terrible. So much life. Who could do such thing?' He clasped his hands and stared off across the square. 'Molly dead. I cannot believe.'

'Goodbye, Gino.' The Italian wandered back to his countrymen, again expressing his grief in a theatrical manner, but now using his native Italian so that he sounded almost operatic. Fess watched him go with a wry smile. So much for his attempt to cloak his relationship with Gino and keep the thrust of his enquiry secret. He turned and began to make his way home, his thoughts again fixed on the murder. It was clear that Gloria and Paula knew much more that they could, and eventually would, tell him. Meanwhile, it appeared increasingly as though he was investigating the murder of two women, Mary and Molly, who had led separate lives. He wondered which of them had worked at Ball and Welch and which of them had attended classes at the Working Men's College. He probably needed to find out. It was getting dark as he made his way through the streets, and lights began to appear in the houses he passed. Coming along Faraday Street, he saw that the Worthingtons' house was in darkness, but some light came from the curtained window of their daughter's place. He drew comfort from the hope that she had taken charge.

He was about to round the corner towards home when, on a whim, he continued down tree-lined Barkly Street until he was outside number fifty. The house had a narrow frontage with two small windows on either side of the doorway. He knocked and waited, but there was no movement from inside the house. Suddenly he felt very tired. It had been a long and demanding day: he had every right to be tired and should be at home with his family instead of hanging about on this doorstep. Just as he turned to go, a husky voice came from behind the door. 'Oo's there?'

'Senior Constable Jordan, Carlton Police. Is that you, Mrs Cutmore?'

'Who else d'yu reckon 'd be 'ere?'

'May I come in for a minute?'

'Do I 'ave any say in it?'

'It's probably better that we have a quiet chat inside, rather than shout through the door so all the neighbours can hear.'

Ma Cutmore at last opened the door and he was confronted by a scowling woman of very small stature in a grey woollen cardigan and long skirt. Her pugnacious, round face, with its folds of skin, put Fess in mind of a bulldog. 'Why are you after us all the time?' she snarled. 'First y'ound me son, so 'e 'as t'go t'Sydney, and then y'grab Ferret. 'ave y'come fer me now?'

Fess edged past her into the corridor but could see that this was about as far as he could expect to go. 'I just wanted to ask you if you had heard or seen anything last night.'

Ma Cutmore folded her arms across her chest and sneered at him.

'Y'mean anything unusual? I 'eard a few squawks, a few shouts from The Narrows. Nothin' unusual 'bout that: it was Saturd'y night, for God's sake.'

'When was this?'

'How'd I know? Tryin' to sleep, I was.'

'Did you see Ferret?'

'I went to me bed early. I always do. Maybe 'e was 'ere. Maybe not. I dunno. Ferret was 'ere this mornin' 'til your blokes took 'im away.'

'What about Nifty Naughton? He has a room here, too.'

'What about 'im?'

'Is he in? I'd like a word with him.'

'Well ya can't.' Ma Cutmore seemed pleased. 'He went on Saturd'y and I ain't seen 'im since.'

'When did he leave?'

'Dunno exactly. Before all the fuss, I'd say.'

'Do you know where he went?'

'Nifty don't consult me on where 'e goes.'

Fess tried for the final time. 'So you saw nothing unusual?'

Ma Cutmore looked at him with a gleam in her eye. 'Didn't say that.'

'So?'

'Looked out me window sometime – don't know when. There was Basher O'Shea, walkin' up and down the street, like he was guardin' the place.'

'What? Out the front?'

'Me window's at the front.' She sneered again. 'That's all I c'n tell ya.'

6

Fess sat in his felt-covered armchair, staring into the embers of the fire. He stirred when Bern returned to the room but did not shift his gaze. 'You must be all in,' she said. 'You've been on the go since around three this morning.'

'It's good to sit here quietly with the kids out of the way. Happy with the day?'

'Yeah, I'd say so. At one stage I thought Carmel was going to be let down by her father, but she didn't see it that way. She told me he was standing at the door of the church, looking as though he was in a guard of honour.' Bern gave him her grin. 'You charm your way round both the women in this family.'

'Y'know, it was strange. Watching her in the line of girls coming towards me, I suddenly saw a young woman — not the girl that was here the night before.'

'She's growing up fast. So are your sons, but I think you may not have noticed that.'

'What do you mean?' Fess asked, and his gaze shifted from the fire to the serious face of his wife.

'We have to decide whether we can afford for Kevin to stay on at school next year.'

'I reckon we must somehow. I don't want my kids leaving as early as I did.'

Bernadette nodded her agreement. 'He's getting restless, though.'

'What?'

'I don't know. Just something in his manner these days. He's not nearly as forthcoming as he used to be. You're not the hero you were, either. They tell me we're going for a picnic on the Yarra, as the boys refused to go to the beach with you.' She gave him a small smile that mixed puzzlement with sympathy. 'You really are keen on the beach, aren't you?'

'Yeah, I s'pose I am.' Fess rubbed his chin and looked back into the embers. 'Those beach holidays were the best part of growing up for me.' For the second time that day he was reminded of his family's trips to the seaside. It wasn't just the pleasure he took in the sand and the sea. The excitement began as soon as they boarded the tram for Flinders Street Station, his father carrying the battered portmanteau that contained their clothes, and his mother anxious they would miss the train. After they found a seat, he went with his father to inspect the engine, puffing steam into the gloom of Princes Bridge. He enjoyed seeing the world rush by as they ran down the bay and felt like he was making his escape. He never thought to question what it was he was escaping from.'

'You were lucky you could afford them.'

'Dad said that taking us for a holiday to the beach and staying in a guest-house was his way of making up for spending so much time on his job. I guess there being only the three of us helped. We went about three times, and I reckon he couldn't afford to keep it up.'

'Fess?' He recognised her tone; it was the one she used when she wanted his agreement for something she was about to do and was not confident he would agree.

'Yes,' he said, sitting up and turning to look directly at her.

'I thought I should call on the Worthingtons. I know Mr. Worthington quite well from going to King and Godfree's, and they are almost neighbours, living round the corner.'

'No, you shouldn't go.' Fess surprised Bern and himself with the vehemence of his response. 'I'm sorry, I just don't think it's a good idea,' he added more calmly.

'Why ever not?'

Fess took up the poker and stirred the embers before putting on another small log. 'I'll turn in soon. Do you want to stay up?'

Bernadette continued to look questioningly at him until he sighed and said, 'The more I find out about that girl, the more puzzled I am by the life she led. It's almost as if she were two people. She did have two names. At home she was Mary and at Gloria Ryan's place, where she waited on table, she was Molly. Her parents know nothing about this and I don't have the heart to tell them what I've found out. They're sure to expect me to keep them in the picture, but I don't know what to say to them.'

'So, if I go, you won't need to.'

'I can't make you an honorary policewoman. No, it's something I'll have to do.'

'Why do you always have to be the one? You order your men to get you out of bed in the middle of the night. You insist on getting involved with a case that's really one for Russell Street. This time you're taking it even more to heart than usual.'

He shook his head and gave a rueful smile. 'I s'pose I am. Jim Thomas, the bloke from the C.I., reckons it's too close to home for me.'

'He might be right. You know I don't want us to stay in Carlton, but …'

'Let's not get into that. Not right now. Not tonight.' Fess emphasised his words with a few vigorous jabs of the poker.

'I was just going to say this case might help you to see why I feel this way.'

'Just because a woman is killed in a laneway not far from where we live?' Fess scoffed.

'That's not it at all. You've just been telling me how the Worthingtons don't know everything about their daughter, as though this is some rare event. Once they enter their teens, even before, perhaps, no parent knows everything their children get up to. Neither they should. It's part of growing up and being adult. It's also a danger time. It's a time for trying things and for making mistakes. Sometimes those mistakes can be tragic, and that's more likely in a place like Carlton. That's why I want us to go to a country town. We have to accept there will still be dangers, but they're fewer and less threatening than here. Can't you see that?'

'But Bern, my duty is here.'

'Sergeant Doyle doesn't want you to stay; he's made that plain. I'm sure you'd be happier in another place with a different boss.'

'There's unfinished business here. Can't you see there's no escaping that?'

'Isn't there? Must you stay for duty, or are you a prisoner of your desire to show you can outdo your father? That's what you need to escape.'

THE SUN-NEWS PICTORIAL MONDAY, JULY 13, 1925

WOMAN STRANGLED IN CARLTON

The Narrows Claims Another Victim

Man Held For Questioning

In the early hours of Sunday morning, the body of a young woman was found in one of the lanes that form the notorious 'Narrows', off Elgin Street, Carlton. She has been identified as Mary Worthington, brutally murdered within a few short steps of her family home in Faraday Street.

Senior Detective Thomas, who has taken charge of the case, said that it appeared Mary Worthington had been strangled but, beyond that, the body had not been mutilated. Dr. Ronaldson, the Government Pathologist, will conduct his post mortem today.

Two men have already been interviewed and one has been held for further questioning. A search is under way for a third man who was seen loitering in the vicinity on the night of the murder. Senior Detective Thomas said that the purpose for this dastardly crime might have been theft, but he does not at this stage rule out other motives, including the possibility that Mary, having witnessed the committing of another crime, was silenced in this barbaric fashion.

Police To Spare No Effort

Senior Detective Thomas says that no effort will be spared to track down the perpetrator of this diabolical attack and called upon members of the public to assist in bringing the criminal to justice. He is anxious to trace the murdered woman's movements during Saturday night. Any persons who remember seeing Mary Worthington are asked to lose no time in placing their information in the hands of police.

A Career Cut Short

Mary, who lived with her parents, George and Valerie Worthington, was pursuing a successful career in the Dress Department of the Ball and Welch department store in Carlton and bettering herself through night classes at the Working Men's College. She has been cut down before her outstanding potential could come to fruition. Mr. Worthington, a highly respected resident of Carlton, is well known as the Manager of King and Godfree, where he has served for many years.

The Narrows

Whilst many of the back lanes of Carlton have long hosted S.P. bookies, two-up schools and sly grog dives, the tangle of lanes known as 'The Narrows' has seen more than its share of crime. More recently, the area has become known as 'Vendetta Country', the place where the back-street gangs feud with bricks and bottles. Now it has sunk to a new level of depravity — the site for the murder of an innocent young woman from a good family. This latest outrage raises further questions about the safety of our streets for law-abiding citizens. Do the local police have the capacity or the will to carry the fight to those miscreants who roam in gangs and commit their crimes with apparent impunity? It is another black day for the reputation of a suburb that was once held in high regard.

'Have you seen this?' Sergeant Doyle tossed *The Sun* newspaper across his desk. '*The Argus* and *The Age* are no better — short on facts, so they put the knife into the Carlton Police. You need to make an arrest pronto.'

'You know it's Basher O'Shea we're hunting,' Fess replied. 'He's certainly capable of the crime. So far he's been hard to track down. He's no longer at the last address we had for him and no one seems to know where he's gone.'

'This network of informers you've been spending so much of your time cultivating, where are they now?'

'My men have been asking around. I've been working with the C.I. man, as instructed.'

'Oh yeah, that reminds me. It seems the C.I. aren't interested in a formal secondment. Happy to have all the help we can give them, but no secondment for you. I reckon they've heard about your wimpish methods of fighting crime. They don't muck about like you do. Neither should we. I've been telling you that.' He scratched his ear, a sign that Doyle was embarrassed about something. It didn't happen very often. He fiddled with several of the sheets on his desk before saying, 'I've had a message from Russell Street that the Acting Chief Commissioner is not too happy with the rise in illegal betting and wants us to clamp down on the S.P. bookies. I presume he's going to clamp down on the cards and roulette in the gentlemen's clubs himself.'

Now Fess understood the embarrassment. It was only a few weeks since Doyle had repeated his suggestion that there was no need to pursue the bookies. 'They do no real harm,' he had said.

'You could start with Ginger Foster. He's had it coming to him for a while. The gee gees are running at Geelong tomorrow, so that'll be your chance. Put on a show when you do it. That way the word will get around. Meanwhile, get Basher in here and get him charged.

Then the papers will have something useful to write about.' Doyle waved his hand, dismissing Fess. 'And take that rag with you.'

Fess found the Plain Clothes room empty; his men were out trying to find Basher. He glanced again at *The Sun*. Sharing the page with the account of Mary Worthington's murder was a report of the incident that had occupied the C.I. on the night Mary was killed. 'GELIGNITE EXPLODES AND FOUR SHOTS ARE FIRED INTO PORT MELBOURNE SHOP — MOTIVE A MYSTERY'. The article gave details of the shooting followed by the explosion, described the people and places involved and ended with the tantalising comment that Detective Sergeant Mufahey, who was leading the investigation, had suggested the motive might be jealousy or revenge. Fess could not see those passions as the motives for Mary's killing. He couldn't see it as being a clumsy attempt to steal from Mary, either. Her bag had been left in the lane where Clarry found it. If Basher was the murderer, it was much more likely he had been hired to intimidate Mary, maybe even to rough her up, and had gone too far. But who had hired him, and why?

He unlocked the cupboard that stood against the wall and took out Mary's bag. Opening the catch, he emptied the contents onto the table. The small purse was unlikely to have held more than the few pounds that Clarry was able to turn into grog. Fess used his thumbnail to flip open the pill-box. Inside was a fine white powder. He moistened his little finger and took up a small sample which he probed tentatively with the tip of his tongue. Mary Worthington a cocaine user? It was hard to believe, but he wasn't mistaken — this was snow all right. Thoughtfully, he returned each of the items to the bag, pausing over the unopened envelope. He would be within his rights to check on the letter from the Working Men's College, which Mary had told her mother was confirmation of her enrolment, but his reluctance to open another person's mail went back to the time when, as a young lad, he had opened an envelope addressed to his father and had to suffer his fury. Fess pushed the envelope back into the bag and returned it to the cupboard.

It was still quite early when he left the Station, the main activity in Drummond Street being at the chaff and grain yard, where drays, drawn by steaming draft horses, were disgorging their loads. Fess knew that Sam Cohen liked to start early, even though the majority of his customers came later in the day. Coming off Lygon Street, he was met by that aroma of soap, hair oil and stale tobacco so characteristic of a barber's shop. Sam sat reading a newspaper in the iron-framed, horsehair padded chair in which his customers received their shave or haircut. 'Morning, Mr. Jordan,' he said, dropping the paper and scrambling from the chair as if caught in the midst of some forbidden act. 'Come for a trim to your beard, or something more ambitious?'

'Here for a quiet word, Sam.'

Sam's dark eyes became sombre and he used his hands to smooth the creases in the white cotton coat he wore. 'Nasty business. I've just been reading about it.'

'It's not what you've read, Sam. It's what you've heard. That's what interests me. You know that.'

'To tell the truth, not much. Though I hear you're looking for Basher O'Shea.' Sam fiddled with the tortoiseshell comb he always carried in the breast pocket of his jacket. All his other implements — brushes, razors, scissors and combs — were laid out on the bench that ran below the wall-mirror in front of the chair. 'They say he was outside the Albion on Saturday, working for Jockey Harrison, but no one seems to have seen him since. The word is he had to go out a bit to find somewhere that'd put him up. I haven't heard where but I don't reckon he's done a runner. Not his way.'

'Of course. How stupid of me.' Fess laughed. 'He's standing guard for Jockey Harrison these days, isn't he?'

'That and a few other things.'

'Yeah?'

Sam came to stand by Fess, looking through the window at the people on the footpath making their way to work. 'They say he didn't like the way some people tried to order him around, so he's not in with any of the gangs these days. Likes to do things on his own.'

'You don't know who else he's working for, do you?' Fess asked.

'No. They say he told Jockey he had another job on Saturday night. Didn't say who'd hired him or what the job was.'

'You haven't heard anything about what did happen on Saturday night?'

'In The Narrows? Not a thing. Seems to have come out of the blue.'

'Thanks, Sam. You'll let me know if you do hear anything.'

❦ ❧

Mickey Ryan did not like to start early. 'What d'ya mean barging in on me at this ungodly hour? Just about to start me brekkie.'

'Now be reasonable, Mick,' Fess said as he grinned at the scowling face and tousled hair that confronted him. 'I haven't barged in. In fact, if you leave me standing on your doorstep like this, people are going to talk.'

'Orright. But there's nothin' 'ere.' He stood aside to allow Fess through the door into the passage and gave a cheeky grin. 'I hear you've got a nice pair o' candlesticks I might be able to find a buyer for.' When Fess did not return the grin he added, 'D'ya want a cuppa? I'm just makin' one.'

Despite Mick's unkempt appearance, the kitchen was in good order, with a clean linoleum floor and a well-scrubbed table, set for two: a pair of empty bowls, a milk jug, a sugar bowl and a packet of Kellog's Toasted Corn Flakes, with its picture of an attractive young woman clutching a sheaf of green corn stalks. On the bench by the wall, next to a modern electric toaster, was a bread board carrying a freshly cut loaf. Further along the bench, a brand new electric jug was coming to the boil. Mick went to a cupboard from which he took a cup and saucer, placed them with the two already on the bench, switched off the jug and swirled some of the water from it around a china tea pot, before spooning in tea leaves and adding more of the boiling water. 'Robur OK with ya, or d'ya only have Twinings'?'

'Thank you, Mick.' Fess sat at the table. 'Got the place looking much better than when I last visited you.'

'Under new management.'

As if on cue, a female voice floated in from the passage. 'Who is it, Mickey?'

'Nobody important. Best y'stay in bed,' Mick replied. 'I'll bring ya tea in a sec.'

'You treat yourself well,' Fess said. 'How did you come by all this new gear?'

'Ya know the answer. Bought them in a pub. Cheap, they were. Would ya like me to get ya some?'

'I think your toast's burning,' Fess said and pointed to the smoke issuing from the side of the toaster.

'There, see what ya've made me go and do.' Mick flicked the blackening toast onto the bench.

'I'm afraid this isn't a social call.'

'Ya surprise me.'

'You know your pal, Ferret, stumbled upon a dead woman in The Narrows on Saturday night.'

'Lotta good that did 'im. Nicked 'im next day. That's the thanks 'e got for 'elpin' you cops.'

'Mickey, can't you have a word with him? He's just making it too easy for us these days and Pentridge is good for no one, particularly at his age.'

'Won't listen. Got 'is pride. We all 'ave.'

'You know we're looking for Basher O'Shea?'

''eard somethin' like that. Also 'eard you're givin' Ferret grief. Ya can't believe 'e'd have anythin' to do with it?'

'I don't, but the C.I. aren't so sure.'

Mickey took up the pot and poured the tea into the cups and added milk to two. 'Ya can fix your own. There's milk and sugar if ya want.' He walked from the kitchen carrying one of the cups.

When he returned he looked hard at Fess and said, 'What about Nifty Naughton?'

'What about him?'

'Livin' at Ma Cutmore's place these days, y'know. There's a bloke who likes the sheilas.'

'Ferret said nothing about him.'

'Would ya, if ya was Ferret?'

Next on his list was Spy Webb at his bicycle shop in Elgin Street. Fess' path took him directly past the Worthingtons' house and, on reaching their door, he hesitated. There was nothing he could tell them that would bring any comfort. But he would like to see if he could learn more about Mary. Tentatively, he knocked. The door was not opened as speedily as it had been the previous day, but George Worthington again stood before him in his shirtsleeves. This time, though, he wore a loosely knotted black tie. 'Ah, Senior Constable Jordan.' Fess was surprised when the stern expression on George's face seemed to lighten. 'I thought it was another reporter.'

'Giving you a hard time? I'm sorry about that.'

'Come in,' George replied. 'Only doing their job, I s'pose. I wish they didn't push so hard. Valerie can't bear it. She's hidden away in the bedroom. Elizabeth's a great help but she has her own family to look after. She'll be around here soon though, I expect.' They walked into the front room, and Fess gained the impression that George, who was eyeing him uncertainly, was delaying asking the question most on his mind.

'We've made no arrest yet, Mr. Worthington, although — as you may know — there is a man we are seeking to interview.'

'The reporters said you'd held someone for questioning. They said it was the man who found her … told the police about Mary.'

'He was arrested for a totally different crime, but we think there is more he might be able to help us with.' Fess gave George a diffident smile. 'I don't want to take up your time unnecessarily, but I'm still baffled as to why Mary came to be where she was.'

George sighed. 'I understand she didn't stay with Paula Ryan.' He caught Fess' quick glance and added, 'Mrs. Ryan was here yesterday evening. I found her a bit hard to take, but Val appreciated her coming.'

'Did you know that Mary sometimes liked to be called Molly?'

'No, I didn't, but Mrs. Ryan kept calling her that and then correcting herself. It was one of the strange things about her.'

'I feel it would help if I could somehow get to know Mary a little better. Would you mind allowing me to see her room?'

'I don't object but I don't see how it could help.'

'I'm not sure, either. I'd just like to try.'

'You've gone to a lot of trouble for me already. It's up the stairs.' Fess gestured for him to go ahead. The room was small with a single curtained window, rose-patterned linoleum on the floor and just sufficient room for a narrow bed with a pink quilt and an ancient teddy-bear resting on the pillow, a slim wardrobe and a chest of drawers surmounted by a framed mirror. Fess opened the door of the wardrobe and found several navy dresses with a Ball and Welch monogram on the breast pocket, plus a number of simple day dresses and an inexpensive overcoat. A beret and a broad-brimmed hat sat on an upper shelf. There were no clothes of the quality Mary was wearing on Saturday night.

Fess pulled out the top drawer of the chest of drawers and, finding it contained a collection of underwear, quickly shut it again. What did he hope to get from this morbid search? He was turning to leave, when his attention was caught by a lacquered jewel-box on the chest. He opened it and saw inside a number of unpretentious brooches and necklaces. Underneath them was a photograph, the kind taken by street photographers, except this one appeared to have been taken at a dance and included four people: Mary, wearing her fetching smile and a velvet evening gown with a low-cut neckline, was beside Paula, who wore an equally revealing chiffon dress. They were flanked by two men, one of whom Fess recognised immediately, the other unknown but somehow vaguely familiar.

He took the photograph from the box and showed it to George. 'Do you know these people?'

George took his time examining the print. Eventually he said, 'Mary of course; except I've never seen her looking like that. The other girl is Paula, I'm pretty sure, though I've only met her once. I don't know the men.'

'You don't know them, but have you ever seen either of them?'

'No.'

Fess knew Nifty Naughton. He wasn't about to ask George where his daughter had met Nifty. Not yet, anyhow. 'May I take this photograph? It might help in finding if anyone saw Mary last night.'

'Yes. I suppose so. I've never seen that photograph before.' He hesitated. 'The reporters wanted photographs, as well. I could give you one of those.'

'No, this one will do very well and I am interested in the men, seeing you don't know them.'

'You won't give it to the papers?'

'I will give it to no one, I assure you.'

❧ ❧

There was now nothing to delay Fess from calling on Spy Webb. Whilst the path by which Senior Constable Jordan had come to be called 'Fess' was unclear, there was no doubt about how Spy Webb earned his name. At first he would have been Spider, the contraction to Spy coming when his nocturnal tours of Carlton became better known. Sometimes he was on the lookout for an attractive figure or trim ankle. Often he could be found in the shadows under an uncurtained window, hoping for a more revealing glimpse of the female form. Twice he had been had up as a Peeping Tom. Several times, when women had lost underwear from an outside clothesline, he'd been suspected of snow-dropping, but no charges were laid.

Fess found that his attitude toward Spy swung from impatient disgust to begrudging sympathy. Severely malnourished as a child, rickets had left him with a puny frame and a grotesque appearance. Small children were frightened of him, but the bigger ones often mocked him, sometimes egged on by parents who liked to demonstrate their disgust with him. He must find it difficult to earn his living.

When walking the streets and skulking in lanes, Spy sometimes saw things that were of little interest to him, except that their value to others allowed him to supplement his earnings from the bicycle sales and repair shop.

Some of the people who paid for Spy's silence were wasting their money. He held an irrational fear of being seen to be involved and would never give evidence that might result in his being called as a witness in Court. Despite his distaste for the man, Fess worked hard to convince Spy that he would never betray his confidence and, from time to time, was rewarded with useful information.

Entering the shop, Fess was confronted by a rack of reconditioned bikes for sale and a large wall-poster of Hubert Opperman enjoying a ride on his gleaming Malvern Star cycle. The jangling bell over the door brought Spy, who limped from his rear workshop wiping his oily hands on a rag which he shoved into a pocket of his grey overalls. 'Senior Constable Jordan. I thought I might be seeing you today. Nothing like the rape and murder of a young woman to get you coppers pulling out all the stops. A terrible business.' The look on his thin face suggested he was far from repelled by the crime.

'No one's said anything about rape,' Fess shot back at him.

The smirk remained. 'Come on now, Mr. Jordan. You're not trying to tell me a pretty young thing like Mary Worthington gets killed in The Narrows without rape being involved? Why hide it? The public's always very interested in rape, and you want that interest when you're after witnesses to come forward. That's why you're here now, I bet.'

'You knew Mary Worthington?'

'Wouldn't say we were close friends …' He paused like an actor weighing his line. 'But I knew her pretty well. Mary liked to walk, too. You couldn't miss her, coming from Ball and Welch or off the tram some nights. Saw her with the others down at Gloria Ryan's once or twice.' He patted down his thinning brown hair. 'Such a pity.' His face was sombre, but his blue eyes contained a spark. 'Mary was such a beautiful girl. The belle of Carlton, you might say.'

'So did you see her on Saturday night?'

Spy shook his head regretfully. 'I was home upstairs reading mags.' Fess knew that Spy's only interest in the magazines he read was to search for more pin-ups to join the collection on the walls of his workshop. 'But I did go for a stroll about nine.' He paused to take in the interest he had kindled in Fess' eyes. 'If she went into The Narrows from this side about then, I might have seen her. It's just across the road, after all.' It was a typical conversation with Spy: Fess having to hide his dislike of the man as Spy dribbled out information and made Fess work for it.

'So, did you see anything?'

'Depends what you mean. I went up to the Uni. Some of those blue stockings in Janet Clarke Hall are pretty as well as a bit careless with their blinds.'

'So you saw nothing that would help me?'

'I didn't say that. It's terrible to think of her lying in that lane, her beautiful fur-trimmed coat getting creased and grubby.'

'How do you know what she was wearing?' Fess asked wearily.

Spy screwed up his face as if checking his memory. 'I couldn't see what she was wearing under the coat, so we'll have to imagine that. The more you imagine, the better it gets. As well as the coat, she had patent leather high-heeled shoes and a cloche hat with elaborate beading. She was carrying that silk bag and her favourite red umbrella with the twisted, barley-sugar handle.' He paused to gauge the effect these revelations were having on Fess and then smiled. 'It was Saturday night. That's what she always wore on a Saturday night. She always had the bag and the umbrella, though, even when she wasn't dressed up. She loved that umbrella, took it with her whenever there was the slightest chance of rain.'

'I'm sick of these games of yours,' Fess growled. 'Stop wasting my time.'

Spy eyed him carefully. 'They say you're after Basher O'Shea.'

'Have you seen him?'

'Not lately. But he'd know Mary.'

'How could that be?' Fess asked disbelievingly.

'He would have seen her at Gloria's.'

'But that was years ago.'

'You're talking about the fuss down there when he was heavying Gloria's neighbour. I'm talking about last week. Happened to be down that way myself and saw him go in there.'

'Which night?'

'Thursday? No. I was around Carlton Gardens that night. Must have been Friday.'

'Thank you, Spy. At last you've given me something useful.' It was also interesting that Spy had confirmed Mary would have been carrying an umbrella, which they had not yet found, but Fess didn't feel like thanking him for that.

7

Fess hadn't intended to visit the Ryans today. That was before he'd seen the photograph or spoken with Spy. Now, his path to Gloria's house brought him to the windows of Ball and Welch in Faraday Street, where he paused. The men's suits and the women's dresses were displayed without flair or energy, reflecting the current mood of the enterprise. Bernadette did most of the shopping for the house and the family, so it had been some time since he was last in the store. Once a thriving emporium boasting twenty-five departments on three levels, the growth of the central city stores, which included a branch of Ball and Welch, had left the Carlton establishment depleted and subdued. He could understand if Mary had been bored by the work.

He found the Dress Department on the second floor almost devoid of shoppers and stood, showing the embarrassment most males display when in a normally exclusive female domain. A gawky, young woman in a uniform similar to those he had seen in Mary's cupboard walked shyly toward him from between the racks of frocks. He didn't need to announce his purpose or his occupation. 'Have you come about Mary?' she asked. 'It's really terrible.'

For a moment he thought she was going to cry, but she recovered herself and he was able to ask, 'Are you the Manageress of this department?'

'Oh, good heavens no.' Fess was relieved to see that his promotion of her had cheered her up. 'You want Miss Rowbottom. She's over there.'

Fess followed the direction indicated and approached a short, grey-haired woman who was standing behind a wooden counter, writing on a lined pad. She eyed him speculatively but said nothing.

'Miss Rowbottom? I'm Senior Constable Jordan from Carlton Police. I gather you are already aware of the most unfortunate death of your assistant, Mary Worthington.'

'Certainly a tragic affair. The streets are safe for no-one these days,' she replied in an accusatory voice that suggested Miss Rowbottom held him responsible for all local crime and this murder in particular.

'It will help my investigation if I can better understand the kind of girl Mary was. Could you tell me how you found her?'

'I cannot see how it will help.' For a moment Fess thought that he faced a refusal to co-operate, but then she continued. 'For what it's worth, she was a bright girl. Too bright, if you ask me. She found us rather too staid here. Still, she was good with our customers, had a good eye for colour and an understanding of fashion. She could have had a good future if she had been able to rein herself in. She had a problem with punctuality, too.'

'Punctuality?'

'Only in recent months. She was sometimes late on the floor.'

'Perhaps her classes at the College kept her up late.'

'I doubt that. She never struck me as the studious type. You're probably right about her being up late, though. I gather she led an active social life, although we don't encourage gentlemen callers.'

Fess thought that was very apparent but took out the photograph and asked, 'Did either of these gentlemen call?'

Miss Rowbottom scanned the photograph disdainfully. 'I do not recognise either of them. As I said, we discourage casual visitors.'

'She dressed very well. Does the store give discounts to its staff?'

Miss Rowbottom gave Fess the patronising glance of someone dealing with a simpleton. 'We do, but even so, our girls could not afford the more expensive of our offerings.' Her face became haughty and she added, 'I can assure you that this department has no truck with the kind of inappropriate gowns displayed in your photograph.'

Fess decided he should leave before being accused of dealing in dirty pictures.

❧ ❧

When he entered George's Terrace, Gloria was in the midst of sweeping the floor. Dressed in a faded floral house-coat with little sign of make-up on her face, she had aged at least a decade since yesterday. 'Oh dear, Senior Constable Jordan, you catch me in my work clothes. I really should change before receiving you.'

'Don't trouble yourself, Mrs. Ryan. I don't need a lot of your time.'

'Have you found the murderer yet?'

He took the photograph from his pocket and handed it to her. 'I'd like you to look at this.'

Gloria subsided onto a nearby chair and wrinkled her brow as she squinted at the photograph. It was clear she had need of spectacles. 'See. Now you know what I was talking about. Aren't they lovely? Was that at the Palais de Dance? They certainly had some good company, didn't they?'

'Do you know either of the men, Mrs. Ryan?'

She took her time replying, her head bowed over the photograph. Eventually she looked up and met Fess' eyes. 'No, I don't think so. Should I? Do you suspect them?'

As Gloria trotted out her questions, her manner changed from caution to something Fess could only describe as relief. Why should she be relieved that these men might be suspects? 'Perhaps Paula will be able to help me.'

'I'm afraid she's not here at the moment. Gone to the market for the day's supplies. Would you like me to send her around to the Station when she returns?'

Fess was about to say he would wait but had a better idea. 'Thank you, Mrs. Ryan. That would be helpful. There is one other thing. You said that you'd told Mary she was welcome to a bed here at any time. Did she leave clothes here?'

'Just some items that she wouldn't need at home. That lovely dress in the photograph and a few other things. I was wondering what to do with them.'

'I'd be grateful if you would hold onto them for the moment.' Fess wondered why he had said this. Was he trying to spare the Worthingtons from more discoveries about their daughter? 'Did she leave an umbrella here?'

'Her precious red umbrella.' Gloria smiled reflectively. 'No, she never left that with anyone.'

'I must be on my way.' He started to rise from the seat he had taken across the small table from Gloria but then settled back. 'There is one other thing. Has Basher O'Shea been to see you lately?'

'Basher?' Fess could see the light in Gloria's eyes depart and her face stiffen. 'Why are you asking about him?'

'It's just that I'm keen to speak with him.'

Gloria was now looking deeply troubled. 'You're saying he's a suspect. How awful.' When Fess did not respond she said, 'I remember you had a low opinion of him, but I found him a total gentleman. Of course, that was years ago. Thankfully, I've had no need of his services lately.'

'I've been told he was here last Friday night.'

'You have been misinformed,' Gloria replied quickly. 'Still …' She reflected for a moment. 'We do have quite a number of non-residents who patronise our café these days. I'm not always in the front of house, so don't see all who come.'

'Maybe Paula will know if he was here.'

This idea did not seem to please Gloria. 'I doubt she'll be able to help you, Senior Constable.' Her face cleared and she smiled. 'You can ask her when I send her around to you.'

❧ ❧

Back in Cardigan Street, Fess did not turn towards the Station but took the opposite direction until he reached the corner across from the City Baths, where he stood waiting. Walking briskly, as was his habit, he had not noticed the cold, but now the breeze blowing up Victoria Street cut right through the tweed of his overcoat. Not the day for a swim. After an uncomfortable ten minutes, he was rewarded by the sight of Paula, standing on the other side of the road, waiting to cross. She was wrapped in a heavy coat, her head protected by a blue scarf that was tied under her chin, and she carried two large string bags crammed with produce from the Queen Victoria Market.

She had her head down and did not notice him at first but, on reaching his side of the street, she scowled at him and said, 'Standin' guard today are you?'

Fess smiled. 'No, Paula, waiting for you. Your mother told me you were at the market.'

'What do you want now?'

'Would you like to rest your load? Those bags look very heavy.'

'You should have waited at our place.' Paula paused

and gave him a shrewd grin. 'But you wanted to see me without me mum.'

Fess took out the photograph. 'I wanted to ask you about this photograph.'

Paula needed only a quick glance to recognise it. 'Yeah, that was taken at the Palais. I prefer Leggett's, myself. It's bigger and they have this beautiful lighting that changes colour all the time.' It seemed that, when roused, Paula had her mother's talent for wandering off with her own thoughts. 'Molly liked the Palais. She liked the crowd better and she had this thing for Ray Tellier and his San Francisco Orchestra. The best part of the Palais is after, at Carlyons.'

'And the two men? Who are they?'

Paula looked at him steadily before she replied. 'Two of the regulars at the Palais.' Her lips curled into a sneer and she added, 'The bloke on the right's Nifty Naughton. I thought you'd know him.'

'Yes, we do know Nifty.'

'So why are you askin' me?'

'What about the other one?'

'He's a pal of Nifty's. Don't remember his name. They're both regulars at the Palais and pretty keen on Molly.' Paula pressed her lips together. 'Most men were.'

'You'd also know Basher O'Shea.'

'What's that thug got to do with it?' She paused and appraised Fess carefully. 'These blokes. Are they suspects?'

'We would like to talk with Basher. I've been told he was at your place on Friday night.'

'Mighta been. I didn't see him.'

'You will let me know if you do see him or anything else comes to mind that might help us?' Paula nodded and lifted her shoulders against the weight of the bags but said nothing.

Fess appeared as though he was about to move on but then looked into Paula's eyes and said, 'Did you know Mary used cocaine?'

'That's what the smart set do these days.'

'You too?'

'Course we did,' she answered gaily. 'Did nothin' for me. It's just for the chumps who need something to have a good time. We made our own fun.' Her face darkened. 'You gotta be careful, though. Some blokes get girls hooked on it and we all know where that leads.'

'Was Mary hooked?'

'Nah. She enjoyed it more than I did. But hooked? Nah. It was just another way she made herself out to be a cut above what she really was.'

Fess nodded. 'Thank you, Paula. Can I help you with those bags? I'm going past your place now.'

Back at the Station he was disappointed when McKenzie reported no sighting of Basher. 'You'll have to try again this afternoon. Tomorrow, though, Sergeant Doyle has ordered me to raid one or two of the S.P. bookies. Apparently the word has come down from on high that we are to shake them up.'

'And Doyle wants you to close down the bookies?' The surprise in McKenzie's voice was apparent.

'That's what he said. I want you to organise a couple of the uniform men to come with us late morning tomorrow. It would be good if they were fairly hefty types. Young Daley looks strong and Williams is burly and can pack a wallop when he needs to. Tell whoever is the Senior on Duty that we need those two for a job ordered by the sergeant. We'll start with Ginger Foster over beside the Vine, but only you need know that.'

'OK, Boss. Whatever you say.' McKenzie shook his head, still disbelieving.

His face changed when Fess asked, 'Do we still have Ferret in the cells?'

'Yeah. The bloody magistrate was ill this morning – slept in more like – so he comes up this afternoon.'

'Good. I'd like a quiet word with Ferret.' He walked to the smaller brick building behind the Station, where a bored constable sat in charge of the lock-up – a set of six cells in a bluestone block attached to the rear of the building. 'Just come to have a chat with Ferret Roberts. Nothing formal.'

'Sure, Senior.' The constable rose from his stool and went to the third cell, which he unlocked. Ferret was sitting on a wooden bench that ran along one wall.

'G'day, Ferret,' Fess said in a cheerful voice. 'I hear you've been held over to this afternoon.'

'What's this about me bein' 'eld for further questionin'?'

Ferret remained sitting, so Fess lowered himself onto

the bench beside him. 'The papers have to say something. I've just called in for a quiet chat.'

'You haven't got Basher yet.' It was a statement not a question. 'I reckon I'd 'ave 'eard if you'd brought 'im in.'

'Ferret, this chat is just between you and me. I don't think you've told me all you could.'

Ferret eyed Fess suspiciously. 'It was risky givin' you the tip on Basher and that ain't done me no good. They say that C.I. coot's still got me in the frame. Reckons I done 'er in to hide me own crime.'

'I know you didn't do it, Ferret. I also know you hate such crimes as much as I do, and you have no time for the hoods and gangsters that infest Carlton these days.'

Ferret nodded his agreement. 'Tell that to the C.I. fellah.'

'What I don't know is why you haven't said anything to me about your fellow boarder, Nifty Naughton.'

Ferret looked away and gave a sniff. 'Ya said this was jist between us.'

'That's right.'

'And if I tell ya what I know, you'll speak up for me?'

'You heard what I said yesterday.'

Ferret still hesitated but then wiped his hand across his nose and said, 'OK. What I told ya about Basher, that's true.' He paused to give another sniff. 'I'd seen the dead sheila before.' Ferret gave a short account of his first meeting with Mary, mentioning the laugh he had heard through the door, but not the smile she had given him. He spoke of hearing that laugh coming from Nifty's room on a few other occasions and then paused again while he figured out the best way to recount the events of the night of the murder.

'Is that all you can tell me?'

'Just gettin' it clear in me mind,' Ferret replied. 'I noticed Nifty stayed in on Saturday night. He never does that. Always goes after skirt on a Saturday. There was one in his room earlier on, I heard them arguin'. At least that's what I thought they were doin', although she laughed as well. Didn't 'ear 'er after a while so I s'posed she'd gone.'

'Was that Mary Worthington you heard?'

'You mean the dead'n? Maybe. Couldn't rightly say. The laugh was a bit different from the one I told ya about. Harsher like. All I know is, when I found the body, I straightway went inside to get 'elp from Nifty, but 'e'd done a bunk and 'ain't been back. At least 'e 'adn't before I was dragged in 'ere this morning. So I came along to report the body and look what good that did me. I'm not saying 'e did it, mind. I'm just saying you should check 'im out. He knows somethin', I betcha.'

'You've no idea where Nifty is now?'

'Nah. Ma Cutmore might know somethin'.' Ferret turned to give Fess a long look. 'If ya can get 'er t'talk.'

'Thank you, Ferret.'

'Remember, ya keep this to yaself. That Nifty's a nasty type. I don't want it gettin' round I told ya anythin' about 'im.'

Jim Thomas didn't hold back when he arrived at the Station that afternoon. 'What've you been doing? I thought you knew the local scene, yet this oaf of a thug just goes into smoke.'

'I still have men looking for him, and I do have quite a bit to tell you.'

Jim settled into a chair opposite Fess. 'OK. Shoot. It better be good.'

'First of all, I've been told that Mary used to regularly wait on table at Gloria's about twice a week. She's had some disagreement with Paula, probably when Paula's boyfriend, name unknown, started to get interested in Mary. Apparently Mary had quite a few fans at Gloria's.'

'Bit of a flirt, eh?'

Fess did not respond to Jim's smile. 'I had another look in Mary's bag and found she had a pillbox full of cocaine.'

'Is this the innocent young girl I've been reading about?' Jim asked with feigned surprise.

'You were the one talking to the papers.'

'I didn't give them the stuff about what a sweet, hardworking girl she was. Anyway, the more press coverage you can get the more likely a witness you hadn't known about will come forward. Piggott's very strong on that.'

Fess shook his head, unconvinced. 'You're not trying to make this case into another Gun Alley murder are you?'

'Piggott used the press brilliantly there,' Thomas replied enthusiastically before adding resignedly, 'but that was the rape and murder of a child.' He pulled out his pipe and tobacco pouch. 'What else have you to tell me?'

'One of my informants saw Basher O'Shea going into Gloria Ryan's place on Friday night. I've asked Gloria and Paula. They say he wasn't there but both of them allowed themselves some wriggle room.'

'I've already told you I wouldn't trust either of that pair.' The pipe glowed as he drew on it.

Fess took the photograph from his top pocket and slid it along the table to Jim. 'You can see the girls are Mary and Paula.'

'The coves look like a couple of silvertails,' Jim said thoughtfully before his head snapped up. 'Wait a moment. I recognise this bloke; he's Nifty Naughton.'

'So you know Nifty?'

'Know him! I was on the case when he shot a bloke in Fitzroy. Everybody knew he did it, but we couldn't get anyone to break the code of silence. Had to let him go. There's not much that riles me more than seeing the likes of Nifty Naughton get away with murder. I'd love to see him hanged for this one.'

'Nifty has a room in the same house as Ferret, the place that backs onto the lane where Mary was found. I had another chat with your friend, Ferret, as well. He's too scared to say much, but I did get him to tell me he'd seen Mary come into the house with Nifty some time back. He also thought she might have been there earlier on Saturday evening. Apparently she had a distinctive laugh and he thought he may have heard it although he wasn't sure. He also said they could have had an argument.

'This is great. Nifty and Mary have an argument, he

strangles her and dumps her in the lane. Lean on Ferret and we can get him to tell us exactly how it was. That way he gets what he asked for yesterday. I sure will speak up for him if he gives us Nifty. Have you brought him in?'

'My men are looking for him, but we have to be a bit careful how we do it. I promised Ferret I wouldn't let on to anyone what he told me. He's much more scared of Nifty than he is of Basher.'

Jim uttered a snort of disgust. 'You're not going to pussy-foot around with Nifty, too. He's well known and must have enough enemies who'd want to see him picked up.'

Fess made a point of not responding. 'I don't know the other man, but there's something about him that rings a bell. You don't know him?'

'Not even any bells. You will pull out all the stops to bring in Nifty?'

'I told you we're looking for Nifty and Basher, but don't expect quick results. Crooks like Nifty are used to going into smoke. You'd better put it out through Russell Street too. He could well have left Carlton.'

'Where did you get the photo?'

'George Worthington let me have a look in Mary's room and I found it there. He hadn't seen her looking like that before but let me take the photograph. He didn't know the men and I didn't bother telling him one was Nifty.'

Thomas eyed Fess carefully and then smiled. 'You do have a way of getting around people, don't you? And you know where to look, as well. I didn't rate you too highly, but we might yet make a team. I go in hard and strong, breaking them down and you come along after, quietly picking up the pieces.'

'You should tell Piggott you've found a new technique. The C.I. could take it up.' Fess was straight-faced. Perhaps too straight-faced.

Thomas again eyed him carefully, but this time without the subsequent smile. 'Oh, Piggott knows all the ways, new and old. We don't have the time in Russell Street to muck about, though — too much to do. Out here in the suburbs everything runs more slowly and you think you can afford the time to play fancy games.'

'Would you like to see local policing in action tomorrow morning?'

'What are you on about this time? Think I have nothing better to do than waste my time in Carlton?'

'We're raiding an S.P. bookie's operation tomorrow. He uses Basher as a bodyguard and I'm confident Basher will be there.'

'Basher manages to give you the slip and then turns up the next day for his regular job? You're kidding.'

'Come and see.'

THE SUN-NEWS PICTORIAL TUESDAY, JULY 14, 1925

THE NARROWS MURDER

—

Detectives Closing In

—

HUNT FOR MISSING SUSPECTS

Public Interest Can be Tool

The search for the murderer of Mary Worthington, the young Carlton girl struck down in The Narrows on Saturday night, has intensified with detectives confident of an imminent arrest.

Senior Detective Thomas said that the C.I.B. are pursuing two separate lines of enquiry. There is evidence to suggest the murder might have been the tragic result of a lover's tiff that exploded out of control. A man known to be linked with Mary Worthington is being sought by police.

Another line of enquiry is centred on a man who is known for his acts of uncontrolled rage and who was seen in the area of The Narrows on Saturday night at about the time Mary was killed.

Hunt for Suspects

Both these suspects have gone missing and are being sought by the Carlton Police, so far without success. Senior Detective Thomas said it is regrettable that the men have not been found yet, but he is confident that they will soon be apprehended. He also said the public outrage that has been aroused by this despicable crime could be useful in gathering evidence. He called upon anyone who might have seen Mary (pictured below) on Saturday night to come forward and assist detectives in establishing her movements on the night of her murder.

Mary Worthington

Pathology Report Awaited

Whilst questions surround the motive behind the murder of the defenceless girl, Senior Detective Thomas refused to speculate on the details of her death, saying that he was awaiting the report of Dr. Ronaldson, the Government Pathologist, which is expected soon.

Tragedy Strikes Again

The Worthington family is no stranger to tragedy. Only a month before the armistice, Mr. George Worthington, the highly respected Manager of King and Godfree's Grocery, and his wife Valerie received the heartrending news that their only son John Worthington, one of the first to volunteer for the Great War and survive the horrors of Gallipoli, was missing in France. His body has never been found. Now their married daughter Elizabeth is their only remaining child.

8

Next morning Fess made sure he saw the paper before he entered the Station. Beside the section on the Worthington family was a photograph of Mary, similar to the one Fess had seen on the morning he first called on them. It was hard to expect anyone to connect the shyly smiling, young girl in the simple clothes with the expensively and fashionably dressed woman they would have seen on Saturday night. Harder still, to see her as the cocaine-sniffing girlfriend of Nifty Naughton.

There was no mention of the gelignite explosion and shooting in Port Melbourne that had shared the page with Mary's murder yesterday. When he had read that jealousy and revenge might be motives for that outrage, he could not see anything like that being involved in Mary's murder. Now he was not so sure.

This time, the item that shared the page was something much closer to home. 'O'SULLIVAN GUILTY' shouted the headline over the story of the trial of Detective Leo O'Sullivan, who had been charged with having conspired with ex-Detectives Fowler and Macpherson unlawfully to obtain money from Terrence Callaghan, licensee of the Londonderry Hotel in Collingwood. For years there had been talk about O'Sullivan, the weekly 'licensing fee' he collected from card sharpers and the bribes he was paid by criminals under investigation, but it had remained only talk. Earlier on in the year O'Sullivan had overreached himself, attempting to have Callaghan pay an extortionate amount for him to ignore two cases of illegal gin found on his premises. Fess thought it would be interesting to hear what Jim thought of O'Sullivan.

Fess folded the paper under his arm, steeled himself and went to the doorway of Sergeant Doyle's office.

'So you've seen the paper today. Yesterday Carlton Police couldn't track down one suspect. Now it's two. I told you to get Basher in here and charged. If a numbskull like Basher has you bushed, what hope do we have of you finding a shifty type like Nifty Naughton?'

'You know it's Nifty we're after, then?'

'Of course I know, despite you trying to keep me in the dark. These contacts of yours? You cultivate them, you go soft on them, but when it matters they keep silent.'

'I'm pretty confident we'll get Basher today, and we have linked him with Gloria Ryan.'

'The woman who runs the doss house for Italians in Cardigan Street? I reckon there's not much she wouldn't get up to. But murder?' Doyle raised his eyebrows.

'I see the jury found Sugar Bag O'Sullivan guilty. That won't go down well with the C.I.'

'Don't try to change the subject. So far the C.I. are loading all the blame for the lack of progress onto us. That's all your fault. Get me a result. Make an arrest.'

* *

When Jim Thomas arrived at the Station, he was in a much better humour than when Fess had left him the previous day. 'Good morning,' he said as he bustled in. 'At last some progress. Just as well the C.I. doesn't have to rely on you.'

'Have you found Basher?'

'While you're uselessly swanning about Carlton, some of us are getting the job done. We have Nifty safely locked away in the City Watch House.'

'Congratulations. Where did you find him?'

At this question Thomas lost some of his jaunty tone, a note of puzzlement entering his voice. 'That's a bit odd. He tried to pull off an armed robbery at some silvertail's house in Kew, where the staff managed to disarm and hold him. When the call came in to Russell Street it went high up the chain. No less than Piggott himself was ordered to drop everything and go out in our only car with a couple of others to bring him in. You might say Nifty was given the Squizzy Taylor treatment. I can't figure out why.'

'Have you spoken with him?'

Again Jim looked a little abashed. 'No. Only found out about him as I was I leaving to come up here.' Brightening, he added, 'Didn't want to miss out on seeing the locals in action. Some time in one of the Watch House cells with the other low life will do Nifty good, and you can join me this afternoon to see how the C.I. go about it.'

'I've been reading how some of the C.I. go about it — your colleague Leo O'Sullivan.'

'Sugar Bag's no colleague of mine,' Jim erupted, his fists

clenched and his face thrust forward to challenge Fess. He took out his pipe and began to light up, giving Fess the impression that on this occasion, instead of playing for time, he was trying to calm himself.

'So you reckon Leo O'Sullivan had it coming to him?'

'Should have been put away years ago.'

'I'd heard the whispers about him. Why did it take so long to catch up with him?'

'Don't get me started,' Jim replied, taking the pipe from his mouth with a gesture that made it clear he was already started. 'Sugar Bag's been at it for years. He was known as a grafter back in his days as a railways investigator before he ever joined the police.'

'So how did he get away with it?'

'If you ask our lords and masters, they'll tell you it's been too hard to get the proof,' he scoffed.

'Surely they're right there,' Fess argued. 'If you've just paid off a copper to escape being charged, you're not likely to want to own up to it, so getting witnesses to testify will always be a problem.'

'Yeah, thank God for Callaghan. But everyone knew what Sugar Bag was up to. The higher-ups are just too lily-livered; they should have snuffed him out, evidence or no.'

Fess chuckled. 'You mean let Piggott go after him?'

'I've told you before,' Jim said with a scowl. 'Piggott finds out who's done the crime, then goes all out, no holds barred, to get a conviction. If you're serious about stopping the crims, it's the only way to go. But you won't get far while you have scumbags that hide behind their police badges to commit their crimes and, worse still, bosses who won't lift a finger to stop them. I've told you before. The higher ranks are riddled with men who were once good coppers but now spend most of their time covering up corruption in the Force, because they're scared to death of being shown up as incompetent and corrupt themselves. They disgust me. Something has to be done about it.'

'Well, well, who would have thought? The man who only goes after results does care about the Force.'

'Well, well, who would have thought?' Jim repeated the words in a derisory tone. 'You have no idea how much of this goes on. Did you see the report in yesterday's paper about coppers in Ballarat charged with grave misconduct? Too little, too late. And the case a couple of weeks ago, when that bastard Les Frazier, the Senior Constable in Charge of the Night Duty Relief in East Melbourne, went down for demanding money with menaces in the Fitzroy Gardens.'

'That was disappointing, I know Les Frazier.'

'Disappointing?' Scorn coated Jim's voice. 'I was the one who put him away. He should have had a much longer sentence, but some of his mates clubbed together to testify to his previous spotless record. Baloney! And this is just the tip of the iceberg.'

'So putting away crooked cops is one of your causes you mentioned when we first met?'

'I'm more bothered about our so-called superiors who let them get away with it, though. And I'm going to do something about that.'

'Without risking your life or livelihood, I suppose.'

'You betcha.'

❦ ❧

Constable McKenzie was surprised when Fess announced that they were to target Jockey Harrison at the Albion. 'But, Boss, you said …'

'Slight change of plan,' Fess stated in a quiet voice that silenced the constable.

❦ ❧

Persistent hammering came from the sheet metal factory beside the Albion Hotel, as Fess and Jim crouched behind the cover of a picket fence on the corner, watching the two hefty constables, Daley and Williams, walk slowly down the other side of the street. The traffic was light: a cart from the factory, several vans and the occasional cyclist. On the footpath there was ample space for the few shoppers returning from Lygon Street and the trickle of men bound for the hotel, so Fess and Jim were able to keep the constables in view. Their stately progress was also being closely observed by the pair standing in front of the hotel. Fess allowed himself a small smile. Basher was there and the first part of his plan was working well. While McKenzie and Schultz were taking up their positions, hidden at either end of the lane at the back of the hotel, the slow approach of Daley and Williams caused the cockatoo standing beside Basher to hesitate over raising the alarm. Jockey would not be pleased if he were made to scamper from the hotel merely because a couple of coppers had walked past.

The policemen did continue past the hotel for another ten paces before their tempo changed and they turned to hurry across the road, bound for the entrance. Basher spread himself to block their way while the cockatoo fled inside. Fess and Jim broke from behind the fence and ran up the street. Williams tried to push Basher aside and received a shove that sent him sprawling onto the pavement. Daley, coming from the other side, managed to duck the punch aimed at his head and get in a quick jab to Basher's midriff that made the man gasp. He reared up, shouting obscenities at Daley and flailing at him with both fists. The young policeman, showing surprising poise and agility, blocked the blows with a stiff forearm or jigged away so that they completely missed the mark. Basher snarled his frustration and became even wilder in his assault, giving Daley the opportunity to land two punches that shook him, allowing Williams to grasp his right arm. Daley tried to pin the other arm, but Basher shook himself free and crashed his knee into Williams' groin. Williams went down again, this time buckling like a breaking wave. Daley landed another blow before skipping out of range. Basher rushed towards him and aimed a kick. It missed its mark as Daley side-stepped and caught the flying boot in a firm grip that swung Basher through the air to crash headfirst in the gutter. Before he had any chance to recover Daley pinned him with his knees and cuffed his wrists. Mindful of the instruction Fess had given him, he also applied fetters to his legs, trussing him like a huge table-bird.

Leaving Jim to help Williams to his feet, Fess hurried into the hotel where Maureen, with a laconic tilt of her head, indicated a doorway at the side of the bar. He threw open the doors of the rooms that lined the passage, unsurprised to find no one sheltering within, reached the back yard and ran into the lane where he found his two constables engaged in an argument with Jockey. When he saw Fess, the bookie turned towards him and said. 'What's going on? I've paid me dues. Where's me protection?'

'I thought Basher gave you that,' Fess replied, with the hint of a grin passing across his face.'

'We let a few others run past but waited for the man with the Gladstone bag, like you said,' Constable Schultz reported. 'There's some cash and we've got his book as well.'

'I hope there was no misunderstanding with Basher out the front,' Jockey said in a concerned tone. 'He can get carried away at times.'

'I think I can reassure you. One of my constables may be a little sore but we won't need to carry Basher away. He should be able to walk.' Fess enjoyed the puzzled look on Jockey's face before leading the procession back through the silent bar to the street where Basher stood sullenly regarding Daley, who gripped him by the arm. Williams appeared better for having vomited into the gutter, and

Thomas completed the quartet, puffing on his pipe and eying Jockey with interest. 'Just the one, then?' he asked in a tone that Fess knew was meant to signal that the C.I. would have achieved a far more comprehensive set of arrests.

'We have the two we wanted,' Fess replied. He didn't say that he had no interest in turning the raid into a purge; he thought Thomas should by now be getting to understand how he operated, without the need to explain. 'I enjoyed your performance, Daley. Done this sort of thing before, have you?'

The constable gave a modest smile. 'Not much lately, but before I joined the Force I used to train at Flannery's Gym and had a couple of prelims at the Stadium. I saw Basher there a few times. He's just as wild but not nearly as quick as he used to be.'

'You move well. Played any footy at all?'

This time a rueful expression replaced the smile. 'I'm hopeless if there's a ball involved. Cricket, footy, whatever …'

'Pity. Carlton could do with a good ruckman.'

'They could do with some good forwards and backs, too,' Jockey interjected. 'You wouldn't want to bet on them, though.'

'Stick to the horses, eh?' Jim said as he walked over to snap open the Gladstone bag, now held by Constable Shultz. 'Not a lot in here.'

'A bit early in the day,' Fess replied and Jim narrowed his eyes to scrutinise him through the smoke from his pipe. Yes, Thomas was catching on. No need for the punters to lose too much money by delaying the raid until later in the day.

❦ ❧

When Basher was brought into the interview room, Fess and Jim were already sitting on the other side of the table. The chains on his legs had been removed, but the handcuffs remained and Constable Williams had hold of his arm. Basher gave no sign of his previous aggression, walking slowly and slumping onto the wooden chair opposite Jim.

'I am Senior Detective Thomas and you already know Senior Constable Jordan.' Basher made no response but his eyes slowly moved between the two men, and Fess could tell he was worried by the presence of the Detective. 'I'm not here to question you about your part in this morning's circus. That'll come later.' Jim paused and leaned forward across the table. 'I'm investigating the murder of Mary Worthington, sometimes known as Molly, last Saturday night.' Again Basher made no response but he blinked, and Fess could see a slight tightening of the muscles in his face and neck. 'We have two witnesses that place you at the scene when she was murdered, and from what I hear, it's just your kind of crime. What've you got to say for yourself?' Thomas was using his usual tactic of going beyond the known facts.

Basher blinked again before replying. 'They say she caught it in The Narrows. Yeah?'

'You know the spot. You were there.'

'I wasn't in The Narrows. Whoever says is lyin'. You're just 'avin' a go to fit me up. Any sheila that goes in The Narrows is pushin' 'er luck.'

'But you were in Barkly street, weren't you, Basher?' Fess interjected.

'I mighta been. Passin' through, like.'

'No, you weren't passing through.' Ferret had described him as skulking behind a tree and Ma Cutmore said he looked like he was guarding the place. 'You were waiting. Waiting for Molly to arrive at Nifty's place. What were you s'posed to do? Scare her off? Is that it? Or was it something more you had in mind?' Fess had not raised his voice, but his tone was unremitting and his eyes bored into Basher. 'She tried to run away and you chased her into The Narrows. You didn't mean to kill her but you couldn't hold back.'

'No, no, no!' Basher tried to stand up and was immediately pushed down by Williams. Basher's face was more animated than Fess had ever seen it and he was breathing in short gasps. 'You've got it wrong. OK, I was s'posed to warn 'er off, tell 'er to stay away from Nifty. But the skirt never turned up. I missed 'er at …' He paused. 'I kept goin' between 'er place and Nifty's but I didn't lay eyes on 'er, so I scarpered.'

'You missed her at …' Fess waited for the gap to be filled and, when Basher merely blinked at him, he provided the words himself. 'Gloria Ryan's place?'

'I didn't say that.'

'You didn't have to,' Jim interjected. 'It's written on your face. Why did she put you up to it?'

'I ain't said nothin' about 'er.'

Fess thought it was as if Basher was rehearsing his defence for later — for Gloria. Or perhaps it wasn't Gloria. 'Are you telling us it wasn't Gloria? Was it Paula who wanted Molly warned off?'

Basher looked from Jim to Fess and then back again, his face increasingly confused. Eventually he brought his lips together in a tight line before insisting, 'I ain't said nothin'. Ya can't say I 'ave.'

Jim erupted. 'You're in it up to your neck. You're s'posed to warn her off, rough her up even, but you can't stop, so you drag her into the narrows where you rape and then suffocate her.' Jim saw the startled look on Fess' face and gave a quick nod of his head. 'Then you go into smoke so we can't find you for days. More evidence of your guilt.'

'I didn't know you was wantin' me. I've been at me sister's in Seddon. She's been sick an' I was lookin' after 'er kids. Ask 'er, why don't ya?'

'You look just like a nanny. I don't care where you've been. You're as guilty as sin. You'd better tell us who put you up to it or it'll be all the worse for you.'

Basher glared at Jim, struggled against the constraints of his manacles but said nothing.

'Constable, take him away and keep him locked in a secure cell while we prepare to charge him.'

Williams looked at Fess, who nodded his assent. They had hardly cleared the room when Jim turned to Fess. 'We did well getting him to admit he was after Molly. You think it was Paula who put him up to it?'

'I think we need to talk with Paula and Gloria again. But what's this about rape?'

Jim gave an apologetic bob of his head. 'Oh, yeah. Sorry about that. I forgot to tell you the Government Pathologist's report came in this morning. Mary was raped. She put up a struggle during which she wasn't strangled but suffocated with a pillow or a scarf or something like that – Ronaldson wasn't sure what. You shouldn't be surprised by the rape, though. A girl as pretty as Mary isn't likely to be killed in The Narrows without being raped as well.'

Fess fingered his beard for a moment 'You're the second person to tell me that. But whoever did it took the trouble to lay her out in a dignified fashion. Not the typical behaviour of a rapist.'

'You telling me you can't see Basher doing that?'

'There's so much that says Basher did it. But you're right; I can't see him tidying up afterwards. And, for all his faults, Basher seldom lies. He's not smart enough to make up stories. Maybe he was sent to warn off Mary and, when he couldn't find her, went to look after his sister's kids. I told you he could be amiable some of the time. We do need to talk with the Ryans.'

Jim leaned back in his chair. 'What's it matter? My money's on Nifty. He raped Mary in his room, suffocated her with a pillow, carried her through the back yard of the house and dumped her in the lane after Ferret had gone off to pinch the candlesticks. It all fits. Probably, when putting her body in the lane, he arranged her clothes like they were when we found her.'

'What about her bag?'

'He had to get rid of that, so he threw it further down the lane and hoped someone would take it away so we'd suspect theft. Pity for him it was useless Clarry who found it. Now we need to go to the watch house and confront Nifty.'

'OK, but Ryan's place is on the way. You did want to leave Nifty to stew for a bit. Another half hour or so?'

'You think Paula wanted to break up the romance between Mary and Nifty?'

'We know they fell out over him. Gloria's used Basher before. Maybe Paula thought she would have a go.'

'It'll be a waste of time, but you're a persistent bugger, aren't you?'

This time, when they reached Argyle Square there were no bocce players to be seen, but the cool weather had not deterred the older members of the Carlton Bowling Club, who had turned out for their Tuesday afternoon competition. They were well rugged up against the breeze, the bulkiness of their clothing further impeding them as they stooped to send the bowls along the green. Until now Fess had given no thought to what he would do when it came time for him to toss it in. He didn't know why the thought came to him now but he did know it wouldn't be bowls. Surely he would find a more interesting and more comfortable pastime when he was eventually put out to grass.

9

Again Fess knocked before entering the green wooden door. The café area was much quieter than when he and Jim had visited on Sunday afternoon; most of the boarders must be at work or out looking for a job. Only one table was occupied by two men Fess remembered seeing playing bocce last Sunday. Paula looked up from her position behind the small counter near the door. She was more presentably dressed than on the previous two occasions he had seen her, wearing a black silk blouse with ruffled collar and cuffs and smoking a cigarette in a bone coloured holder. 'Mum's not here,' she said flatly. 'It's her day for afternoon tea with her old friends from Malvern and she's left me to mind the place. I don't know when she'll be back.'

'That's all right, Paula. It was you we wanted to see.'

'Oh, yeah?' Her initial expression of surprise seemed genuine but soon turned to a defensive pout. 'What d'ya want me for?'

'We want to ask you what you said to Basher,' Jim demanded.

'That won't take long.' Fess could see her relax and knew they had made the wrong start. 'I haven't spoken to him. I don't speak to him. He gives me the creeps.'

Jim continued to stare accusingly at her. 'But he was here?'

'I already told him,' she said nodding toward Fess. 'I dunno. You'd have to ask Mum.'

Fess decided to try a different tack. 'I understand you and Mary had a falling out.'

'Cripes, you're not too well informed. Who told you that?'

'She wouldn't go dancing with you last Saturday, so you had to go to the pictures on your own.'

'I told you Molly had somethin' else on. She's … She was a pal, but I didn't own her. Nobody did.'

'So you didn't mind when Nifty dropped you for her?' Jim asked.

Both men were surprised when Paula threw back her head and gave a laugh that began in her chest and rose in pitch and volume as it travelled up to her throat and out through her open mouth. 'You've been talkin' with Nifty, have you? You blokes are all the same. You haven't got a clue.' She rose and walked from behind the counter. 'Come over here,' she said indicating the nearest table. 'Sit down and let me tell you a few of the facts of life.'

They did as they were bid and, when they were settled opposite her, she continued. 'Molly and I like a good time, and for that you need a bloke in tow most times. A lot of them are chumps with tickets on themselves, who think you can't help but fall for the line they spin. You play along and soon they start moonin' after you and for a while that's fun. But you know it won't last, you wouldn't want it to, anyway. Old timers like you two and Mum think we poor, little girls can't look after ourselves and have to be protected. Tosh. It's the blokes who need protection, if only they knew it. Yeah, I had a fling with Nifty, but I was gettin' tired of him. You know he's a back-lane tug with smart clobber and a fancy tongue; no future there. Molly got interested — she had this thing about him bein' a crook. I don't reckon she'd met many before, and she thought it made him more exciting. God knows why. But Molly wasn't one to be tied down either — good on her — so Nifty wasn't the only one sniffin' around. He didn't know it, but she was more interested in what he got up to than the cove himself.' She laughed again, this time, more a reflective chuckle than the full-blown guffaw she had given earlier. 'That's where she was on Saturday night.' The amusement in Paula's eyes died and she looked down at the table. 'At least that was where I thought she was. Something went very wrong? Are you sayin' it was Basher?'

Fess thought of the account of Mary in the newspaper. How different Molly was from the young woman her family knew as Mary. How could they not know or at least suspect? Perhaps they did but were reluctant to admit it to themselves and quite unwilling to share their fears with him. 'You go to night classes with Mary at the College?'

Again Paula gave the hearty laugh that shook her whole body. 'There's not much you get right, is there? I'm no student and, anyway, Mum keeps me too busy here to go off to classes. I make sure I've got Saturdays off. Not many classes on a Saturday night.'

'So how did you and Mary become friends?'

'She dropped in here one night lookin' for work. I think one of the girls at Ball and Welch had been doin' a bit here and told her about us. Mum took one look at her and gave her a job. We got to know one another and started goin' to the pictures on a Saturday. That's when she began to stay overnight with us.'

The door behind her creaked and, looking over her shoulder, Paula said, 'Here's Mum, back from sippin' tea with the toffs.'

'Here again so soon. Have you gentlemen come to tell us you've arrested poor Molly's killer?' Gloria was wearing a silk afternoon dress, similar to the one she had worn on Sunday, but this one had a swirling floral pattern in claret and magenta, and was topped by a slightly frazzled fur jacket. On her head was perched a confection of net, sparkly beads and a piece of silk from her dress. She sank into the chair Fess had vacated and gave a sigh. 'It's a pleasant trip from Malvern, but you have to change trams and it gets a bit tiring for me these days.' She gave a coy grin. 'I should spend some time on the beat. That keeps you policeman fit and strong, doesn't it?'

'He was askin' about Basher,' Paula announced. 'He hasn't been here, has he?'

'Basher?' Gloria sat up straighter and eyed them cautiously. 'Why are you asking about him again?'

Fess took a chair from the next table and sat next to Gloria. 'He's told us that he was given the job of warning

Mary to stay away from Nifty last Saturday night. We all know how Basher warns people.'

'And did he warn her? Do you know? Did he see Molly, the poor dear? Perhaps she didn't listen to him and went ahead anyway. Do you know what happened?' Gloria put up her questions like a smokescreen — an ineffective one.

'So it was you that put Basher up to it,' Jim interjected.

'I warned Molly. I told you the last time you were here. I told her that man Naughton was no good and would only bring her grief.' She glanced disparagingly at her daughter. 'You can't tell these young people anything, though. They think they know it all.'

Fess didn't bother pointing out that, on his last visit, she had denied knowing Nifty. 'So you thought you'd use Basher to threaten her, to warn her off.' He knew he was using Jim's approach, the method he deplored, but excused himself — Gloria was so adept at being scatterbrained.

Gloria gave a convincing simulation of annoyance. 'I keep telling you, but you won't listen. I could see nothing good could come from Molly's flirtation with Naughton, but she paid no attention to my warning.'

This time Fess was not going to let her get away with it. 'Yesterday you told me you didn't know him.'

'I don't,' Gloria replied blandly before giving her indulgent smile. 'Paula has told me about him.'

'Aw, Mum, you know you were more concerned about Molly not turnin' up here so often.'

'Don't be nasty, dear. Aren't you just a little miffed that Nifty preferred Molly to you?'

'Baloney. She loved leading them on but she didn't give a fig for Nifty, or anyone else if it comes to that. I was miffed with her because gettin' up to no good with Nifty meant she wasn't around to go out with me.'

'Paula, are you sure you don't know anything about what Mary planned to do with Nifty on Saturday night?' Fess asked.

'No. I asked her but she wouldn't say. You can bet they weren't going to the flicks or out dancin'. Nifty had somethin' on and Molly wanted to be part of it.'

'And that's what led to her death,' Gloria announced, sniffing into a handkerchief she had drawn from a pocket. 'I'd say that nasty Naughton man had a hand in it. I tried to warn her she was making a great mistake. I only wanted what was best for her.'

'Don't be such a bloody hypocrite.' This time it wasn't Fess, but Paula who was accusing her mother. 'You were fussed you were losin' your favourite waitress, the one the blokes really went for. So you hired that back-street thug to frighten her and, thanks to you, she's dead.'

'No, no, no,' Gloria wailed. 'Basher told me he couldn't find her. None of this is my doing.'

It was with a sense of release that Jim and Fess returned to Cardigan Street and walked toward the corner where Fess had spent such a chilling ten minutes the day before. 'What a pair,' Jim scoffed.

'You know, there's an honesty underneath Paula's cynicism,' Fess replied. 'With a mother like Gloria, it's hard to see where she gets it from.'

'Another one of the Carlton low life you have a crush on. At least she's way better looking than the others you've shown me.' Jim began to feel for his pipe and added, 'We did get clear how Basher was put up to it. What we really need is a witness who was in The Narrows. My money's still on Nifty, though.'

They turned at the corner and silently began to walk up the slope to Russell Street, passing the bleak walls of the old gaol on the other side of the road. It had been closed last year, but that had done nothing to dispel the air of melancholy that clung to the bluestones. Ned Kelly, its most famous prisoner, had achieved the status of a mythical hero, but what of the others whose lives had been ended by the hangman's noose? Fess thought of the Gun Alley murder. The execution of Colin Ross for that murder must have been one of the last held at the gaol. The case had been of great public interest only three years ago but, despite the efforts of his barrister, Thomas Brennan, to cast doubt on the verdict, Ross was never mentioned now. Fess had read Brennan's book and found its claims hard to ignore. Certainly it cast doubt on the methods used by Jim's hero, Piggott. It appeared he had decided early on that Ross was guilty and bent all his efforts to find any evidence that would sustain the charge, ignoring anything that went against it. The Court's reliance on the word of a number of dubious witnesses was also very troubling.

Was Jim going down the same path? From the very start, he'd been keen to nominate someone as the murderer and go after him. First it was Clarry Garton, then Ferret Roberts followed by Basher O'Shea and now Nifty Naughton. He had a grudge to settle with Nifty as well, feeling he'd been cheated of his conviction for that previous murder. All he lacked was a witness, and he sounded like he would settle for anyone, no matter how dubious, just like his hero had done.

Fess looked again at the gaol and remembered the item he had seen in Friday's paper, where it was announced a contract had been let for the construction on the site of a college for the training of young women in domestic economy. What had originally caught his attention was the comment that it was to proceed as rapidly as possible to relieve unemployment in the building industry. A pity that more money couldn't be spent on police buildings. Now, as he looked again at the dismal walls, he thought that a gathering of young women bent on domestic economy might help overcome the gloom. He certainly hoped so.

Still in silence, they crossed Victoria Street and passed the front of the gaol before coming to the City Watch House. The watch house was a dressed stone building of imposing proportions with an arched entry mounted on decorative columns, the arched design repeated at each of the upper windows. High above the door stood a square tower with mock dovecotes at each corner. Were it not for the barred windows and the iron studded door, it could be mistaken for the home of a wealthy citizen or a museum.

Immediately on entering, they took a passageway sharp left into the receiving room, where the Watch House Keeper was at his desk behind a high wooden counter. 'G'day, Charlie,' Jim said jovially. 'Here at last. I told you I'd be coming. Can one of your blokes get this Naughton cove out of the cell for us?' Without waiting, Jim led Fess down another passage that led to a small room with a single window set high in the stone wall. The air in the room was stale and dank.

Soon afterwards Nifty was brought in, looking altogether different from the man Fess was used to confronting. The sharp suit, often in a cloth that carried a prominent stripe, was gone. So, too, were the brightly patterned tie and the pork-pie hat, pushed to the back of his head by the Brylcreamed cow-lick that sat above his narrow, sneering face. Also missing were the brawny and slow-witted thugs who usually accompanied him. This time the man beside him was brawny and possibly slow-witted, but dressed in a police uniform. Nifty wore fawn dungarees and an open-necked shirt, which was made from a coarse material and several sizes too large for him. He was unshaven. 'Fess Jordan! What brings you here? Not your usual territory.'

'I might say the same to you, Nifty.'

'Just a misunderstanding. I'll soon be out of here.' His clothes might be different, but he remained as cocky as ever. Apparently, it would take more than a change of clothes and the squalor of the crowded holding cell to undermine his arrogance.

'Sit down, Naughton,' Jim commanded. 'I'm Senior Detective Thomas. We've met before. This time we're investigating another murder, the rape and murder of Mary Worthington.'

Nifty turned his head to appraise Jim before answering in a bored voice. 'Oh yeah? She the one in The Narrows?'

'Don't play silly games with us,' Jim growled. 'We have witnesses that place you at the scene.'

Fess slid the photograph across the table in front of Nifty. 'You called her Molly.'

'They're two of the girls from Gloria Ryan's place. I remember seeing them at the Palais but I don't remember the photograph. So she's the one who's dead.'

'I've already warned you,' Jim said, standing so that he looked down on Nifty. 'We know Mary used to come to your room. We know she was there just prior to her death. You raped her, suffocated her and then dumped her body in the lane at the back of your place before scarpering.' He sat down again and the anger in his tone was replaced by world-weariness. 'Do us all a favour. Stop wasting time and admit it. You might be able to get away with manslaughter if you get a good lawyer.'

'She wasn't in me room. That was another bit of fluff.'

'Oh, yeah. What's her name?'

'That wouldn't be fair to the lady, given her circumstances.'

Fess could see that Nifty was beginning to enjoy himself. He was no stranger to police interviews and relished the contest, confident he could handle most interrogators.

'Strange how you know the day Mary was killed. We haven't told you that.'

Nifty's face tightened and he swallowed before saying, 'Yeah, well I haven't been in me room since Saturday, so I thought that was when you meant.'

Fess changed tack. 'You used to go to Gloria Ryan's place.'

'Once or twice. That Italian food ain't real bad. You should try it.'

Jim stirred, impatient with what he saw as a useless digression, until Fess said, 'No, Nifty. You went there often to see Paula. That was until you turned your attention to Molly, as you call her. You don't go there now. Molly came to you.'

'Y'know how it is. Be a bit nice to them and they think they own you. Me, I like to move around. Haven't been near those two for weeks.'

'And this bloke.' Fess pointed to the second man in the photograph. 'Who's he?'

Nifty appeared relieved to get off the subject of his relationship with the two girls, and became expansive. 'He's a cove from the Palais. A regular there who's got tickets on himself. Last year, when Squizzy went into smoke, he even made a play for Ida, Squizzy's wife, who kept comin' to the Palais without her man. Had to move on when Squizzy got back, o'course. Had a go for Molly, but I don't think she was too keen.'

'Does he have a name or are his circumstances sensitive as well?' Jim asked, reasserting himself.

'I reckon he was Hal or somethin' like that.'

Jim stood up again. 'Let's get back to this murder you've committed. You did a bunk straight afterwards. It's obvious you're as guilty as sin.'

'I was with the skirt who was with me earlier. She'd gone back to her place and I had to wait until her husband had gone. He works nights.'

'Come off it. You won't even give us her name. She's no use to you.'

Nifty tilted his head and sneered at Jim. 'She will be if I really need her. You don't want to know her name. She's married to a cop.' Nifty shook himself as though bored and changed the subject. 'You're barkin' up the wrong tree comin' after me. I'll tell ya, though. When I came out of my place, Basher O'Shea was skulkin' behind a tree. Now, if this Molly was done in The Narrows, you should ask Basher what he was doin' there.'

After Nifty had been led back to his cell, Fess turned to face Jim. 'If you want to pretend to a suspect that you know more than you do, that's up to you. It's when you tell the suspect something I've passed on to you in strict confidence that I get annoyed.'

'What are you on about?'

'Nifty will know it was Ferret who told us Mary had been in his room, and Ferret wasn't sure she was there on Saturday night.'

'It could have been Ma Cutmore who shopped him.'

Fess shook his head wearily. 'Don't give me that. Ma tried her best to give him an alibi. It wouldn't surprise me if Nifty spoke with her before he shot through.'

'I told you I don't play the games you do. If you have a problem with Ferret, you've only yourself to blame for breaking his confidence by speaking to me. I made no promises to him. I used what you told me.' Jim shrugged and gave Fess a conciliatory grin. 'Look on the bright side. Nifty will have no chance to get back at Ferret when he's been hanged. All we need now is a confession or, failing that, a witness who saw him carrying her into the lane. I'd even settle for someone who saw him in the lane at about the right time.'

Fess grasped his chin and gave his beard a reflective rub. 'I can see why you say that but I know Nifty. He's a cold-blooded killer, but he doesn't bash or strangle people. He leaves that to the thugs he usually has with him. No, Nifty relies on his gun to frighten and coerce people or, when the mood takes him, even to kill them, as you've seen.'

Jim shook his head vehemently. 'This is different. He wasn't cold-blooded here. Just the opposite. His passion got the better of him. He had a falling out with his girl and lost it. That malarkey about the policeman's wife! And naming Basher, like pulling a rabbit from a hat. I'm beginning to feel sorry for Basher. No one minds dobbing him.'

'I'm not convinced it was either of them. There's something not quite right.'

Jim stood up. 'You can have your doubts. I'll take Nifty.' He walked back into the receiving room with Fess trailing pensively behind him.

'Ah, there you are.' The Watch House Keeper was surprisingly pleased to see them. 'Thought you'd like to know I'm about to let your man out. Piggott rang through to say the charges have been withdrawn: the witnesses don't want to front up.'

'What?' Now it was Jim's turn to frown. 'Surely they haven't been got at?'

'I don't reckon anyone gets at Piggott or Fitzwilliam.'

'Fitzwilliam?'

'Y'must have heard of him,' the keeper said patronisingly. 'Gets his picture in the papers. Stafford Fitzwilliam. He was the toff whose house Naughton broke into.'

'I think you mean Sanford Fitzwilliam. He's the former solicitor and current socialite,' Fess said.

'A pal of yours?' Thomas sneered. 'Do you socialise at the races or is it over cards? They say he takes everyone's money. You must stand out among the silvertails.'

'We met during the strike. I did get to know a bit about him.' Fess did not go on. There was a lot more he could have said about Sanford Fitzwilliam, but now was not the time. 'What are you going to do now?'

'I'm not going to have that arrogant bastard go into smoke again. I'll keep him in here under suspicion of murder. A few more nights in the cell will take the smile off his face.'

Fess nodded thoughtfully, and it was unclear whether

he agreed with Jim or was considering some other possibility. 'Nifty knew the charges would be dropped. I wonder how he could be so sure.' He turned to the keeper. 'You said the witnesses didn't want to come to Court. Did they say why?'

'If they did, Piggott didn't tell me.'

Fess nodded thoughtfully again. 'Perhaps we should ask Fitzwilliam if he knows why Nifty should disappear on the night one of his girlfriends is murdered and turn up at Fitzwilliam's home, waving a gun around, and why he handed him over to the police, only to back out the next day.'

'There's no future trying to rattle the cage of a man like that.' Thomas shook his head vigorously. 'He's obviously got connections.'

Fess pressed his lips together and gave Thomas a rueful stare. 'I didn't think you'd be so easily scared off by someone like Fitzwilliam. I guess it's the connection with Piggott. You wouldn't want to come uninvited into one of his cases, even if the set-up does look fishy.'

Jim waved his unlit pipe at Fess. 'Don't give me that crap. 'I'm happy to ring Fitzwilliam and tell him one of his old pals, Fess Jordan, would like a chat. It'll be a waste of time, but you like these pointless chats, don't you?'

'In that case I'll be on my way.' Leaving the watch house, Fess wondered whether Jim would follow through and he would have the opportunity to meet Fitzwilliam again. Probably his involvement in their murder investigation was coincidental, but it did open up new possibilities.

He did not turn back towards Carlton but continued on past the City Court and around the corner to the main building of the Working Men's College. Standing together and built from similar rough-hewn sandstone, it appeared to Fess as though the College building was an adjunct to the Court. Or should it be the other way around? On entering the wide doors of the building, he saw a room to his left that carried no sign but contained desks and cabinets, suggesting it might house the administration for the College. When he walked through the open door a fresh-faced girl rose quickly from her seat at one of the desks and came toward him. 'Senior Constable Jordan, Carlton Police,' Fess said to her.

'Is there a problem?' she asked anxiously.

'Not that I know of,' he replied in a friendly voice. 'I would like to make some enquiries of whoever is in charge of the evening classes in shorthand and typewriting.'

'Oh, good.' Her worry dispelled, she gave him a sunny smile, perhaps like the one Mary was known for, and added, 'On odd occasions, some of our students can get a bit out of order on one of the streets or at one of the pubs, and the police get involved. You need to speak with Mr. McPherson in the building across Bowen Street on the first floor.' She turned her head to consult the large round clock that was mounted on the back wall of the office. 'The day classes are over and the evening ones don't start until seven, so he might not be there.'

'Thank you. I'll try my luck.'

Fess walked along the cloister-like corridor and emerged

onto the bustle of the small city street that was Bowen Street. His region ended at Victoria Street, so the College was not within his area of responsibility and he had not had any reason to visit before. He found it strange that the College buildings should be scattered along a city street. The University, with its gracious buildings set in spacious grounds, was altogether different.

The ground floor of the building he entered contained a number of empty classrooms. Climbing the wooden steps to the first floor, he could hear the staccato sound of a single typewriter. The typing was not continuous but broken into short bursts that came to him like sporadic machine-gun fire. He walked toward the sound, his boots loud on the bare boards of the corridor. Reaching the source of the noise, he looked in on a sizeable room where four rows of continuous benches carried an array of closely spaced typewriters. A dapper man with slick, dark hair, wire-rimmed glasses and a pencil moustache, dressed in a hand-knitted maroon cardigan with a white shirt and a conservative tie, sat behind one of the typewriters toward the end of the second row. 'I was hoping you were the Remington man,' he said when he saw Fess. 'He often looks in on a Tuesday and today students have been having trouble with this machine; it tends to jam when you type an "a" and an "s" one after the other. Do you know how many separate parts there are in a standard typewriter?'

'I'm afraid I don't. Are you Mr. McPherson?'

'Indeed I am. You won't find anyone else up here at this time of the day.'

‘I am Senior Constable Jordan from Carlton Police.’

‘It’s often occurred to me that shorthand and typewriting skills would be a great asset in the Police Force, with all the material you have to take down and report on. What do you think?’

‘You make a good point,’ Fess responded diplomatically. ‘There are a number of skills and capabilities that would make us more effective. Finding the time for training is a major problem, though.’

‘We could mount a special course for you. We’re very happy to do that sort of thing. In the case of the police it would be a public service, although of course, there would be a fee. We could tailor it neatly to your needs.’

Fess thought Mr. McPherson looked rather like a tailor’s assistant. ‘Meanwhile …’ he inserted quickly so as to forestall the entrepreneurial Head of Shorthand and Typing, ‘… meanwhile, I am here to enquire about one of your students — Mary Worthington. I understand she attended your shorthand and typing classes.’

‘I thought you might have come for that,’ Mr. McPherson said mournfully. ‘We don’t have many police calling up here.’

‘Do you mind telling me a little about her? Was she a good student?’

‘Ah, there is no simple answer to that simple question.’ McPherson shook his head ruefully. ‘She made such a promising start last year in the shorthand classes; could have been one of our top students. But I really think it came a bit too easily for her and she became bored.

Certainly her performance and her attendance started to tail off, but she did pass and took on typewriting this year with her old vigour. The boredom, if that is what it was, set in even earlier though, and she missed many classes. We hadn't seen her at all in recent times and I wrote to her just the other day to suggest she withdraw from the course. It's a waste of her money to pay the fees. I did hope she might return one day. She was a very engaging young lady.'

Here were the contents of the letter Fess had been so unaccountably squeamish about opening. Here was more detail of Mary's path to becoming Molly.

10

When Fess turned the key in the lock of his front door, he was looking forward to his seat beside the fire with his family around him, each of them telling the stories from their day. Before he had the door closed, Bernadette appeared in the entrance to the living room and he prepared for the light kiss on the lips that was her usual welcome. 'About time,' she said. 'Your dinner's in the oven.' She hurried down the passage to the kitchen, leaving him to look in on the living room, where his younger children, Michael and Carmel, were reading beside the fire. More accurately, they had been reading but were now gazing toward him with troubled faces.

'Well, how is everyone?' he boomed, much too heartily.

'OK,' Carmel said without conviction, looking at him from under her eyelashes. Michael remained silent. What had the boys been up to this time?

When he entered the kitchen, Bernadette had her back to him, leaning forward to take his dinner from the oven. The family had eaten earlier, as they so often did: arriving home at this hour was not unusual for him. The frosty reception was. Bernadette rose and turned toward him, holding a heaped dinner plate in an oven glove and looking at him with the same troubled gaze he had received from his daughter. They really were looking like one another these days.

'Where's Kevin?' Fess asked.

She set the plate of rabbit stew down at the head of the table with a vigour that caused the cutlery to rattle. 'Out the back in the sleep-out.'

'A bit chilly out there, isn't it?'

Bernadette tossed her head in exasperation. 'I had to put him somewhere. Where else was there?'

There were always difficulties when the occasional family drama required the children to be separated. There was simply not enough room in the house. When they first arrived, it was impossible. His mother insisted on retaining the larger front bedroom for herself and maintaining the living room in pristine condition, immediately ready for that rare event, the arrival of unexpected visitors. This was not the whim of an elderly lady; she had insisted on the inviolability of that front room from the first day she had entered the house with her husband and young son. The smaller bedroom was all that was left for the five of them. Fess had employed the knowledge gained as a builder's labourer and called on some of his old friends to help him erect a sleep-out on the back verandah. His mother had not been happy about it, but Fess had talked her round. The sleep-out was cold in the winter and hot in the summer but remained water and windproof, and the boys became used to it.

After his mother's death two years ago, they had been able to leave Carmel with a room to herself and move into what he still thought of as his mother's room. His grandfather, Florence Jordan's father, had been a successful manufacturer of leather goods. Although his grandparents died before Fess had the chance to remember them, he seemed always to have known that his mother had married below herself when she became the wife of a policeman and was forced to live in a small rented cottage in Church Street. Never was she to be called Florry and never did she call Fess anything but Edward. She was the last ever to use that forgotten name.

Soon after his father was promoted to Sergeant and began his lengthy tenure in charge of the Carlton Station, Florence inherited a sufficient sum from her parents to enable her to buy the house in Murchison Street, which she lived in until her death. As the wife of the Sergeant-in-Charge, she made claim to 'a certain position' in the community and explained to her son that maintaining such a position placed certain requirements upon her. Florence did not mix easily with her neighbours but cultivated a group of other 'well-to-do' women who, from time to time, came to the house for an elegant afternoon tea served on the Royal Crown Derby that had been acquired for such occasions. On returning from school, he would be paraded before the guests, his memories of these events combining shy awkwardness with perfume, large hats and glittering jewellery. Florence had always been well-groomed but now became well-dressed as well. Fess thought his tall and stately mother the most beautiful and the most elegant of women.

Florence tried to instil into her son that he, too, was a person of substance and should be treated appropriately. His father saw things differently: that his son needed to become a person others admired and respected because of his courage, strength and stamina. In other words, he needed to become like David Jordan, and his father spared no effort to see he did so. Young Fess was blessed with a queen for a mother and a hero for a father. It was only when he reached his teens that he began to gain a more balanced view of their strengths and weaknesses. Now, as a parent himself, he was continuing to do so.

Bern had not been born into a 'family of substance' and saw no need to follow her mother-in-law's ideas in anything. There was a tension between them that remained, even after death. She certainly felt no need to maintain a position and Fess had tried to lighten the atmosphere by telling her he was delighted she spent so much less on clothes and appearance than his mother must have done. With three children he could not afford it and had only recently come to realise how much his parents had saved by having only one child. Bern didn't seem to see the funny side.

When Fess did not respond to her justification for the marooning of Kevin in the sleep-out, her exasperation broke the walls of her reticence and her words tumbled out in a spate. 'Kevin didn't come home after school today. I was getting frantic. Then one of your constables brought him home. He'd been caught stealing in Mansons' Bakery. I don't know whether they've charged him or not.

The constable was very vague about the whole thing and Kevin won't say a word. I told you yesterday he was restless and now we have this.' She tossed her head and gave a humourless smile. 'Michael says he knows nothing about what happened, but I don't believe him.'

Fess wondered how many interviews he had conducted where he had later used those exact words. He nodded and said, 'Let me eat this excellent stew, and then I'll have a chat with Kevin.' He took his time over the stew, watched with silent impatience by his wife. He must have been about Kevin's age when he took those sweets. Probably all boys had a go at it. Wiping his lips, Fess said, 'Thank you for that, my dear,' and rose to go into the sleep-out.

'You won't …,' Bernadette said and then stopped herself. 'Never mind.'

The light in the sleep-out was not switched on and Fess, blinded by the brightness of the kitchen, could not immediately see his son. Eventually he realised that Kevin lay on his bed with his overcoat used as a blanket. 'There you are,' Fess said gently. Kevin made no reply but lifted his body by propping on one elbow and regarded his father suspiciously. It had always intrigued Fess that those accused of having committed a crime were the ones who often wore the suspicious expression when confronted by a policeman. 'I hear you were caught stealing,' Fess said conversationally.

'Just a couple of cakes.'

Pleased to have a response, Fess decided to see if surprise might help. 'When I was your age I took lollies.'

He could see from his son's wide-eyed face that he had achieved the surprise he was seeking. Now he had to build on it. 'Yeah, the other kids at school said the son of a policeman didn't have the guts to do it. I reckoned I didn't have much choice. Was it like that for you?'

Now it was Fess' turn to be surprised. Kevin straightened up and was gazing at Fess with what looked like admiration. Bern was right. It had been a while since he was able to get such a response from his son. 'Were you ever caught?' Kevin asked with obvious interest.

'No. I only did it once before I saw it was a mug's game.'

Now Fess saw the rapport fracture. 'Huh,' said Kevin scornfully. 'You reckon being a copper isn't?' He lay back on the bed staring at the window. 'What are you going to do to me?'

Fess was irritated, not with his son, but with himself. The man with the reputation for being able to get people talking couldn't manage it with his son. 'We police wait until we have the whole story before we decide what to do.' He wished that was really true, an image of Jim waving his pipe, flashing through his mind. 'So why don't you tell me what happened?' He tried for a tone midway between asking and requiring.

'Yeah, a policeman.' Kevin's tone was one of resigned regret and Fess was not clear what lay behind his words. For a moment he thought that was all he was going to get, but then Kevin continued in a flat voice. 'I went into the shop. I saw two cakes I liked on the display stand. I took them and ran but tripped over in the street and Mr.

Manson caught hold of me. He took me round to the Station and one of the constables — I don't know his name — he brought me home.'

'Thank you. That's a good start. But you haven't told me why you decided to do it. Spur of the moment? A dare, like me? Some other reason?'

'I just did it.'

Fess could not avoid a feeling of disappointment that his son should be so inept. Manson chose to display some of his cakes on a display stand, deliberately to catch the customers' attention, and the shop was often crowded. It should have been child's play — he noted the irony of the words — to pinch a couple of cakes without anyone noticing. But Kevin had been spotted and then tripped up in trying to escape. He must have been goaded into it just as Fess had been all those years ago. 'Nothing else you want to tell me?'

Kevin shook his head, gazing intently at his father. Fess hadn't obtained the full account he was seeking and could see there was more to tell, but he would get nothing more tonight. Perhaps a night in the sleep-out would bring the result Jim hoped to get from Nifty's night at the watch house.

Breakfast in the Jordan household next morning was a sombre affair. The children had nothing to say while giving their cereal and Vegemite toast remarkably careful attention. Bernadette who, the night before, had alternated between urging Fess to take a tougher line with Kevin and complaining at his not pushing Michael to tell what he knew, continued signalling with her eyes that there was still time for him to extract the full story before he departed. He had tried to calm her by saying, 'Let me see what they have to say at the Station,' but this only raised other fears.

'Will he have to go to Court?'

'I very much doubt it. But let me see.' He did not say he was troubled by how he should treat the matter when he did go to the Station. He couldn't ignore it, of course, but must be careful not to involve himself if the police were to take the case further. Bern didn't need to hear this.

❧ ❧

Fess arrived early at the Station but made little progress in finding out the details of Kevin's crime. They said that Constable Johnson, who had brought his son in yesterday afternoon, was not on duty today and Sergeant Doyle had taken over the matter himself. They treated him with the cautious sympathy usually offered to those who were known to be in trouble with the sergeant, and Fess assumed that Doyle had seen his son's crime as another opportunity to give him a hard time.

There was as yet no sign of Doyle so Fess turned his attention to the day's newspaper.

THE SUN-NEWS PICTORIAL WEDNESDAY, JULY 15, 1925

MARY WORTHINGTON RAPED AND SUFFOCATED

Government Pathologist's Shocking Report

TWO MEN HELD FOR QUESTIONING

Following a detailed examination of the body of Mary Worthington, the young woman murdered in Carlton on Saturday night, the Government Pathologist has reported that she was brutally raped before being suffocated, perhaps with a pillow or scarf. These findings deepen the horror of the crime that has shocked the city.

Underworld Figures Involved?

Police have now detained the two men the C.I.B. were seeking to interview, and both have been held for further questioning. Senior Detective Thomas declined to confirm the identity of those held but said that both of the men had known Mary Worthington. He refused to give any further details of their connection with the dead woman but said that the findings of the Pathologist made the police all the more determined that the rapist and murderer should be brought to justice. When it was put to the Detective that the men were well-known within the criminal community, he said he was unable to release the names of the men at this stage.

Nevertheless, rumours are circulating that one of the men is a former boxer who has previously faced charges for assault and for rape. The other man, they say, is well known for his involvement in the gangland of Carlton.

Code of Silence

Senior Detective Thomas did say that it was not uncommon for a code of silence among criminals to hinder police in pursuing their investigations. He said the appalling nature of the rape and murder of Mary Worthington demanded that the perpetrator not be allowed any protection by the criminal underworld. It is absolutely vital that anyone with information that might assist police come forward without delay.

Family Shocked by Latest Revelations

Elizabeth Robertson, the remaining child of George and Valerie Worthington, speaking on behalf of the family, said that her mother and father were shocked by the findings of the Pathologist, and so distraught that they were unable to speak with the press. She asked that her family be given the opportunity at the funeral, which will be held tomorrow at the Carlton Methodist Church, to farewell Mary with the dignity that she deserved.

Fess shook his head and fingered his beard. Jim certainly knew how to use the press. No doubt, he had fed them the confidential contents of the Pathologist's report and the details of Nifty's and Basher's detention, but he had covered himself by ensuring the press used his name only on the issues where he could safely be seen to comment. It was a nice touch, invoking the code of silence. The way he had done it was code itself — code for reminding possible witnesses of C.I.'s practice of paying for information leading to a conviction. Piggott's admirer and apprentice was using all the wiles of his master.

Fess was brought from his reflection by the loud voice of Doyle commanding the Duty Constable, 'Get Senior Constable Jordan to present at my office right now.'

He thought about waiting for the constable to summon him but decided this was an empty gesture. 'Morning, Sarge,' he said as he reached the doorway.

'What the hell have you been playing at?' Doyle demanded as he looked up from his spider crouch.

'What?' said Fess, nonplussed.

'I told you to pick up Ginger Foster, not Jockey Harrison. Can't you get anything straight?'

Jockey must have been up-to-date with his payments, just like he said. 'Sorry, Sarge. I thought you were just giving me a for-instance, not an order.'

The message got through to Doyle. 'I gave you no order to pick up Ginger. Don't try that one on me. But I expect, when I make a suggestion in this Station, it gets acted on. You've been here far too long not to understand that.'

'It was a way to get Basher as well. You know we arrested both him and Nifty yesterday.'

'You might have got Basher but you didn't get Nifty. The C.I. had to do that on their own. I've been speaking with them. Not too impressed by the way you want to go off on side issues. It's like dog's balls that Nifty raped the little tart … Don't give me that look. She hangs around with the low life and sniffs their snow. She's not the little angel her parents would like.' He scowled at Fess. 'As I was saying, Nifty couldn't get what he wanted from her, so he raped her, smothered her and dumped her in the lane. There's only one thing we need now and that's someone who's willing to say they saw him do it. The C.I. understand that and I see in the paper this morning, Thomas is doing his best to get a result. It's your job to help him, but all you want to do is drag him down to Ryan's and now out to Fitzwilliam's place. How many times have I told you your obsession with Fitzwilliam has to stop?'

Before Fess could reply, a heavily accented baritone voice from the front of the Station reverberated down the passageway and into Doyle's office. 'I see Senior Constable Fess Jordan.'

The much softer response from the Duty Constable was not intelligible, nor was it deemed acceptable. 'Then I see him with Sergeant. I pay taxes. Is my right.'

'Sort that out and come straight back,' Doyle snapped.

Fess walked up the corridor into the reception area, where he was confronted by Joseph Manson, the baker. Manson was short and stocky, with wide shoulders and almost no neck, as though he had been sawn from a solid block. His square face held small, deep-set eyes and was topped by cropped black hair. In his shop, he wore a white jacket with a high collar and a navy-and-white striped apron that made him look more like a butcher than a baker. For his visit to the Station he had abandoned the apron, giving him the appearance of a barber or a medical orderly.

'Senior Constable Fess Jordan. You can't sweep this under your carpet. This I will not allow.' He shook his head adamantly. 'Your men; they drag their feet and do not go after the thief, and now I find the reason: his partner is your son.'

'Come through, Mr. Manson,' Fess replied in as diplomatic a tone as he could muster. 'Let's see what can be done. First we need to speak with Sergeant Doyle.'

He led Manson back to Doyle's office and said, 'Sergeant, I understand you've taken personal control of the investigation of the robbery at Mansons' Bakery yesterday. This is Mr. Manson.' He stepped aside and the baker pushed into the room, grasped the visitor's chair that spent most of its time unoccupied in the corner, set it opposite Doyle and plumped himself down. Doyle recoiled so that he was sitting straighter on his chair than Fess had ever seen him. Manson filled the space on the desk with his elbows and leaned forward to confront the sergeant. 'We are told, we citizens, that there is the same law for all. Now we have two.'

'Two? I don't understand you, Mr. Manson,' Doyle growled.

Manson took his elbows from the table, but only so that he had the space to ram home his points with a stabbing finger. 'Pinchas Goldstein, the butcher, he bores the street with his story: how he has two old silver candlesticks taken from his house and very next day the famous Senior Constable Fess Jordan plucks the thief from the air like magic, and the candlesticks he returns safe and sound to Pinchas Goldstein. What a story.' He shook his head and his face took on the expression of a stage tragedian. 'But what of poor Joseph Manson? Two cunning brats enter his shop. One distracts with his theft of the cakes while the other makes off with the cash in the till. But Joseph, he foils their plot. He captures the one and knows who is the other. Where are the police? Where is the hero, Fess Jordan? Hiding away. And why? Because he deserts his post and tries to save his son. Wait until I take this to the newspapers.' Manson subsided, exhausted by his passion. He leaned back in his chair with his small, dark eyes continuing to flare at Doyle.

'Mr. Manson, you are right.' Doyle gave the surprised baker a twisted smile. 'I was just saying the same thing to the Senior Constable.'

'You were?'

'We cannot allow any thief to hide behind his father. That is why I have dismissed Senior Constable Jordan from the case and taken it over myself. As the Sergeant-in-Charge of Carlton Station it is my duty to do so.'

Manson had now recovered from his initial surprise at Doyle's conciliatory opening. 'But you do nothing. There is no arrest. My money is still missing. Why for Pinchas Goldstein and not for me?'

Doyle stood up. 'I am in charge now. You can be sure things will move much faster. He came from around his desk. 'But I must ask you to allow me to get on with the job. Senior Constable Jordan will show you out.' He offered his hand to Manson who turned toward the door, following Fess. 'And come back here when you've seen Mr. Manson out,' he snapped at Fess.

When Fess returned he said to Doyle, who was back in his spider position, 'I haven't been able to find out what actually happened yet.'

'Let me enlighten you.' Doyle began to recite as if from an incident report. 'Yesterday afternoon at about four, Constable Johnson on his beat attended a disturbance in Lygon Street where the proprietor of Mansons' Bakery, Mr. Joseph Manson, had apprehended a schoolboy, who had stolen two cakes and run from the shop.' He paused and a contemptuous smile came onto his face. 'He should have escaped easily but was outdone by an old bird on the pavement, who tripped him up with her stick.' When the stern expression on Fess' face did not alter, Doyle wiped his smile and returned to the flat voice in which he had given the early part of his report. 'On returning to the shop it was discovered that another boy, who was also in the shop, had used the diversion to go behind the counter and take from the till the sum of approximately four pounds and six shillings, or so Mr. Manson alleges, and escape out the back door. The first boy was brought to the Station where he identified himself as Kevin Jordan of Forty-Two Murchison Street. When escorted to his home by Constable Johnson, his identity was confirmed by his mother, Mrs. Bernadette Jordan. She was informed of what had occurred and the lad was given into her custody.'

'She was informed of some of what had occurred,' Fess said venting his irritation.

'All that pertained directly to her son.'

'So what about the other boy?' Fess asked.

'This is where it gets tricky,' Doyle admitted. 'One of the customers in the shop identified him as a member of the Rawson family from Dorrit Street.'

'Following the family tradition. Bert and one of his older boys are still in Pentridge for stealing those bales of wool, aren't they? Did someone go round to the house?'

'Of course. Johnson went there, but only Dora was home. At least, that's what she said. Reckoned the kids were still all out and hopped into Johnson for waking her up. She'd been sleeping off the grog she had for lunch. He didn't think he should force his way in, so came back empty handed.'

Fess suddenly recollected something Kevin had mentioned the other day. 'If you check I think you'll find there's a Rawson in my son's class at St. George's.'

'Yeah, we have. His name is Billy Rawson.'

'So why is that tricky?'

'Well, the customer that said it was one of the Rawsons knew the boy because she lives only a few doors away. When Johnson tried to get her formal statement, she began to think of the consequences for her if it got around she'd dobbed in young Billy, so she changed her tune and said she couldn't say who pinched the money.'

Fess scratched his chin under his beard. 'Now I begin to see. You need a positive ID or he's home free. Your best bet is Kevin.'

Doyle nodded and his eyes gleamed. 'A job for his father, I'd say. I'll give you until tomorrow to deliver.'

Fess was about to go but turned back. 'Just a thought, Sarge. Why not send one of the men to St. George's School and, with the permission of Father O'Donohue, have him interview this Billy Rawson? Get him to turn out his pockets. It occurs to me that he may be a little different from the usual thief. Home may be the least safe place for him to hide cash and, anyway, he may want to show off his loot to some of his classmates.' He had to admit that it did look like Kevin was acting as a decoy — that would explain why he was so ham-fisted in taking the cakes — but maybe Billy had dared him to do it, not telling him of the rest of his plan.

Doyle nodded. 'Concentrate on getting a witness or two who can give us Nifty, and get your son to tell us what we need to satisfy Manson.' He did not say what he had in mind for Kevin and Fess didn't ask.

11

When Fess came away from Doyle's office, the Duty Constable was hovering. 'There's a Mrs. Robertson here to see you.'

'Mrs. Robertson?'

'Yes.' Seeing that Fess still showed no recognition of the name, the constable said, 'She's the sister of the murdered woman.'

'Oh, of course. Bring her in.'

Elizabeth Robertson was a pleasant looking woman in her late-twenties. She lacked the outstanding beauty of her younger sister, having inherited more of the comfortable look of her father. Today she wore a black coat and a circular grey hat with a narrow brim, her pale lipstick the only sign of colour. She looked around the clutter of the cramped Plain Clothes' room with the eye of a housewife well practised in maintaining a clean and tidy house.

'We're a bit cramped in here,' Fess said as he gathered up some papers from a chair and gestured for her to sit. Taking a chair for himself from behind the crowded table, he asked, 'How is the family coping? I'm sure it must be hard.'

'The reporters have been too much for Mum and Dad,

pestering them and telling them all sorts of stories just to get their reaction. They're like vultures.'

'I know what you mean. Fortunately for me, Detective Thomas has been handling the press. I expect you've come to find out what progress we've really made? You may have seen in this morning's paper that we are questioning two men. We don't believe they acted together but we have evidence to suggest that either one might be guilty. We're exploring those possibilities now, but I can't give you the details of our suspicions at this stage, when that is all they are — suspicions.'

He gave Elizabeth what he hoped was a kindly smile and added, 'I know it must be dreadful for you and you'll be anxious that your sister's killer should be brought to justice, but I must beg you to be patient.'

Elizabeth dipped her head and her face took on more colour. 'Actually, my parents asked me to call in to see if you can tell us what you've found out about Mary. It's not the murder so much that's troubling Mum and Dad. In a way they've accepted it as a horrible accident — Mary was in the wrong place at the wrong time. What they want to know is how did she come to be there? We know she didn't go to the pictures with Paula Ryan, like she told Mum and Dad. And how did Paula and Mrs. Ryan really fit into her life? Mrs. Ryan keeps coming to visit and, each time, she says some strange things. Now the reporters are saying Mary knew these awful people you've arrested.'

'Were you and your sister close?'

'Mary thought I was too dull.' Elizabeth lifted her head

to look directly into Fess' eyes. 'She was much brighter than me, clever and full of energy. I think she wanted more from life than she was getting. She certainly didn't want to settle down and have children like I've done. I don't think my parents could see it, but she changed: became more secretive.' She paused to take a handkerchief from her bag and wipe it across her eyes and nose, even though there was no sign of tears.

'Might it be that Mary had other interests, other involvements that she hadn't talked about?'

'Is that what you've found?' Elizabeth asked quickly.

'We have learnt a little about Mary. I believe that, when we learn more, we'll know how she came to be where she was and who killed her. I'm not trying to dodge your question, but this week one of my sons landed himself in a spot of bother; nothing too serious, but enough to involve the police. Why am I telling you this? It came as a complete shock to my wife and to me. His brother knew much more than we did but, of course, hadn't said anything. Do you know anything that you would be reluctant to tell your parents?'

Elizabeth took a deep breath and pressed her hands together. 'I never told them how angry I became with all the attention they gave Mary.' She paused, as if taken aback by her own outburst, and then continued in a quieter voice. 'My mother has always been keen for her children to "better ourselves", as she puts it. Dad calls it "going up in the world". I settled down to a life not all that different from hers, and you know about John. Mary was Mum's last chance and my sister used that to live a much freer life than I was ever allowed. Mary was clever, too. Mum let her stay over at the Ryans' place when she told her how Mrs. Ryan had all these friends among the well-to-do. Mum hoped she might give Mary a chance to make her mark there, as well.'

'Did you know that Mary sometimes liked to be called Molly?'

Elizabeth lifted a hand to her lips. 'There was that night I saw her in the street.'

'What?'

'Oh, sorry. One Saturday night a few weeks ago, I was walking down Grattan Street and looked up to see a woman coming towards me. I didn't recognise her at first. She looked so smart in a gorgeous coat and hat, but I saw she was carrying a bag and an umbrella just like Mary's. It was only when she came close that I saw it was Mary. She tried to pretend she hadn't seen me, but I wasn't going to let her get away with that. When I called her name, she said, "You must be mistaken. I'm Molly," and hurried off. I was so flabbergasted that I just let her go.'

'Did you take it up with her later?'

'Of course I did, but she denied the whole thing.' Elizabeth paused and Fess guessed from her expression that she was reliving a painful memory. 'Mary had an extraordinarily infectious laugh. You couldn't help but join in. That is, if it wasn't you she was laughing at. At times she could be very cruel with that laugh. When she told me I was wrong, she laughed at me and Mum joined in, telling me what a fool I was to mistake someone else for my own sister.'

'Did you know that Mary had dropped out of her course at the College and worked some evenings in Mrs. Ryan's café?'

'I should have been able to work that out for myself. Some of her stray comments make sense now.'

'What were they?'

'Hard to remember the detail. Saying how boring life was at home, at work, at the College. How she was looking for a job that had some excitement in it. How Paula had a lot more fun than she did. That sort of thing.'

'Is there anything else you think might help us?'

'No, I don't think so. She certainly had become more secretive, so, apart from that night in the street, all I have is stray impressions and odd comments like I've already mentioned. I think she had a new boyfriend who was not the kind of man to introduce to Mum and Dad. Whatever he was, Mary found his sort of life exciting.' Elizabeth paused to look directly at Fess. 'Perhaps he was one of the two in the papers?'

'The funeral is this afternoon?'

'Yes. I'm dreading it. There'll be all those people we hardly know. And the reporters too, I expect.'

'Are Holdsworths conducting the ceremony?'

'Yes. Dad knows some of the people there. They're just across the street from King and Godfree.'

'They're very experienced. Tell them of your concerns and I'm sure they will see that things are done in a way you and your parents will be happy with.' He wriggled in his seat. 'Now if you will excuse …'

Elizabeth understood and started to rise from her chair. 'What should I tell my parents?'

'I'm reluctant to advise you there. You know them much better than I do and will understand what may best give them some respite.' He saw the worry on her face and took pity. 'Why not tell them a few of the more easily digested things and leave the hard ones until we have the complete picture? I hope that won't be too many days off.' If he had been a stranger advising Michael how he should treat his parents, would he have given him the same advice? But Mary wasn't Kevin and he wasn't George Worthington. George had been in the same store for forty years and, unbeknown to him, his daughter had gone out looking for an exciting release from her boring life. Perhaps they weren't all that different.

Jim telephoned to say that Fitzwilliam had agreed to see them. 'Took me some trouble, I don't mind telling you but, yeah, he said he could fit us in at six o'clock tonight at his place in Kew. It'll be a waste of time as far as our investigation's concerned but it could be fun seeing how one of the toffs lives.'

'Nifty still your prime suspect?'

'Of course.'

'And have you had anyone come forward after your piece in the paper this morning?'

'Nah. No luck there, yet. I don't suppose you've heard anything more.'

'I have to admire the way you worked those reporters. Piggott must have been proud of you.' Jim did not reply and, looking again at the newspaper, Fess saw that lower on the page was a follow-up on the case of Leo O'Sullivan. 'THREE YEARS FOR O'SULLIVAN' it said. 'I see your colleague Sugar-Bag got three years.'

'Should have been longer,' Jim growled. 'What's worse is that the judge said nothing about how he'd been allowed to get away with it for so long. That's going to change though.'

'What do you mean?'

'Wait and see.' Jim cleared his throat. 'Things to do. I can't keep chatting all day. Fitzwilliam lives in Walmer Street, off Studley Park Road, beyond the bridge. There's no way I can get the car, so watch out for me on the tram from half past five.'

'Yeah, I know where he lives.' Fess wished he hadn't admitted that knowledge. The boys hadn't been happy, either, when he made them tramp that extra distance on one of their river picnics, just so he could look at the fine house in which Sanford Fitzwilliam lived.

'You haven't yet told me how you know the silver-tail. It'll help pass the time on the trip out to see him. See you then.'

Fess hung up the phone, his thoughts back at the time

of the police strike and its damaging aftermath. It was almost two years since the strike, but he often revisited his memory of those days.

Jim had been right about Nicholson. Despite the enthusiasm within the Force when Alexander Nicholson had been announced as the new Chief Commissioner, the first internal appointment for some time, there was growing frustration and disillusionment as their pay and conditions, known to be the worst in Australia, showed no improvement under his leadership. They said he obtained the position only after he assured the Government that he wouldn't need the increased funding and resources that his two predecessors had called for, and Victoria continued to have the lowest ratio of police per head of population in the country. The absence of superannuation for all those who had joined after 1902 rankled deeply. Fess had been lucky, one of the last batch of recruits to qualify. He sympathised with those who missed out and could understand the cynicism his men sometimes showed when he was urging them to improve their performance.

In the week before the strike the 'spooks', as they were called, had paid a surprise visit to Carlton. The Beat Constables were furious that these Special Constables, appointed to catch out any who were slacking or derelict in their duty, should descend upon them. On the morning the strike began, Nicholson secretly reassigned his spooks to other duties. Why he kept the reassignment secret, when one of the triggers for the strike had been his introduction of these men, continued to baffle Fess.

When the agitators gave orders for the men not to report for duty and Doyle received the call for some of the Carlton Police to report to Russell Street, Fess was relieved that he chose only Beat Constables and left the Plain Clothes men in Carlton. He felt guilt, a little like his guilt over the Great War, when the constables returned battered and angry, not so much with the leadership as with the citizens who confronted them. They had to cope with the jeers of the strikers and the assaults of the mob, intent on brawling and looting. Several of them had to be treated at the hospital but none were badly injured. The chaos in the city reached a crescendo on the Saturday evening, with two hundred in hospital and seventy-five thousand pounds worth of goods looted. Fess was relieved that there was little contagion in Carlton and they were spared the presence of the hastily recruited and sworn-in volunteers known as the Special Constabulary Force, each one provided with a baton, an arm-band, a hat-band, carrying the letters S.C.F., and no police training or experience.

The respite from the S.C.F. did not last. The first indication of the change was the appearance in the Station of a tall man of military bearing, wearing an elegantly cut three-piece, grey suit, with a white shirt and knitted silk tie, kept in place by a diamond cluster pin. He carried a silver-topped walking stick and a black bowler hat, which he removed as he entered. 'My name is Mr. Sanford Fitzwilliam and I would like to speak with Sergeant Doyle,' he announced in a voice that carried the accent of an English public school and the conviction that his wish would be immediately acted upon.

Fess had not seen Fitzwilliam's arrival, but the Duty Constable, who carried the message that he was required in Doyle's office, spared no detail and was particularly impressed that the visitor had remained closeted with the sergeant for such an appreciable time. Doyle usually dismissed visitors very quickly.

Fitzwilliam, comfortably ensconced in the visitors' chair, turned his head as Fess appeared in the doorway. His face was pale with smooth skin and a thin, precise moustache, as though he had just come from the barber. His deep brown eyes carried an intensity that suggested to Fess the real Sanford Fitzwilliam was looking out from behind a handsome mask. Did he sense this immediately or did that impression develop later? Fess found it hard to say. He was sure that he was immediately wary of Fitzwilliam, and they say first impressions are indelible. They certainly were for Fess.

'Come in, Senior Constable Jordan. Mr. Fitzwilliam is here to offer the help of the S.C.F.,' Doyle drawled. 'I'm allocating two of his men to your section.'

Fitzwilliam had risen to offer his hand to Fess and continued to hold it as he said, 'Senior Constable Jordan? Are you the son of Sergeant David Jordan?'

'You knew him?'

'Indeed I did. Some years ago I maintained a practice as a barrister. Your father and I often met on opposite sides as I sought to defend some poor fellow who had the misfortune to fall foul of the law.' He tilted his head back and drew in a breath, before smiling gently and adding, 'I met with a degree of success and also formed a great respect for your father – a man to whom I could relate. At times we were able to trade information to our mutual benefit.'

Trying hard to mask the dislike he had taken to the man, Fess said, 'Given your profession, I'm surprised we haven't met before.'

Fitzwilliam chuckled in a way that Fess found oddly sinister. 'Oh, no chance of that. I gave up my life of crime many years ago. I found it more lucrative to become adviser to some of our large companies and, more recently, have dabbled in business myself. Semi-retired, you might call me, with a number of charitable and social interests. One of my charities is involved with the criminal element, though. The poor fellows serve their time, pay their debt to society and then return to the community with no money, no job and often nowhere to live, so they are forced to take up their former criminal life. The only way to have these people turn their backs on crime is to find an alternative way for them to achieve their desires. Helping Hand is our attempt to give them a better chance.' He paused to take in the impact these words had on Fess, who remained impassive. 'Rehabilitation of the criminal is an urgent need in our society that receives far too little attention, wouldn't you say?'

Fess had expected that, by now, Doyle would have grown impatient with being left out of the conversation.

That was his usual style. Instead he smiled affably and said, 'It's always a pleasure to meet an old friend of David Jordan.'

'That's true,' Fess agreed without enthusiasm. 'But I think my section won't need any help from the S.C.F., thank you.'

'I can understand your reluctance,' Fitzwilliam replied. 'But now we have Monash taking the lead I believe the S.C.F. will be an important addition to the regular Police Force. You know Sir John.'

'Not personally. No.'

Fitzwilliam's face showed sympathy that Fess lacked this connection. 'Fine chap. Fine chap. You'll know he's heading up the Citizens Committee the Government put together to deal with the strike. I'm on it as well. We needed to get some organisation behind these Special Constables that have been appointed. That's why I'm here. Sir James McCay will eventually take charge.' Fitzwilliam paused to rub his chin. 'Actually, I don't think that's public knowledge just yet. Keep it to yourselves for the time being,' he said with a conspiratorial smile. 'Meanwhile, Monash has asked me to head up the S.C.F. contingent in Carlton and Fitzroy. I won't intrude, though. As I've just been explaining to Sergeant Doyle, you're the men on the spot, no question. I do have some knowledge and some small involvement in Carlton, but I'm here only to liaise, oil the wheels as it were. My S.C.F. chaps will come under your command. All volunteers. Give more power to your elbow, I'm sure.'

Fess looked to his sergeant for support and was both surprised and disappointed when Doyle said, 'It's all been authorised by the Chief Commissioner. I'm allocating two of them to you, so you better make good use of them.'

❧ ❧

At first Fitzwilliam had been as good as his word, making rare appearances at the Station. Fess had not liked the look of the men who were foisted upon him and was unmoved when they complained at being given menial jobs with very little responsibility for what they called 'real police work'. Meanwhile, he had been seeing what he could find out about this man who had so confidently imposed himself and his men. Many people were willing to pass on what they knew, mainly rumour and hearsay that Fitzwilliam seemed to throw off like the bow wave from a liner, but few had anything of substance. Bernadette contributed a number of stories from her reading of the social pages and the gossip columns.

Fitzwilliam's origins were unclear: they said he came from a titled family in Scotland, had served in the Royal Scots before entering the law and had come to Australia under some kind of cloud, the details of which varied. Some said shady legal practice, others an affair with a titled lady, and yet others spoke of financial problems. He first came to prominence in Melbourne, successfully defending a number of well-known criminals by demonstrating surprising holes in the prosecution case or producing witnesses the police had unaccountably overlooked. They also said that Colin Ross wouldn't have been hanged for the Gun Alley murder if Fitzwilliam had his brief, but by then he had retired from the bar.

His wealth appeared to grow at a rate that suggested income from sources other than his practice. Some said he inherited from the family in Scotland. He was known to be a keen and successful gambler, often seen in the members' reserve at the track, and his involvement in high stakes card games was legendary. His success at cards was built upon a sharp intelligence, a charming inscrutability and an ability to hold his nerve when under pressure. There were whispers that his 'life of crime', as he jovially expressed it, extended beyond the courtroom to more direct involvement, but nothing concrete had come to light. He charmed his way into Melbourne society, where some of the less savoury rumours about him only added to his lustre, and married into an establishment family. More recently he had become very establishment himself, retiring to his mansion in Kew where they said he oversaw a number of business interests, including a substantial property portfolio. He often appeared in the social pages and, as he had already said, was frequently named as a patron of various charities. He had said that he had some involvement in Carlton, but Fess could find no record of a business that named him as owner or proprietor.

Fitzwilliam did appear when the two men allocated to Fess were discovered attempting to break into a jewellery shop. Almost before they had locked the men in the cells, he was there.

'Spot of bother with a couple of my chaps, I hear.'

'Caught red-handed trying to rob a jewellery shop,' Fess replied.

Fitzwilliam nodded. 'Sure they weren't just testing out the security of the place? Some shopkeepers are very lax.'

'This one wasn't. Your men were found trying to prise the bars from one of his windows.'

'Oh dear.' For the first time Fess saw him look disconcerted. 'In our need to get the S.C.F. up and running we couldn't check as thoroughly as we wished. Now what is to be done?'

'Quite straightforward. They will come to Court tomorrow. I don't know if they have a record, but I'm confident they'll get a stint in gaol. Not only have they committed a crime; they have also betrayed the trust placed in them.' Fess inwardly winced as he heard his own words. He sounded so prissy.

Fitzwilliam pursed his lips. 'You're right, of course, old boy. But ...' He paused to regard Fess with a knowing smile. 'We have to look to the bigger picture. The public has been shocked by the police strike and needs to have its confidence restored in our guardians of the law. They don't distinguish between the regular police and these S.C.F. chappies. D'you follow me?'

'What are you suggesting?'

Fitzwilliam drew in a breath, leaned forward and in a voice that suggested he was sharing an important secret said, 'I think our lords and masters would be best pleased if we said as little as possible about this unfortunate incident and let the men go with a caution.'

'That's hardly an example for the regular police or the volunteers.'

'I told you how I admired your father. He was a man who could see the bigger picture and understood priorities. He knew when it was best to forego immediate success in the interest of the longer term. A lesser sentence, or no sentence at all, in exchange for something — information perhaps — that would be of more use to him in the longer term.'

Fess strove to contain his anger, feeling the colour mount in his face. 'You dress it in fancy words, but what you're suggesting is something very different and I don't like it at all.' He spat out the words as though ridding himself of a nasty taste.

'No, you misunderstand me. As I've already told you, I have the greatest respect for your father. To lose him in the way we did was a tragedy that affected me deeply. I valued his advice and hoped he would attain the advancement he deserved.' Fitzwilliam shifted in his seat and smiled at Fess in a way that did little to calm him. 'He was so fortunate to have you follow him into the Force. I think it's the greatest blessing for a man to have his son follow his calling. I was overjoyed when my son began to study the law, but he didn't stay the course.' He shook his head sorrowfully and added, 'I've managed to marry off my daughters most successfully, but he's been a great disappointment to me. I found him a position in real estate, but he failed at that as well. Now he helps me with my little business enterprises, but I have no confidence he'll be able to take over from me and allow me to retire fully.' Fess felt his anger begin to ebb away, replaced by impatience with this long account that had no bearing on the issue at hand. Fitzwilliam still had not finished. 'The thing is, he was the one who employed these chaps to do some work for us in Carlton. They were at a loose end when that job finished and he suggested I recruit them into the S.C.F., give them something useful to do — might even lead to sound careers for them in the Force. It's most embarrassing.'

'I'm afraid the more you tell me, the more important it is that you stand aside and let the law take its course.' More of the pompous language, but this man drew it out of him.

'You're not a betting man?'

'I don't follow you.' Now he was starting to copy Fitzwilliam's phrases.

'Why don't I give you a surety of, say, fifty pounds? You hold it as a stake. If these two fellows offend again, they are tried and you keep the stake.'

'And if they don't offend again.'

Fitzwilliam chuckled. 'We'll just have to wait and see, won't we? It could take a long time of course, but I'm in no hurry to claim the stake.'

'I don't accept bribes.'

'Of course you don't. I just wish you had some of your father's flexibility.'

'What are you saying?'

'I'm desperately trying to find a way in which your concerns can be met and we can avoid damaging public confidence in the police.'

'The S.C.F. is not police.'

'Ah, the nub of our problem. You have a view of the police that, I'm afraid, recent events have made out-of-date.'

'If it's out-of-date to go soft on men who commit a crime and breach the trust put in them, then you're right.'

'It seems there is nothing I can say to persuade you. A pity.'

Fess interviewed the men who, it turned out, already had criminal records, but their stubborn refusal to answer any of his questions suggested to him that they were either too fearful or had been well paid to remain silent. Then Doyle intervened. 'I've decided to let those S.C.F. men go with a caution. It's not in the best interest for charges to be pursued.'

'You're not going to let them off scot-free, surely?'

'They'll be sacked from the S.C.F. I have Fitzwilliam's assurance.'

'Why are you toadying up to him?'

Doyle leaned forward, his eyes flashing. 'Don't you talk to me like that, Senior Constable.' He relaxed back in his chair and gave a scornful grin. 'You have never understood the value of being owed a favour by a powerful man. Your father did.'

Fess remembered the men he had met at his father's funeral. He turned on his heel and left Doyle's office.

Goaded by his anger, he undertook extensive enquiries, which showed the men who were released were known to have been involved with one of the Carlton gangs, but he could find nothing to connect them with Fitzwilliam or his son. The S.C.F., under the leadership of Sir James McCay, became the path through which new recruits entered the Force but, as far as Fess was aware, Fitzwilliam played no further role and did not come to the Station again. He was still very active in the community, though. His charity work continued to include attempts at the rehabilitation of criminals, but Fess could find nothing untoward in these activities. Bernadette kept him informed of the many times Fitzwilliam appeared at charity balls, premier racing events, concerts and garden parties, always in the best of company.

Ever since, Fess had remained vigilant for any sign of Fitzwilliam's involvement in Carlton. He was named as the owner of several properties where the tenants had been engaged in criminal activity, but if you held every property owner responsible for crimes committed by his tenants, the gaols would hold some very respectable inmates. A few times he heard the Fitzwilliam name mentioned in connection with one of the gangs, just as it had been with the crooked S.C.F. men, but always these leads petered out like a dry creek. Whenever he thought he might be closing in on Fitzwilliam, the trail disappeared as if the man had been warned and was able to cover his tracks.

Had pursuing Fitzwilliam become an obsession with him? Bernadette thought so. But, if Fitzwilliam was the kind of man Fess believed him to be, unmasking him would strike a major blow against the criminal gangs, far more influential than chasing the low level criminals that occupied so much of his time. It would be his crowning achievement. Nifty Naughton had disappeared straight after Mary's murder. Why had he then chosen to attempt to break into Fitzwilliam's house, and why was he so confident Fitzwilliam would not press charges? There had to be a link between them. This was the best opportunity he'd had to chase down Fitzwilliam for a long time. But what was the link and what, if anything, did it have to do with the murder?

Jim was certain Nifty was the murderer, but nothing quite fitted together. If Nifty had murdered her in a fit of passion, as Jim maintained, why would he leave her in the lane so close to his room? If he decided to cover his tracks by trying to make it look like a mugging, why did he dump her bag down near Elgin Street without taking her money, and why did he so respectfully arrange her body? What they had learnt from the Ryan women suggested that Basher was the more likely murderer and he had been seen nearby. But the same questions arose. And where was her precious umbrella? Someone must have taken it. But who, and why?

12

Fess became conscious of a figure hovering in the doorway. 'Ah, Constable Daley. Why are you loitering there?'

'You looked like you were concentrating hard on something, Senior, and I didn't like to interrupt.'

'What is it you want?'

Daley glanced over his shoulder before answering in a low voice. 'I've just come back from St. George's School. Sergeant Doyle sent me up there to speak with Brother O'Donohue. The brother asked me to pass on a message to you.'

'Didn't the sergeant tell you I can't be involved in this business?'

Again Daley looked over his shoulder before coming further into the room. When he spoke, his voice was even lower than before. 'Brother O'Donohue was very particular. He said he wanted to speak with you as a parent and not a policeman. He asked if you could go to the school after the children leave this afternoon.'

Fess nodded. 'Thank you.'

'I haven't reported to Sergeant Doyle yet. I don't think I need to tell him about Brother O'Donohue's message.'

Daley's expression made it clear that this was a question not a statement.

'It's up to you, of course.' Fess paused before adding, 'I do think that discretion plays an important role in policing.' Daley's face brightened and Fess said, 'We seem to be bumping into one another quite a bit lately. You interested in taking on Plain Clothes?'

'It does seem more interesting than the beat.'

❧ ❧

When Fess' mother sent him to Sunday School at the Methodist Church in Palmerston Street, he was taught by Mr. Fotherington, a young man who worked at the State Library and spent each Sunday spreading God's word. His only other interest was architectural history. Mr. Fotherington told Fess that the three semi-circular arches at the entrance to the bluestone church, the small windows and the squat tower were all aspects of the Norman style in which the church had been built. Having left the Sunday School as soon as he was allowed, these architectural details were among the few things that Fess could remember from Mr. Fotherington's teaching. Now, as he stood across the road from the church, all that appeared to have changed in the intervening years was the demolition of the white picket fence that had surrounded the church on three sides and the creation of a rockery garden along the eastern side.

Although there was still some time before Mary Worthington's funeral service was due to begin, a crowd had already gathered. The square, black bulk of Holdsworths' empty hearse stood in the road between the leafless trees. The wreaths that lay beside the steps leading to the entrance provided the only colour to soften the bleakness of the scene. The sky was overcast, but at least the rain had held off and it was not too cold.

Among the silent crowd, some of whom were already entering the church, Fess could see several men he identified as reporters and one photographer with a large camera. Fess had come because he thought the family might need some protection from the press and other onlookers, but his concerns now seemed unwarranted. The great majority of the mourners who passed him were local residents and shop-keepers; George Worthington had spent a lot of time at King and Godfree and was well known to many. The Misses Fortescue from the haberdashery shuffled by, both of them wearing broad-brimmed, black hats and long, black dresses that swept the footpath. Miss Rowbottom, from Ball and Welch, followed soon afterwards, accompanied by the young lass he had first spoken with when he went there. The stony-faced Manageress gave a stiff nod of her head as they passed, while her companion, clutching a handkerchief in her gloved hand, offered him a shy smile. It was a surprise when Bernadette came along. She too looked surprised when she saw him, gave him one of her enigmatic smiles and quickly passed by. After his outburst over her suggestion she visit the Worthingtons, she had obviously decided not to consult him about her attendance at the funeral.

A voice beside him hissed, 'Look at them — hypocrites.'

Fess turned to find Spy Webb who, as he so often did, had appeared from nowhere. 'What do you mean, Spy?'

Spy spat contemptuously into the gutter. 'Hardly any of them would know her and none of them would care. They click their tongues and say I spy on people. What are they doing now? They'll sit in that church and look solemn, when all they've come for is to enjoy the spectacle and be glad it isn't them.'

'No, Spy, that's far too hard. Many of them didn't know Mary, that's true, but they do know the Worthingtons — George, at least. They want to show their sympathy and support.'

'The things they write in the press. Most of it's sentimental rubbish,' Spy growled.

'Yes?'

'Mary was a beautiful, flesh-and-blood woman, not the immaculate saint they make her out to be. She could have a nasty streak at times, like all of us.'

'Why do you say that?'

'Just last week I was following her down Faraday street after she came out of Ball and Welch. She turned around and said, "Go away, Spy. Stop following me, you pest." I was taken aback, I don't mind telling you. She's known I've paid attention to her before and she seemed to like it — a bit flattered, I s'pose. I said to her, "You know I mean no harm." "Of course I know that," she said. Then she gave this scornful laugh and said, "If you were a real man I might have something to fear, but you're missing there, aren't you?" and she gave that laugh again. A man can take a lot, but to be laughed at like that …' He spat into the gutter once more.

'You stopped following her, then?'

Spy gave a derisive chuckle. 'She thought I did. Went right past her place and into Barkly Street. Not sure which place she did go into; I was too far away.' He looked at Fess from under his eyebrows. 'Could have been Ma Cutmore's. I don't know.'

'Which day was this?'

'I thought you might be interested. I see Nifty Naughton's in the frame. One day last week — Tuesday or Wednesday, I'd say.'

Fess wondered whether this was one of Spy's embroideries. He was quite capable of them. 'So, are you going to the service?'

'No. I'm not going to sit there with all those hypocrites giving me the eye. I have my own private memorial for her, at home.' Spy turned away and scuttled up the lane at the back of where they were standing.

Fess glanced at his watch. It was time for him to go to St. George's School. He chose a route that avoided Lygon Street and Mansons' Bakery. Instead he walked all the way down Drummond Street, past the Station, past the chaff and grain yard and past the once grand houses, most of which were now subdivided and poorly kept. His thoughts turned from Mary and the funeral to Brother O'Donohue.

Daley hadn't told him what he found when he went to the school and he hadn't asked. It was already stretching things to encourage the young constable not to tell Doyle of the message from O'Donohue. Strange that Doyle had sent Daley. Perhaps he thought the earnest young man might do better than the older ones; O'Donohue certainly was no lover of the police and had little time for Doyle.

The Head of St. George's Primary School, Brother Francis O'Donohue, was born and grew up in the slums of Dublin, surviving childhood long enough to escape into the Church and, via the Church, to Australia. He was a large bear of a man who had apparently raced to the age of sixty and remained there ever since: they said he hadn't altered a bit in the twenty years he had spent at St. George's School. A grin was never far from his round, ruddy face and he often gave a wheezing laugh that shook his entire frame and left him searching for breath. Sometimes his smile expressed sympathy, sometimes regret and, occasionally, even displeasure. Perhaps it was because of his normally sunny appearance that, when he did frown, there was no mistaking the chill in the air. He loved the children and they knew that, but his bulk and height, his booming voice and the direct line he appeared to have to 'The Man Upstairs', as he frequently described his God, meant that they, and many adults as well, became overawed in his presence.

When Fess stepped onto the verandah that abutted the three classrooms of the school he could hear the Head in one of the rooms, complaining to a cleaner about her work. 'Now, Ada m'dear, it will not do. We cannot have our lovely children in rooms that are as dusty as a country road. I can't keep my eye on you all the time, with all the children and the teachers to watch over, but The Man Upstairs, He can. Remember that and have Him smile on you as you do His work. I know there are other women who want to take your place, but we wouldn't want that now, would we?' he chortled.

Ada, a slight woman with faded, ginger hair and a stained apron, nodded her already bowed head.

'Quite right. So you be getting on with it now, while I speak with my visitor.' He turned away from Ada and extended a large hand. 'Mr. Jordan. Good of you to call.' Fess noted that Brother O'Donohue had not used his police title. This was no indication of forgetfulness. Despite the impression he sometimes tried to give, he was far too fly for that. 'Come along and let's have a chat.' He led Fess along the verandah, the hem of his ankle length, black cassock swinging in time with his stride, until they reached the door of the end classroom, which was empty. 'In here will do,' he said as he entered and walked to a table that stood in front of the closely-packed desks. 'A great service on Sunday,' he said with a broad smile, and gestured to Fess to take a seat opposite him. 'Young Carmel looked a picture. You must have been so proud.' The Head continued to beam at Fess. 'It was very good to see you there. We miss you when your duties call you away from Mass. I know The Man Upstairs grieves when any of His people can't make it to Mass.'

'You asked to see me, Brother, as a parent, not a policeman.'

'Young Kevin, he's become a fine, big lump of a lad.'

Fess hadn't given it a lot of thought but could see that Kevin was probably big for his age and all the Jordans were strongly built. 'He's run into some trouble, though,' Fess replied. 'It's not easy being the son of a policeman.' He shouldn't have taken this line. Better to wait for Brother O'Donohue make the running. That's what he normally would have done.

'We had one of your constables here today. I liked the cut of his jib. I'd reckon you have a good'n there, not something I often say. I sent him straight off, though. Begging your pardon, but we don't want police in the school: it gives the children the wrong idea. We need them to feel a policeman is there to be a friend, a protector, not to frighten them, wouldn't you say?' He gave Fess a knowing smile, confident of his agreement.

'Even children have to face the consequences if they've done something wrong.'

'Yes, of course.' Brother O'Donohue's smile widened and he leaned forward. 'And we need the parents to face the consequences too, don't we?'

'Is that why you asked me to come here?'

'After your constable had gone, I had a chat with young Kevin. You need to do the same.'

'I've already done that,' Fess replied, striving to keep the irritation from his voice. What right did this man have to lecture him on what should be done about Kevin? 'I suspect he's fallen into bad company, been foolish and needs to put things right.'

'Bad company, you say. You'll be meaning the little lad, Billy Rawson.'

'In a family like that it's hard to see him having any chance.'

'Ah, but that's where you're wrong.' Brother O'Donohue's grin filled his face. 'Where I grew up there was a lot of bad company, but we still had a chance. A slim one, maybe, but still a chance.' He chuckled to himself, perhaps recalling a distant memory, and the folds of skin between his jaw and his clerical collar jiggled like the wattles of a turkey. He passed a hand across his lips and the chuckle subsided. 'But I shouldn't be delaying you; you have important work to do.' He reached into his pocket and took out some coins, which he pushed across the table to Fess. 'These should properly go into your charge.'

'What?'

The Head held up a hand as if quietening a noisy class. 'After your constable told me what he was after doing, I took it upon myself to have a chat with the lads, Kevin and Billy.'

'So, this is the money taken from the bakery.' Fess had been right that Billy would keep his haul with him.

'I don't know where it came from. All I know is that it was in young Kevin's pocket.'

'Kevin?'

'He said he'd earned it doing jobs after school — very commendable. He couldn't seem to remember where he'd done the work and who paid him. None of my business, really, and I shouldn't have taken the money but, there it is, I did. And now I'm giving it to you, his father.'

'He'd got it from Billy Rawson?' It was clearly a question, not the statement Fess might have made only a few minutes ago.

'Do you know young Billy?' Brother O'Donohue enquired in a conversational tone, as if referring to someone who might be a mutual acquaintance.

'Kevin's mentioned him. Said he was in his class.'

'A slip of a lad. The whole family's on the small side and I don't think he gets a lot to eat.' He paused to look into Fess' eyes. 'Young Kevin would have him for breakfast.'

'Are you saying Kevin is the leader in this theft?'

'He's a bright lad, your son. His classmates take notice of what he says. I s'pose he takes after his father in that regard.' Again the Head paused. 'But lately I've been watching him and haven't liked what I've seen. You mentioned bad company before. If you don't mind me saying so, I think young Kevin needs some good company to set him straight.'

'Are you saying I'm not setting my son a good example?' This time the hostility burst through in the crackle of his words. What did this man know about being a father, a real father, not the pretend fathers they had in the Church?

'Quite the opposite,' he replied, benignly untroubled by the anger Fess was showing. 'You said it wasn't easy being the son of a policeman. Of course, you've had that yourself already. But policeman or no, it isn't easy growing up with a father who sets high standards and, worse still

…' — his laugh shook his whole body — '… actually lives up to them.' Fess watched him closely. O'Donohue would have known his father in his earlier days in Carlton but he wouldn't know anything about their relationship. Or would he? Recovered from his bout of laughter, he continued. 'Sometimes I'd say I was better off with my dad. He showed me what not to be. I had nothing I had to live up to and could choose.'

'Like Billy Rawson?' The question was out before Fess knew it. He needed something to say as his mind struggled to take in what he was being told. 'I'm sorry. None of my business.'

'That's it.' This time the smile was the one Fess felt sure was given to the child with the correct answer. 'The trouble with Billy, though, is that he needs a mite of encouragement to find a better way. I'm trying, with the help of The Man Upstairs, to see what I can do. If you can get Kevin to see sense, that would help a lot. And not just with Billy.'

'Are you saying Kevin is a bad influence in the school?'

'He's an influence. He could be such a good influence. I've talked with the lad and he's been quite open with me. The boys often are. Begging your pardon, he needs to be open with you. That's what we need.'

It was only when Fess stood in the street outside the school that he thought to count the coins he held in his hand. They amounted to four pounds. Had Billy Rawson kept only six shillings?

Fess stood in the gloom at the tram-stop while his thoughts remained with the words of Brother O'Donohue. He had as good as accused Kevin of being the ring-leader of some children's gang that Fess knew nothing about. How could this be? Earlier he had been asking the same question of the Worthingtons and incredulous that they were so ignorant. He gave a wry grin. At least Kevin hadn't coined a new name for himself. On the other hand, how would he know if the other kids had a different name for him? Boss? Killer Kev? He had to get a grip on himself and work out how he was he going to handle Kevin. How was he going to get him to talk with him, to be open with him as the Brother had said? He needed to kick off in a way that immediately encouraged Kevin to talk. Perhaps the direct question: you didn't tell me you stole money as well as cakes. No, too direct, too accusatory. He needed something that was less challenging. What about this: you didn't tell me Billy Rawson was involved. No, that might just make Kevin clam up, not wanting to let his accomplice down. Come to think of it, he wouldn't have much respect for his son if he did admit Billy was involved. And what about the police investigation? He should have no part of that and yet he now held most of the stolen money. He was so immersed in his thoughts that he almost missed seeing Thomas, who had to wave at him from the dummy when the tram was about to move on without him.

'Asleep on the job? I thought you were about to let me go on by.'

'Yeah, sorry. Had a few things on my mind.'

‘Not just Mary Worthington and Nifty Naughton, I’d say.’

‘No. My son, Kevin, has got into bad company and done some shoplifting. I know I should stay out of it, but I keep being dragged back in.’

‘It’s a bugger when your role as a policeman collides with your personal life. Hasn’t happened to me yet, but I’ve seen others.’

‘What’s really upsetting me is that I had no idea what he was up to. No idea.’

Jim smiled and said, ‘I thought you must be stewing over this interview you made me set up with Fitzwilliam. You promised to tell me all about him on the way out there. Now’s your chance.’

The conductor shouted, ‘Mind the curve,’ as the tram swung into Elgin Street for the long run out to the bridge on the Yarra, and Fess embarked on an account of his dealings with Sanford Fitzwilliam, leaving out any mention of his father.

When he had finished, Jim beamed at him. ‘I remember. The only time I’ve seen Senior Constable Jordan steamed up. You told me the people you hate are the cowards who roam in gangs and, even more, the rich men who hide in their posh houses, raking in the profits from the robberies, prostitution and drug peddling they get others to do for them. You think he’s one of them. That’s why you’re so keen to see him. It’s not about the murder at all. You want to tie him in with Nifty.’

‘No, you’re wrong. I keep telling you we don’t yet have

a clear picture of what went on that night. There are too many loose ends that don't fit. And I want to find out why Nifty would try to break into Fitzwilliam's house. He's not into house burglary and he stays in the inner suburbs.'

'I don't believe you, but that doesn't matter. It took me a lot of trouble to line up Fitzwilliam, and it will be interesting to see his place. It'll help pass the time while I wait for some witnesses to come forward and tie up the case against Nifty. Your contacts have given us nothing.'

'Apart from those sightings of Basher and the earlier links we've established between Mary and Nifty, no one seems to know anything. That's another odd thing that doesn't fit.'

'That's why you need some reward money to loosen a few tongues. It's a pity we're so limited in what we can offer.'

'Yeah, Piggott is famous for buying witnesses to support his case.'

'Cobblers,' Jim spat at him. 'He offers rewards for information. We should do the same. The reward the Government offered in the Gun Alley case made all the difference. I don't see them doing the same here, though,' he said gloomily.

Fess was ashamed of himself. His attempt to stir Thomas was nothing more than petty revenge for the man pointing out something Fess didn't want to admit, even to himself. Why did he continue trying to pursue Fitzwilliam? Apart from those two thieves from the S.C.F., he had found nothing of significance to link the man with any criminal activity in Carlton. It was true that he would dearly love to unmask the rich men who hid behind the gangs and profited from them, but was this his reason for persisting in his pursuit of Fitzwilliam? He hadn't told Jim what Fitzwilliam had said about his father. No matter what really drove him though, this was the most promising lead he had yet found, and he must follow it through.

He shouldn't have told Jim of his problems with Kevin. To be fair though, Jim hadn't taken the opportunity to make some crack. Not like the first night, when he barrelled straight into him, laughing at him for getting out of bed to stand watch over the body, mocking his dedication and even suggesting his father's death had been a useless waste. But that was Jim's style — go in hard and be aggressive. As you came to know him, there was more to him that that. Perhaps the aggression, the cockiness that came over so strongly at first, was his way of covering a lack of confidence. Perhaps the pipe was there as a prop. His own technique was very different: say as little as possible and get the other person talking. Ask questions, listen carefully to the answers and show you are listening. But the object was the same.

He had been irked when Jim told him Piggott was his hero.

Everybody knew Piggott and his reputation for going in hard, getting a result, whatever it took, and not worrying too much about the niceties. No question he was effective, but at what cost? Piggott wasn't the first to take this approach to policing — a war against crime where winning was everything. If Jim had known David Jordan, perhaps he would have been his hero. Fitzwilliam had as much as said that he knew of cases where his father had gone outside the law to get a result. How did he put it? Something about being able to see the bigger picture and understanding priorities. If he were honest, it was those snide remarks that gave Fess such an intense dislike of Fitzwilliam. He had reason to suspect him, but it was the intensity of his dislike that drove him on what had been such a fruitless pursuit so far. The real problem for Fess was that Fitzwilliam's insinuations were probably true. He had decided long ago that he wanted to be a different kind of policeman. Now, when he looked back, he had to question what had really led to this decision. Was it that the methods his father used had already seemed wrong to him, or was it that he just wanted to do things differently? Perhaps it was both.

The silence that had come between them was broken when Jim said, 'I'm not saying your approach is always wrong. I bet I wouldn't have got some of those people to tell us what they did. And you do it so craftily. Most people don't realise what they've told you until it's too late. They say you were once a priest. Is that where you learned how to do it? Is that how you got your name?'

'Good heavens, no. To tell you the truth, I only became a Catholic so I could marry Bern.' Fess was proud of his reputation, happy that few people knew how he had come by his name and amused by the outlandish stories that claimed to explain its origin. Very few people had the cheek to ask him directly, and already he regretted his reply. Besides, if he did tell him, it would be such a let-down. It was back in primary school, when he was called Edward by most people, they had a history lesson about Edward the Confessor. Straight afterwards he became Edward the Confessor to the other kids, but it was too much of a mouthful and soon became Confessor and then Fess. It had been Fess ever since. He couldn't tell Thomas this.

Jim continued to look at him expectantly but, when Fess added nothing more, he shook his head and said, 'We're nearly there. Remember I'm the officer in charge of this investigation, so I take the lead. I ask the questions and you stay on a close leash. I don't want you sounding off at him. He has a lot of powerful friends.'

13

They stepped down from the tram when it reached the terminus and made their way up the slope and over the bridge across the Yarra, following the road that curved into the leafy outskirts of Kew. The sun had now set and their route was beside dark bushland, through which they could see the lights of the houses on the ridge. They crossed the road and took the first street to the right, past several imposing houses that looked over the bush toward the city.

'This is it,' Fess said when they reached the edge of a large block that contained a sprawling single storey house surrounded by a dense garden, in which the bare branches of tall, deciduous trees stood above the slate roof like a series of stretching hands. A verandah, supported by elaborately carved wooden pillars, ran along the front of the house.

Jim was not looking at the house, his attention entirely taken by a bright red car with a soft hood, standing in the driveway that led to a brick garage at the rear of the property. 'The latest Buick three-passenger Master Six,' he said with awe in his voice.

'I can't see Fitzwilliam driving this. I would have thought he'd have something much grander,' Fess replied.

'You know, it has electric starting and lighting. It must be something to drive. Do you think if I was nice to him, he'd let me take it for a spin?'

'You can drive?'

'O'course I can. Been able to for years.' He caressed the side of the bonnet with his hand. 'There's a beautiful engine under there.'

'Beautiful? I reckon cars are ugly things. Give me a cable tram or a steam engine any time. There's some romance about them.'

'We'd better get inside,' Jim said with regret. 'We're right on time and I wouldn't want to keep your pal Sanford waiting.' They mounted the steps and sounded the bell beside the oak front door.

The door was opened by a maid in a starched apron who appeared to expect them. She did not ask their names or their business but offered to take their hats and coats, which she placed on the wooden hall-stand that already held a number of hats, coats and umbrellas. She invited them to sit on the velvet cushioned chairs, which kept company with the hall-stand, and then she disappeared through a door at the end of the hall. Across from them a tall grandfather clock kept stately time. Jim paced up and down uneasily while Fess took one of the seats.

'Come and have a look at this,' Jim commanded in a stage whisper. Through a door to the right of the hall they looked into a drawing room, brightly lit by a crystal chandelier, which hung from a ceiling rose formed from a circle of fern leaves. Nobody was in the room, enabling them to stand in the doorway and scan its contents. At the far end, a bay window was screened from the street by a claret-coloured velvet curtain with gold silk cords and tassels, not unlike a smaller version of the stage curtain Fess had seen at His Majesty's when he and Bern had celebrated their tenth wedding anniversary with a rare night out, alone and together. A richly woven Axminster carpet in autumn tones covered most of the floor, leaving a margin at the edges to display the complex pattern of the parquetry. A fire burned in the marble fireplace that dominated the centre of the room. Two leather couches faced the fire with matching armchairs at either side and, in front, a low polished table that carried a large silver cigarette box and lighter, together with several flat brass dishes — ash trays perhaps — and a small copper statue of a mounted horseman. In the far corner of the room stood a walnut-encased grand piano. Closer at hand was a glass-fronted cabinet containing a large array of bottles and glasses. On the walls, oil-paintings and wall-hangings portrayed a variety of highland scenes.

'Wow! Isn't this really something?' Jim said.

'Yeah, very sumptuous.' But to Fess' eyes it was artificial, designed to impress, rather than to live in.

The door to the room on the other side of the hall was open but, without light, they could make out only the shapes of a long dining table with matching chairs and a wooden dresser along the far wall. Any temptation to explore further was doused when a tall, heavily-built man appeared. He had slicked-down brown hair and wore the precisely knotted dark tie and the black three-quarter coat of a gentleman's valet. 'Evening, gents,' he said, the slight coarseness in his voice at odds with the formality of his dress. 'Mr. Fitzwilliam's expecting you. Come with me.' He took them down a carpeted corridor that changed direction twice as it passed a number of closed doors and one room, in which another large man looked up from arranging some chairs around a circular table that held what looked like several decks of playing cards.

Reaching a panelled door, their attendant knocked softly and leaned forward to grasp the brass knob and open the door. He stood aside and, with a nod of his head, indicated they should enter. Sanford Fitzwilliam rose from behind a mahogany desk. 'Good evening, gentlemen. Please come in.' Another bay window behind the desk was covered with art-silk curtains displaying a Japanese design, and the other three walls were lined with glass-fronted, walnut book shelves. To judge by the bindings, many of the books were legal texts and law reports. Jim entered first and Fitzwilliam, now standing before the desk, offered his hand and said in a friendly tone, 'You must be Senior Detective Thomas. Fred Piggott speaks highly of you.' He wore a navy blazer over a white silk shirt, open at the neck to reveal a bright blue cravat. 'And Senior Constable Jordan! I wasn't expecting you.' Fitzwilliam looked genuinely taken aback, and it was a moment before he extended his hand again, showing the gold link that secured the French cuff of his shirt.

'Senior Constable Jordan is assisting me with his knowledge of the Carlton area,' Jim said.

After a moment's hesitation Fess took his hand and felt the firm pressure of it as Fitzwilliam's brown eyes stared into his. 'Haven't had the pleasure for some time.' He released Fess' hand and said, 'Now, gentlemen, please make yourselves comfortable.' He indicated two plump armchairs that faced the desk before returning to the high-backed chair on the other side. He sat back and smiled again at both of them. 'I'm sorry to have to bring you out here at this time of day but I was fully committed until now and have a group of friends coming for a spot of cards shortly. When Fred Piggott said it was important for your investigation that you speak with me, this was the best I could do.'

Jim shot a quick look at Fess, who continued to gaze at Fitzwilliam, apparently unmoved by the revelation that Jim had not made the appointment himself. Jim cleared his throat. 'It is good of you to give us your time,' he said deferentially. 'We are here because the man who attempted to burgle your house is suspected of committing a murder only two nights before.'

'Is he now? I didn't realise the fellow was of that ilk. My son was the one most in danger. The wretch bailed him up with a pistol and demanded money. I wasn't home at the time — had to be at a fund-raising dinner with the Governor — and just arrived back in time to ring the Acting Commissioner. Fortunately, Jenkins and Holloway were able to deal with him before he could do any damage.' Seeing that his listeners were not with him, he added. 'Jenkins is the chap who brought you to me and

Holloway is my butler. Stout fellows, both of them, and alert too, thank goodness. They told me the blighter had a pistol but I must say I thought it was for show. Didn't pick him as a murderer. Just as well they were able to subdue him before he had a chance to use it.'

'Yes, it was,' Jim agreed. 'A nasty character, Nifty Naughton, who should be punished for his crime. A pity you were unwilling to proceed with the case against him.'

'You know how it is.' Fitzwilliam shrugged his shoulders and blinked his eyes. 'He took nothing and no damage was done. Don't like appearing in the courts and having the family name in the papers.' He paused and then, perhaps mindful that his name frequently appeared in the press, added, 'Not associated with a sorry business like an attempted robbery.' Again he paused to gauge their reaction and, with Fess in particular still looking sceptical, he sighed. 'I can see that I must "come clean with you," as they say. My men Jenkins and Holloway are products, successful products, of my charity Helping Hand. That's the one that works on the rehabilitation of former criminals. For a start, they're most anxious about appearing in Court and having a barrister parade their former crimes.' He gave a small smile. 'Barristers can be so cruel and spare no one when defending their clients. Secondly, and perhaps less defensibly, they don't want word to get about that they've been involved in apprehending a criminal. Now I know the nature of that criminal I'm more inclined to share their concern about the possibility of revenge being taken.'

Fess, who had not yet said a word, suddenly interjected, 'I think we must respect their positions,' causing both Jim and Fitzwilliam to snap around to face him. 'But before we go, seeing you were not here and your men are understandably reticent to speak, might we have a few words with your son, please?'

'Surely. That's if he's at home. Never know from one moment to the next where the blighter's going to be.' He lifted his voice and called, 'Jenkins!'

The attendant, whom Fitzwilliam must have known would be waiting directly outside the door, immediately opened it and stood in the doorway. 'Mr. Fitzwilliam?'

'Is Hal at home, do you know?'

'Saw him a bit earlier. D'you want me to chase him up?'

'If you would be so kind.'

As Jenkins departed, closing the door behind him, Fitzwilliam returned his attention to the policemen. 'I should have offered you a drink. Forgive me.' He still did not make any offer.

'Quite all right, sir. We should not need to take much more of your time,' Jim replied.

'Senior Constable Jordan, how is your family getting on?' Fitzwilliam smiled affably at Fess. 'The children must be growing up now.'

Fess stiffened. How did Fitzwilliam know about his problems with Kevin? No, of course he couldn't. Just an eerie coincidence. But he did seem to know about the family. Or did Fitzwilliam know that Fess had been trying to investigate him and wanted to show that two could play at that? 'It was my daughter's first communion last Sunday,' Fess eventually mumbled.

'An important day for the family, I believe. Strictly C of E myself, but I envy you having such a strong family behind you.'

What was this man getting at? There was something in the way he spoke that made Fess feel he was threatening him. But how? The door opened again and Fitzwilliam's son strode in. He was tall like his father and had his narrow eyes and lips. He wore a brown leather jacket over tweed trousers, with a yellow woollen scarf draped loosely around his neck, and held leather gauntlets in his hand. He paid no attention to the visitors and spoke directly to his father. 'Yes, Dad, what is it?' he asked in a tone roughened by impatience. 'I'm about to take off for a drive.'

Fitzwilliam looked up without blinking. 'These men are Senior Detective Thomas from the C.I.B. and Senior Constable Jordan from the Carlton Station. They are investigating a murder they suspect was carried out by that chap who broke in here and threatened you the other night.' He broke eye contact with his son and said to the policemen, 'Gentlemen, my son Hal.'

'Oh, yeah?' This time Hal did acknowledge the presence of Fess and Jim, turning to face them. His tone was dismissive and uninterested, but there was something about his eyes that caught Fess' attention. 'Who'd he murder?' he asked them.

'The dead woman's name is Mary Worthington,' Jim replied in the flat voice of police procedure.

'You knew her as Molly,' Fess added as though aiming to help his memory, and took the photograph from his pocket, leaning forward to place it on the desk so that Sanford Fitzwilliam could clearly see it as well. 'That's Mary between you and Paula Ryan, with Naughton beside her.' He turned his head to look up at Hal, who remained standing in front of the desk. 'We understand you had some interest in Mary.'

'Interest?' It was his father who asked the question. 'Clearly there are matters you have been withholding from me. We need a full explanation of your dealings with this Naughton man and with the unfortunate woman it appears he has murdered.'

Hal sauntered over to the side wall and leaned back against the bookcase. His face wore a grin, but some of the arrogance had slipped away. 'OK. OK. I thought I could spare you this, but it seems I can't. Yes, I met Nifty Naughton at the Palais when he was with Paula and Molly. We had some fun together and, yes, I did flirt a bit with Molly. She was that kind of girl. I've never heard her called Mary. I'd seen in the paper about the girl murdered in Carlton, but it never occurred to me she was Molly. I haven't seen her for ages. Naughton's a different matter. First of all, let me say that I didn't know the kind of man he is. I'd met him. Saw him at the Palais a few times. That photograph must have been taken on one of those occasions, though to tell the truth, I don't remember it, and hardly knew him. Jenkins and Holloway have opened my eyes to the type he is. You get all sorts at the Palais and you don't ask for their police record before having some fun with them. It's part of the attraction of the place.' Hal paused for a moment before saying, 'He didn't break in here the other night.'

'What?' Sanford interjected, his eyes like coals.

Hal waved a hand as though he could wave away his father's anger. 'He was waiting for me in the garden when I came home. He told me he was in bad trouble and needed a whack of money so that he could skip interstate. I refused at first and he pulled a gun on me. That's when I told him I was carrying very little — the truth, as it happens — but could get some more from the house. I came inside in a manner that was sure to alert Jenkins and Holloway that something was amiss, and they did the rest. Naughton hadn't thought we'd have that kind of protection. He's good at terrifying chamber maids and the like, but he didn't know what hit him. I wasn't keen for anyone to know of my connection with Naughton — particularly you,' he said with a nod to his father. 'When Jenkins and Holloway realised who it was, they began to worry about payback, so we agreed to throw him out without telling anyone. Trouble was, you came home and took over, calling the cops in.' He sighed as though dealing with a meddlesome child. 'We tried to spare you all this.'

'You don't seem very upset by the death of an old flame,' Jim said.

'I guess I'm finding it all hard to believe. First Naughton and now this. It's like something from a gangster movie, not real life.'

Sanford rose to his feet. 'Gentlemen, I don't wish to be

rude but I must prepare for my friends. I'm appalled by these revelations from my son, but at least I believe you now have what you came for, some confirmatory evidence that will strengthen your case against this Naughton monster. The sooner he is hanged the better, I would say.' He turned his head to speak directly to Fess. 'You may recall my telling you what a disappointment my son was to me. He hasn't improved any. I try to find useful things for him to do, but he prefers the hedonistic life – smart cars, women of dubious reputation. It brings him into contact with some unsavoury characters. I can now understand why Naughton came here, hoping to get the money for his flight from justice. Jenkins will show you out.'

Immediately the door swung open and Jenkins stood, ready to escort them. 'Goodnight, Mr. Fitzwilliam, and thank you for your cooperation,' Jim said. He looked for the possibility of a departing handshake but, finding none, walked smartly to the door.

Fess lingered. 'Where were you on Saturday night?' he asked Hal as he stood close beside him.

'Saturday?' He appeared to have trouble remembering back those few days. 'Yes, of course. I tried my luck at the new place in Footscray – the Orama. Just opened last week. Saw a few people I knew but didn't really like the crowd there.'

'We may need to speak to you again,' Fess said, addressing a space midway between the two Fitzwilliam men, so that it was unclear which of them he meant. Neither responded, and he joined Jim who was waiting anxiously for him.

Jenkins closed the door, leaving the Fitzwilliams to conduct a conversation Fess would dearly have liked to overhear.

They had barely reached the steps of the verandah before Jim hissed at him, 'What the bloody hell are you playing at, keeping me in the dark? How long have you known Hal Fitzwilliam was the other man in that snap?'

'About twenty seconds before you. When I was sitting there, as ordered, silently watching you question Fitzwilliam, it occurred to me that the man in the photograph had some of the look of Sanford Fitzwilliam. Was that what might have rung a bell when I first saw the photograph? I was far from certain. That's why I asked if we could speak with Hal — so I could check if the bell rang any louder. As soon as he walked in, I knew. Did I have to produce the photo before you saw it, too?'

'I'll say this: we wouldn't have made the connection if you hadn't wanted to pursue your old pal, Sanford.' Jim paused in the driveway and used his hand to make a covetous survey of the body-work of the Buick. 'I reckon you've spoilt any chance I had of driving this beauty, though.'

'The tram's much better. Come on,' said Fess, making for the street. When Jim joined him, he asked, 'So, where did you learn to drive?'

Jim paused to get his pipe alight before stuffing the pouch back in the pocket of his coat. 'My uncle's a mechanic — a good one. He looks after some great machines and I used to help him when I wasn't working.'

'Did you ever think of following him?'

'He wanted me to, and it would've been great.' Jim drew

on his pipe sending a cloud of smoke into the air around them. 'But they pay apprentices even worse than the police and I wasn't too keen to be working for a relative. Not that I had anything against Uncle George,' Jim hastened to assure Fess. 'He's a good bloke.'

Back in the street, which skirted the bush above the river, the night had fully closed in and the stars in the cloudless sky were icicle bright. 'I reckon we have what we need,' Jim said. 'With Hal as our star witness and the others to support him, we can't fail.'

'I wish I had your certainty. Sanford managed to put a big gap between himself and his son. For a man who has the knack of knowing precisely what is going on around him, he was surprisingly ignorant of what his son was getting up to.'

'Come on ...' Jim stopped, smothering his words in a cough and then drawing on his pipe again.

Fess knew what Jim had been going to say. Soon he would be home, and he still had little idea of how he was going to handle Kevin. 'If you put together all the stories we've heard – from Ferret, Nifty, Gloria, Paula, Basher and now Hal Fitzwilliam – they all carry some truth, but I doubt any one is fully true or tells us all we should know. They're all tangled together, but not properly connected. A can of worms, if ever I saw one. There has to be a way we can fit them together and, when we do, I'll be confident we have the murderer.'

'You still want to entangle Sanford in your can of worms, don't you?'

‘That would be a bonus. There was nothing we learned tonight that helps me there, though.’ Fess could hear the rueful note in his admission. ‘No connection with Nifty.’

They continued on in silence, Jim puffing on his pipe and Fess wrestling with the best way of dealing with Kevin. Perhaps he could begin by saying something like, ‘Brother O’Donohue asked me to call and see him today. He said he wanted to speak with me as your father and not as a policeman.’ No, that sounded too pompous. Kevin would probably just give him that truculent stare he wore so often these days. Perhaps he should show Kevin the money and ask where he obtained it. No, that was starting off in too accusatory a fashion again. He needed something that brought them together.

When they came over the bridge a tram was just arriving. It stopped to allow the few passengers who had travelled the whole distance to alight and then began the manoeuvre that Fess never tired of watching. Tonight it was doubly welcome: it might help him explain to Jim his discontent with their investigation. ‘Take a look at this,’ he said, the enthusiasm in his voice catching Jim’s attention. ‘Watch the way the two of them work together with the tram itself.’

As Jim watched, the conductor, standing on the front platform of the car, lifted the pin that coupled the draw-bar of the car to the matching fitting on the dummy. The grip-man released the brake sufficiently to allow the dummy to roll down the slight incline that had been built into this portion of the track, with the uncoupled car trailing behind. 'Watch carefully now,' Fess called. 'As the dummy approaches the cross-over, there's a system of rods that changes the points and diverts the wheels and grip to the other rails.' As if in obedience to Fess' rapt description, the dummy swung onto the return set of tracks, after which the gripman changed the points back so that the car overtook the dummy and, further down the track, swung across to take up a position behind it.

Meanwhile, the conductor, standing on the leading platform with his hand on the gooseneck brake handle, waited until the precise moment the car had straightened on the return track before applying just sufficient pressure to bring the car to a standstill. He then stepped down onto the road, ran around to the other end of the car and coupled the car to the dummy by lifting the chain that had been supporting the draw-bar and, as the dummy slowly approached, guiding the draw-bar into the wide bell-mouthed fitting on the dummy. When the dummy bumped lightly against the car he dropped the pin into the coupling and secured the draw-bar. He then lifted a heavier safety chain attached to the dummy and placed it over a hook attached to the car. Having completed the coupling, he walked two or three steps back to the grating in the road beside the track, bent down and lifted a handle that caused the rope to be deflected into the jaws of the grip.

'We can get on now,' Fess said, his words difficult to hear over the noise made by the rope now running over the pulley wheels of the grip. The conductor then hurried to the rear of the tram where he released the hand-brake and, as if in celebration of his performance, gave two quick tugs on the strap that operated the bell in the canopy of the car. The gripman released the brake lever on the dummy and drew the grip lever towards his body, allowing the tram to move forward on its return journey. 'There you are,' purred Fess. 'Not a moment or a movement wasted. All in harmony, connected together. We need to feel the same way about our investigation.'

'If you say so,' Jim replied flatly. 'Personally, I'd settle for someone willing to say they saw Nifty do it. Let's hope putting the word out will bear some fruit, although I'm less concerned we need it now we have Hal's testimony.'

'You'll be speaking to Nifty again tomorrow?'

'You betcha. I'm looking forward to telling him what Hal had to say about him.'

'I'll have to leave that to you. I have some local matters I must deal with first thing.'

Jim gave Fess an appraising glance and surprised him by saying, 'No rush. Let's get him out of the cell around ten tomorrow.'

They lapsed into silence for the remainder of the journey, Jim contentedly puffing on his pipe while Fess continued to struggle with what he should say to Kevin. It would be so much easier if he were not a policeman and was free just to play the role of father. He remembered the scorn in Kevin's voice when he said, 'Yeah, always a policeman.'

Fess stood to leave the tram when it reached Nicholson

Street. 'I'll see you at the City Watch House ten tomorrow,' he said in farewell to Jim.

'Yeah,' he replied taking the pipe from his mouth. 'I hope you can sort out that other business.' He looked away, as though embarrassed, but then added, 'I need you to be fully focussed on getting Nifty's confession.'

The quickest way home for Fess was to walk up Barkly Street, taking him right pass Ma Cutmore's place. He hesitated but then knocked firmly on the door. Again, he had to wait before he heard the sound of shuffling footsteps and the husky voice asking, 'Oo's there?'

'Senior Constable Jordan, Mrs. Cutmore.'

'You again?'

'Just need another minute of your time.'

The door slowly swung open and Ma Cutmore stared bleakly at him. 'Come t'arrest me now, 'ave yer? Ya've got Ferret and Nifty. I'm the only one left.'

'I'd just like a quick look in the room that was Nifty's.'

'C'n I stop ya?'

'I'd rather you didn't try.'

'It's down 'ere. But I told ya last time, 'e ain't been 'ere since Sat'd'y night.'

The room was in darkness with the blind down and the air stale. Ma Cutmore switched on a lamp that stood on a narrow chest of drawers by the door. The room was somewhat larger than Fess had expected, with a low table in front of a padded two-seater couch along one wall. On the table were two glasses, a large, circular ashtray, overflowing with butts, and a bottle of Old Court Whisky. A single bed was made up neatly with pillow and blanket but no eiderdown. Fess went to the tall cupboard in the corner. In the long mirror on the door he could see Ma Cutmore watching him closely.

He opened the door and found a collection of coats and suits hanging inside. On the floor of the cupboard were several pairs of shoes and, on the upper shelf, two of the pork pie hats Nifty favoured. Fess pushed aside the coats but found nothing else at the back of the cupboard. He took down a battered suitcase from above the cupboard, but it was empty.

'Wotcha lookin' fer?' Ma Cutmore asked.

'You haven't seen an umbrella anywhere about have you, Mrs. Cutmore? A red one.'

'Nah. Could do with one of them meself.'

Fess looked under the bed and behind the couch, but there was no sign of the umbrella. It did appear that Nifty had taken very little with him and, apart from the indication that two people had been enjoying a drink sometime before he left, that was all Fess learned from his visit.

14

Bern was in the passage before Fess had the door fully open. 'I've been waiting,' she said unnecessarily.

Fess said nothing as he went through the routine of stowing his hat and coat before removing his jacket and hanging it in the wardrobe. Bern followed behind, rather like a dog waiting for her master to throw her a ball. He turned and leaned over to kiss her gently on the lips. 'Good evening, Mrs. Jordan. Are you well?'

'It's not good, is it? Michael told me.'

'Ah, you got him talking. What did he tell you?'

'He said the police had been to the school, because it wasn't just cakes that had been stolen, but money, as well. I couldn't get much more out of him but...' She wrinkled her nose in a way that Fess always found attractive and only saw when she was deeply puzzled. 'I somehow gained the impression that Michael is sort of envious of Kevin. Disapproving but envious. When I tried to find out more he clammed right up.' She turned her gaze directly on Fess. 'What have you found out? Do you understand what's going on?'

Fess grasped her shoulders with both hands and bent his knees so that their faces were aligned. 'It's complicated. I want you to be patient while I speak with Kevin again.'

'But ...'

'No buts. Trust me.'

'Fess you can be so irritating. I was going to ask you what we do now. The children are in there in front of the fire, wondering what you're going to do, what you're going to say. Are you going to take Kevin out to the sleep-out straight away? Do you want to eat first? We've eaten already, of course, and yours is drying out in the oven again. What do you want to do?'

'I think the usual family chat first, my dinner next and a talk with Kevin after that. Let me check out the mood.' Fess spoke much more light-heartedly than he felt and led Bernadette into the living room. Carmel, next to the fire, looked up from her knitting through shy lashes. She had been laboriously working on a red and white scarf for weeks, fighting her tendency to drop concentration and stitches while continually ridiculed by her brothers, who were familiar with the speed and skill with which their mother wielded her needles. She wouldn't have made much progress tonight. Michael sat on the floor, toying with his collection of model cars. Fess had given him a beautifully detailed model of a cable tram for his recent birthday, but Michael had been disappointed: he had been hoping for a Studebaker Light 6 Tourer like his best friend George Phillips had been given for his birthday. Jim Thomas wouldn't have made that mistake. Michael looked up at his father with expectant eyes. 'Now the drama begins,' his face seemed to say. Kevin was unmoved. He had pulled his armchair toward the fire and slumped in it with his legs stretched out so that his feet were almost in the hearth. Eventually, he glanced up at his father but immediately returned his gaze to the fire.

'I saw a great car today,' Fess announced jovially as he squatted beside Michael. 'The man I was with, Detective Thomas, is a bit of a car buff and he said it was the latest three passenger Buick with electric starting and lighting.'

'That'll be the Master Six,' Michael replied.

'What colour was it?' asked Carmel, who liked to insert herself into the male conversations whenever she could.'

'Bright red.'

'Mixing with the toffs, eh?' Kevin said in a voice that carried an unmistakable note of scorn. 'In Carlton?'

Pleased to have triggered some reaction from him, Fess allowed the challenge to slip past. 'No, this was in Kew. That's why I'm late; the tram takes a good while to get back from there. I was visiting Sanford Fitzwilliam.' Fess glanced up at Bern to make sure she had registered the name.

She had, of course. 'Was this about the murder?'

'There'd been a break in at the Fitzwilliam home by a man we suspect of having been involved with the murder. There may be more to it than that. We'll have to see.' Fess had done what he came into the room to do and hastened to put an end to the artificiality of the conversation. 'I'd better go and have my dinner before Mum's efforts go up in smoke. Afterwards ...' He paused for only an instant but noticed how all eyes were drawn to him. 'I think it would be good if Kevin and I had a chat.' He could hear the silence as he left the room, followed by Bernadette.

When she had brought his meal from the oven and placed it before him on the kitchen table, she said, as she always did, 'Mind, the plate's hot,' but did not stop there. 'What are you going to say to him?'

'It's more what is he going to say to me? But, if you wouldn't mind, I'd like to get my thoughts arranged. I haven't had much time today, with everything else that's been going on,' he lied. 'How about you go and sit with the kids while I eat these sausages and chew on how to approach Kevin?' Bernadette shot him a surprised look but said nothing and walked back to the living room. He didn't need time to think. He just didn't want to talk with Bern. If there had been time to explain, she would understand; she always did. And he would explain, but after he'd spoken with Kevin.

He rinsed the plate and cutlery in the sink and left them on the draining board before returning to the living room. 'Right, son, let's go,' he said altogether too heartily.

Kevin, who had been the only one not to look at him when he stood in the doorway, did not move and Fess began to wonder how he would deal with a refusal. But then his son rose awkwardly to his feet and Fess turned to lead him to the kitchen. 'Shut the door, please, Kevin. This conversation is just between us.' The boy continued to move slowly so that Fess was already sitting at the table when he entered the kitchen. Looking up at his son, he was reminded of Brother O'Donohue's comment. Kevin had developed into a fine big lump of a lad, almost as tall as Fess. No longer sprawled as he was in front of the fire, he stood straight, perhaps steeling himself for the ordeal of confronting his father, although he didn't look in any way overawed — almost arrogant, in fact, and not the schoolboy Fess knew. 'Come and sit over here,' he said in what he hoped sounded like a neutral voice. He wondered how often he had said that to the people he had interviewed — criminals, witnesses, victims, complainants. The tone varied with each one. What was the right tone for an errant son?

Kevin sat with his shoulders square, his hands together in his lap and his eyes studying his father, waiting for him to begin. It was what Fess would have done: don't commit yourself and let the other make the first move. 'Last night you said I was always a policeman, but that isn't so. There are times when I have to stand aside and let others do the policing. This is one of them.' Kevin continued to watch him carefully but still said nothing. 'When my son is involved in what turns out to be a more serious crime than pinching a couple of cakes, then, as a policeman, I can't be involved. All I can be is a father. So, as your father, I want to understand, properly understand, what you did and, just as importantly, why you did it.'

'You're still a copper, though.' Kevin spoke in a dismissive tone, as though Fess was the guilty party and had been unconvincing in his promise to turn over a new leaf.

For a moment Fess struggled with the anger that welled inside him. To be a policeman was a noble calling and no one, least of all his son, should be allowed to suggest not. But just a minute. Perhaps he was saying nothing about policing and everything about how hard he found it to relate to his father. Brother O'Donohue made it clear he should speak with him as his father not as a policeman. He had challenged him to allow Kevin to be open with him. Was this just the first step? Was Kevin telling him that he always seemed like a policeman, not a father, no matter the circumstances? 'So how are we going to deal with that? How can we get over this problem that I'm always a copper?'

'I don't think you can.' Now Fess could hear no accusation. It was almost as if Kevin was sorry for him. 'It was born in you and you've never broken free of it.'

'If it was born into me, it was born into you, doubly so.'

Kevin did not immediately reply, but Fess could see he was thinking it over. 'Maybe it's what you always wanted.'

'OK, let's accept what you say and find a way to work around it. I know,' Fess said, smiling for the first time in their conversation. 'If I'm always a copper, let me tell you what I know as a policeman. That might be the place to start.' Kevin nodded his head, but his eyes were puzzled, unsure where his father was going and perhaps disconcerted by the lightness in his voice. 'Yesterday afternoon you entered Mansons' Bakery, took a couple of the cakes and left the shop without paying for them. There are plenty of witnesses to confirm that much. But what puzzles the policeman in me is why so many people noticed you, even Mr. Manson, who was busy serving other customers. You must have wanted to be seen. Did you want to be caught? No, you were quick to leave the shop and would have easily outrun Mr. Manson if a feisty old woman hadn't tripped you up with her stick.'

'She didn't trip me up,' Kevin asserted quickly. 'Well, not on purpose like she said afterwards. She shouldn't have had it poking out like she did, where anyone going past could trip over it. She didn't even know what was going on until Manson arrived and then she tried to make herself into some kind of hero.'

Clearly, getting caught had been a blow to his pride. If he had done it for a dare or to show off to his classmates, getting caught would tarnish his achievement. 'So, if you didn't want to be caught, there must have been another reason. That becomes clear when Mr. Manson goes back into his shop and is told that another boy, a much smaller one, had made off with the contents of his till. Mr. Manson says four pounds six shillings was taken. The boy leaves through a back door, suggesting the theft had been pre-planned. But of course it had. The two of you acted together.'

Kevin was now watching him carefully. 'You can't prove that,' he said, not as a quick defensive reaction, but thoughtfully, as though he were a lawyer analysing the case against him. Brother O'Donohue said he was a bright lad. Not many fourteen year olds would have come up with that line. Strange, at what times and in what circumstances you can find pride in your children.

'You're right,' Fess agreed. 'Some of that policeman's way of looking at things has rubbed off on you. We can't even prove that Billy Rawson was the other boy; not to convince a magistrate that is, because, while a number of people said they saw him, none of them are game to stand up in Court and say it was him. You're on your own.' Fess thought of saying, 'We're on our own,' but decided against it: too soon for that. 'And there's another problem for the police: they have to link you to the money that was stolen.' Fess was disturbed to see Kevin begin to relax: he could see that he might yet escape. 'But this afternoon you are discovered to be carrying four pounds that you can't explain. I have it here.' Fess placed the money on the table and looked enquiringly at his son.

Kevin stiffened and said, 'How did you get that?'

'Brother O'Donohue asked to see me this afternoon, as a parent not a policeman. He was very clear on that point.'

'He shouldn't have taken it off me. He's a thief.'

'Did you tell him that?'

Kevin hung his head, looking more his age. 'He wouldn't have listened if I had.'

'I'm puzzled that Billy kept only six shillings.'

'I didn't say that Billy took any money.'

'No, you didn't. If you let me be a father for just a moment and not a policeman, I'm pleased that you're not shopping Billy. Back to being a policeman, though. If Billy didn't take it and then give most of it to you, where did it come from?'

'I earned it,' Kevin replied doggedly. The young schoolboy was emerging more clearly with every exchange.

'Kevin! We agreed only a moment ago that a policeman needs to be able to prove his claims. So do you. Where is your evidence that you earned the money? There is none.' Fess saw the defiant look in his son's eyes and was annoyed with himself. He'd been too smart and overreached. 'So we come back to the two questions I asked at the start. Yeah, it's pretty clear what you did: organised and led a scheme to steal money from the till of Mansons' Bakery with an accomplice as yet unidentified. The case against you is a strong one. But I still don't know why you did it and, speaking more as a father than a policeman, that troubles me greatly.'

'You would never understand.'

'Try me.'

'All right, then.' The defiance remained but was joined by something that bordered on exultation. 'It's fun. It's exciting.'

'Surely going through all this isn't exciting?'

More soberly now, but still with the need to protect his pride, Kevin said, 'This is the first time I've been caught.'

'There have been other times?' Fess had not completed the question before he wished he could take it back or at least remove the surprised tone with which he'd asked it. Here was a clear demonstration that he didn't understand his son and the disdainful amusement on Kevin's face wounded like a spear.

'Shoplifting on your own is so easy it's boring. Some of the other kids are too scared to try, but there's no excitement after you've done it a few times.'

'So you took on something harder?' Fess could see that their roles had been reversed. Instead of him leading

Kevin, now his son was telling his naive father how it was in his world. How could he get back some control in this conversation? And Bern would be devastated.

'Everything else is so boring you have to find something that's exciting. What's exciting for you, Dad?'

Fess did not immediately answer, his thoughts with Mary Worthington. Paula said that Mary 'had this thing' about Nifty being a crook. Was she looking for some excitement in a boring life, too?

'See, you can't find anything. I don't want to end up like you, stuck in boring Carlton. Why did we have to come here in the first place?'

'You'd rather we stayed in Bendigo?'

'It didn't need to be Bendigo. But not in the city. You can do things in the country. That's where I'm going next year after I leave school.'

'You haven't told me about this.'

'You didn't ask. You're always too busy locking up people who have no other way of looking after themselves.'

'Did Billy Rawson tell you that?'

'It's true. You've said it yourself. I've heard you going on to Mum about it. How you wish you could catch the rich people who live off the poor crims. Isn't the bloke you went to see today one of them? Fitzwilliam?'

'Did you get into this because you were sick of being a policeman's son and wanted to break away from that?'

'The son of a copper, grandson of a copper, Grandma always telling me what a fine man Grandpa was. Yeah, I want to make my own way, not follow along the rut you two went down. But pinching things isn't breaking away from anything except boredom; it's having some fun. I keep telling you that, but you don't listen.'

'So what are we going to do about you now?'

'I guess I'll have to go to Court.' His voice was dull, even a little fearful, the passion that had fired his words as he lectured his father now spent.

'Perhaps you will. As I said straight off, that'll be up to the police, not to me.' Suddenly Fess knew what he should do. He wasn't the one to bring Kevin to his senses. He had become the one it was important for Kevin to defy. But there were others. 'I'm here to support you, not to convict you. So is the rest of the family. You need to tell them.'

'What?'

'You have to tell your mother and your brother and sister what you've done and why. You have to explain yourself to them. Each of them has to bear the consequences of what you've done, not just you.'

Fess could see the reluctance with which Kevin faced this unexpected task. 'You can tell them, Dad. I've told it all to you.'

'And you're going to tell it to them now.' He stood over his son, painfully conscious of how young Kevin really was. The truculence and the bravado had vanished, leaving uncertainty and embarrassment behind. 'Come on. We'd best get on with it.'

Slowly Kevin rose to his feet and Fess gestured for him to go ahead. As he followed his son from the kitchen, he was assailed by doubt. Was this the best way? How would Mick and Carmel react? And Bern? What about her? But his greatest doubt was about himself. Kevin had laid out his shortcomings as a father pretty well. Should he leave it all to Kevin or should he be acknowledging this to the rest of his family?

Three pairs of anxious eyes met them as they entered the living room. 'Kevin has been explaining to me what he has done and why he did it. I believe he should share this with you as well, so we can deal with it as a family.' Strewth, he sounded pompous. 'Sit over in that chair,' he said to Kevin, indicating the empty one by the fire. 'I'll camp on the carpet with Michael.' Bernadette went to speak but choked off whatever she thought to say. Carmel's eyes were wide, her knitting spilling onto the floor. Michael's attention had been fixed on his brother from the moment he had re-entered the room.

Kevin gave a final look of appeal to his father who, resisting the impulse to say something to ease his way, nodded for him to begin. 'Well, you all know I took a couple of cakes from Mansons' and was caught when I was stupid enough to trip over an old woman's stick.' He gave a small deprecatory chuckle, but no one joined in. 'I've pinched other things before without any problem.'

'Oh dear,' Bernadette sighed.

'Dad did it, too.' Fess could see that Bern's disapproval had a power completely missing from his own. 'Yeah, he took some lollies once.'

'And straight after, realised how silly I'd been and never

did it again.' He had to say something. He couldn't let Kevin divert attention onto him. 'Go on, Kevin.'

'While I was being chased by old man Manson, someone else pinched the money from his till.'

'You put Billy Rawson up to it, didn't you?' Michael said, and Fess was uncertain whether the accusation was hostile or merely an attempt to appear knowing.

'Let's be clear here,' Fess intervened again. 'I am not involved as a policeman in this.' If only that were true. 'But I know that the police have not yet finally established who actually took the money. Yes, there are suspicions that it might have been Billy who was involved, but Kevin is not saying and, as his family, we should respect that and say nothing ourselves.' Why must he always sound like a policeman laying down the law?

Kevin continued doggedly. 'This afternoon Brother O'D called me in and made me turn out my pockets. He found some money that he gave to Dad.'

'Where did you get it from, Kevin?' Bern knew the answer of course. She just didn't want to believe it.

He shrugged. 'You can work it out. That's the end of the story. Dad says I might have to go to Court, but that will be up to the police.'

'Why have you done this?' Bern had come to the crucial question.

'I've told Dad. I'm bored with everything and this was a bit of fun, a bit of excitement away from boring school.'

'It's not fun for the people whose stuff you've taken,'

Carmel said, surprising them all. Was this the little nun speaking? Fess hoped not.

'What would you know?' Kevin said in the dismissive voice of a boy putting down his kid sister, but Fess could see the colour in his face.

'Mick thinks it makes you a big man in the school,' she sneered. No sign of the nun this time.

'I didn't say that.'

'Yes, you did.'

Fess needed to break this up. 'I hadn't realised how unhappy Kevin was with living in Carlton.' He could see the wrinkle in Bern's nose. 'He wants to leave school and live in the country. He certainly doesn't want to stay in Carlton and become a policeman. We need to talk about that and see what's to be done to help him.' On that first day they met, when Fitzwilliam had told him about his charity, Helping Hand, he had said something about the only way to have criminals turn their back on crime was to find an alternative way for them to achieve their desires. Fess remained suspicious that the main purpose of Helping Hand was to recruit men Fitzwilliam could use in his gangs, but the principle was right. At least, he hoped that was what Bern and he could do with Kevin. 'Meanwhile I have to see what I can do for Kevin in this scrape. None of us want him to have to go to Court. And remember …' He made sure he caught the eyes of both his other children. 'Kevin has told his story just to us. We mustn't let him down by gossiping about it with anyone else. That won't be easy at school, but it must be done.' He stood up. 'Time for bed.'

Less reluctantly than usual, the children went to their beds, leaving Bernadette and Fess staring into the flames from either side of the fire. Had he built this whole thing into something much larger than it really was? After all, shoplifting was hardly a major crime. He'd done it himself, and so did most kids. Kevin had taken it further, though, and his recruitment of others into his schemes had to be stopped. But was he overreacting because his son's major crime was something totally different? He had accused his father of falling into a rut and, worse still, of making no effort to get out of it. Hadn't Jim Thomas said something very similar when they first met?

'It's really my fault,' Bernadette said suddenly.

'What?'

'If I hadn't kept on at you about leaving Carlton, he wouldn't have become so unsettled, so dissatisfied with living here, so convinced all will be well if he could only live in the country.'

'That's ridiculous. It's me he blames, not you.'

'No, it's not blame. It's just that you were such a hero for him and now you aren't. It's good when a father inspires admiration and respect in his son, but every son has to understand his father is a human being with strengths and weaknesses, not some kind of comic book hero. It's a necessary part of growing up. I'm happy he doesn't see you as a hero any more but sad that it's left a hole he's tried to fill in such a foolish way. Now the most important thing we can do is try to help him find his way.'

Fess looked across at her as she continued to stare into

the fire. Did she really believe what she was saying, or was she just trying to make him feel better? Perhaps both. 'Yeah, you're right. It doesn't really matter who's at fault. It's where we go from here that matters.' Now he was trying to cheer her up, but he meant what he said as well.

'What are we going to do?' Bernadette asked with a sigh.

'I know what I'm going to do.'

When he told her, Bernadette smiled at him and said, 'Yeah, that's good. I hope Mr. Manson and Kevin think so, too.'

15

The rich aroma of recent baking greeted Fess when he entered Mansons' Bakery. All of the bread, buns, cakes and pastries were behind the counter except for the cakes in the daily display which was on the customers' side. The shop was crowded so that Manson did not at first notice him standing there. Fess realised that the displayed cakes certainly presented an opportunity for someone to do some shoplifting. Eventually he was noticed and the baker raised questioning eyebrows. 'Could I have a word, please, Mr. Manson?' Fess asked.

'A minute. We're very busy you see.' When the customers had dwindled to a number that his wife could handle on her own, he inclined his head at Fess, inviting him around the side of the counter and through to the bakery proper. Although the baking for the day was over, the clean metal mixing utensils stacked on the scoured benches and the cooking ingredients stored away in their bins, the space was made cosy by the residual warmth of the ovens. Manson wiped his hands on his striped apron and turned to face Fess, who did not pause in front of him, but walked on through a storeroom and into the small back yard, which contained several outhouses and the bakery van, a rather battered vehicle with 'Manson Bakery' in fading brown letters on the side of the cream cabin. 'Why bring me out here? It is cold.' To emphasise the point, Manson folded his thick arms and began to rub his shoulders.

'I didn't want to be interrupted,' Fess replied. 'Mr. Manson, I've told you several times already that I cannot act as the policeman handling your case. I am here today as the father of Kevin Jordan, one of those involved in the theft, and I want to emphasise this by laying aside my police badge.' He took the badge from his pocket and placed it on the running board of the van. Manson was right: it was cold out here away from the warmth of the bakery.

'So?' The baker was growing impatient with what he saw as some kind of silly show.

Fess began to think he might have a point. 'I have this for you.' He took an envelope from his trouser pocket and handed it over.

'What is this?'

'Count it. It's the money that was taken from your shop.' Manson gave a puzzled frown, opened the envelope and had to grasp at it when the coins threatened to spill onto the ground. As he began to count the money, Fess said, 'I don't intend to tell you how I was able to retrieve the money.' He wasn't going to tell him that he'd made up the six shillings from his own pocket, either.

Manson, now in much better humour, said, 'Yes it is the missing. Do you think I care how you were able to do this? I thank you, Senior Constable.'

'Mr. Jordan, if you don't mind. As far as I'm concerned that is an end to my involvement unless and until the police proceed against my son.' This was always going to be the tricky part, and Fess watched carefully to see the reaction his words were having.

'Ah yes, I see.' Manson furrowed his brow. 'Now I have my money returned, you think those boys should go unpunished?'

'I can speak only of my son. I do wonder whether there is a more productive method than taking him to Court, although that is an option on which others will decide.'

Now it was the baker who was doing the careful watching. 'You have the suggestion?'

'Mr. Manson, I thought it might be a good discipline for my son if he came here next Saturday and experienced the hard work that goes into producing your bread, your pies and indeed the cakes he stole.'

'You have a good idea Senior..., Mr. Jordan. I am too busy for the courts and justice is never certain.' He became stern again. 'He must be here by five in the morning. Saturday is our busiest day and the baking must be over before the shop opens.'

'I will see to it.'

'Mr. Jordan, I have sons of my own. They're older now. You are a good father to your son.'

'I wish you were right, Mr. Manson.'

* *

After leaving the bakery Fess continued down Lygon Street, eventually coming to the lofty facade of the Trades

Hall Council building, with its Greek temple portico. Fess thought, as he often did when passing the Trades Hall, of David McGrath, who had been killed here, back in 1915. A genial man with a walrus moustache, he and Fess had joined the Force in the same intake. Fess had gone to Bendigo, but David stayed on in the city, and it was during a bungled burglary at the Hall that he had been shot. John Jackson was hanged for it, but rumours persisted that Squizzy Taylor had been involved, along with one of his early backers. People like that never get near Court, though. McGrath's widow had to bring up their two daughters on her own. At least Fess had been fully adult when his mother became a widow. Continuing across Victoria Street, he soon came to the City Watch House.

The Watch House Keeper was a different one from the other day, but Jim was in exactly the same position, his feet on the desk, smoking his pipe. This time, though, he wasn't in the same rush he had been on Monday. Instead of leaping to his feet, he remained sitting and waved for Fess to sit in the chair next to him. 'Just before we see Nifty, how are you going with the lad? Any progress?'

Fess sank onto the chair and sighed. 'Progress? I feel for the Worthington parents even more than before. I had no idea what Kevin was getting up to. He's been shoplifting, for the excitement of it, he said. Would you believe it? I had no idea. It all came out last night after the head teacher at the school asked to see me and handed over the stolen money he'd found on Kevin.'

'Didn't you ever pinch something, or were you too scared of being caught by your dad?'

'Yeah, but Kevin was building his own gang. I hope I've put a stop to that.' Fess squared his shoulders and looked into Jim's eyes. 'Kevin tells me he wants to make his own way and doesn't want to follow along the rut his father and grandfather went down.'

Jim went to respond but changed his mind, asking instead, 'So what happens now?'

'I've just come from seeing the baker. I went through the pantomime of taking him into his back yard and putting aside my badge so I could impress on him I wasn't there as a policeman but solely as Kevin's father.'

'Did anyone see you?' Jim snapped.

'I wanted this conversation to be private, just between Manson and me.'

'So no one knows about this?'

'Bern knows what I had in mind.'

Jim frowned. 'That's not really what I was asking. What else did you do?' There was urgency in this question as well.

'I gave Manson back the money that was stolen and …'

'You handed him money at a secret meeting?'

'And I suggested that Kevin should work in the bakery next Saturday as a preferable punishment to going to Court.'

'My God, it gets worse. Did he buy that?'

'What do you mean? Yes he did. Told me I was a good father.'

'Senior Constable Jordan, you are charged that on … What's the date today? Doesn't matter. That you sought to pervert the course of justice by offering a bribe to the complainant in the case against your son, who is on a charge of theft.'

'You've been paying too much attention to O'Sullivan's conspiracy case.'

'Old Sugar Bag. You're nothing like him; but how could a man of your rank and experience be so stupid and leave yourself open to such a charge?'

Fess stared at him reproachfully. 'You must have a lot of backstabbing in the C.I. Let's get back to the real world. I'm here to interview Nifty.'

Jim shook his head sorrowfully. 'You always have to protect yourself. You must know that: we all do. You amaze me.' He sighed and turned to the Watch House Keeper. 'Bring him in, please, Bert,' he said and rose to his feet, still in no hurry and still musing over what Fess had told him. They entered the same room as last time, cold and dank as before, and sat awaiting Nifty's arrival. There was the distant clang of a cell door and then footsteps that came closer until Nifty appeared in the doorway and stumbled into the room.

'All right. Take your time,' he said to whoever had pushed him. 'I hope you've come to apologise for keeping me in here, and let me go,' he said, but some of the swagger was missing and his hair was awry. He had the same ill-fitting clothes, which were now stained and crumpled. The watch house was taking its toll.

'Sit down,' Jim said sternly. 'We have news for you — none of it good.'

Nifty took his place opposite them and kept his eyes on Jim, ignoring Fess. 'What's that?'

'We now know you went out to Kew because you needed cash, so you could scarper interstate, and thought Hal Fitzwilliam would be an easy mark. You told him you had to get away because you were in deep trouble. We all know what that trouble was. Just as well Fitzwilliam's men were more than a match for the likes of you, you little creep.'

'Is that what he said?' If Nifty was feigning surprise he was doing it very well. 'Yeah, you'd believe him, too, you coppers. The toff from Kew with the father who knows everyone.' Nifty gave a wide smile that lacked an ounce of humour. 'He's always complainin' about his father, but I bet he's happy to use him now. I didn't go to steal anythin'. I went to get me money back. He owed me.'

'Oh, yeah? Why did he owe you?'

'It was business,' Nifty replied noncommittally. 'I'd paid him for somethin' he didn't supply so I wanted me money back.'

'Business or theft, I don't care,' Jim said, shrugging his shoulders. 'We know you admitted to him you were in trouble. We already know you were with Mary and had an argument with her. You've signed your own death warrant.'

'Hal Fitzwilliam's a liar. And who's goin' t'believe an old lag like Ferret Roberts?' Nifty said defiantly. 'He'd say anythin' that might get him off.'

Fess noticed the hollowness that was creeping into Nifty's arrogant tone. 'Can you tell us why Hal Fitzwilliam would want to have you found guilty of rape and murder?' Fess asked without any of the sarcastic challenge that Jim would have put into his voice. Rather, it appeared that he had some sympathy for the man and was encouraging him to defend himself. 'You need to tell us what really happened. It's your only chance.' Jim shot an angry glance at Fess, who could tell the effect his words were having on the Detective. He hoped Nifty was drawing the same conclusion. He hadn't gone soft on Nifty, though. Perhaps his unsuccessful pursuit of Sanford Fitzwilliam had warped his judgment, but he couldn't resist the hope that he might finally unmask Sanford through his son. In trying to clear himself of the murder, Nifty might give him the evidence he needed. He and Nifty were united in totally different causes.

'Yeah. You're right. Unless I spill the beans those bastards are goin' t'nail me,' Nifty said reflectively and rubbed the stubble on his chin.

'It might be best if you took us through what you did and what you saw on Saturday night,' Fess suggested. 'The real story this time.'

'Yeah, OK.' Nifty's eyes narrowed as he appraised both of them. 'She was at my place early on that night but she left. Went out to meet Hal at Kew.'

'She went to his house?' Jim was disbelieving.

'Nah. Too risky.' Nifty chuckled. 'He had this lover's walk somewhere, just over the bridge after you get off the tram.'

'That'd be the path that takes you to Galatea Point,' Fess said quietly.' When both of the other men gave him surprised stares he added. 'It's through the bush. The Galatea Point path goes along the top of the cliff before dropping down to the river. There's also a path in the other direction that goes to the Boathouse. We go for picnics out there sometimes. There's a great view, but it'd be a pretty cold place this time of year for a lover's tryst.'

The idea seemed to amuse Nifty. 'Yeah, he would have tried it on, too. Reckoned he was irresistible to all women. Not to Molly, though. She thought he was a creep and she could handle his type with no trouble.'

Jim leaned forward, his impatience bubbling like a cooking pot. 'So, if she didn't go for a canoodle, why did she meet him there?'

'We had a business arrangement. I told ya.'

Fess sighed. 'Nifty, I told you this was your only chance, and I meant it. If you're going to get out of this — not be up on a rape and murder charge — you have to come clean with us, totally clean. Choosing bits and pieces won't do the trick.' Fess sounded as though he was cajoling one of his children to own up to something. He hadn't tried that tone with Kevin. Perhaps he should have.

'OK. OK.' Nifty sighed. 'You've probably worked it out, anyway. Hal had a business goin', supplyin' snow. Molly was there to make a payment and take delivery.'

'Are you saying Molly dealt cocaine?'

'No. Well not yet, anyway. She was just the link. Hal didn't like to work with me direct. He said he couldn't risk gettin' too close to people like me.' He gave them a sly grin. 'I mighta got offended, except it looked too good a chance t'miss.'

'You expected her back at your place? That's why you stayed in on Saturday?'

'Yeah. She didn't need to take much more time than the ride out and back. Probably Hal would try to have her hang about with him, even go for a ride in his flash car, but Molly wouldn't have any of that.'

'Did you see anything, hear anything, when she did come back, out in the lane at the back?' Fess asked, his voice sharper than it had been before.

Again Nifty sighed. 'Yeah, not long after nine, 'bout the time I expected her back, I did hear someone callin' out in The Narrows. You often do. When the time got on, I started to worry. After a while I took the risk and had a look in the lane.'

'Very brave of you,' Jim said. 'You found her?'

'Yeah. She was dead.'

'Did you lay her out straight and smooth down her clothes?'

'What? I didn't touch her. All I did was have a look in the pockets of her coat. Big pockets she had on that coat; good for carryin' the flat tobacco tins Hal used for the snow. There was nothin' there so I scarpered. I knew someone had blown us and could be linin' up to go for me, as well.'

'You didn't think about reporting the crime.'

'Wha'd'ya take me for? I knew, given half a chance,

you'd lay it on me and I was right. I needed to go into smoke quick-smart.'

'So why go out to Fitzwilliam's place?'

Nifty gave Fess, who had asked the question, a scornful look. 'Like I told ya, t'get me money back, o'course, from Hal. He was the one who wanted to use Molly, so he hadn't delivered to me. The mug must'a let it slip to some tug and the gang moved in.'

'Which gang would that be?'

'Dunno. You gotta say Basher is best bet but, as far as I know, he isn't in any of the gangs these days. Works on his own. Maybe some of Squizzy's boys. I know Hal was in with Squizzy until he tried it on with his wife down at the Palais when Squizzy was away. Hal was lookin' to use me instead. That's how we got started on this caper. Maybe Sqizzy found out somehow.' Nifty frowned and shook his head ruefully. 'I was a dill to get mixed up with him. He's too keen on usin' the stuff himself and, when he's on it, he talks big and doesn't mind what he says.'

'Hal uses cocaine?'

'Too much. He goes up and down like one of them yo-yos.'

'And Mary, too?'

'Nah. She just played with it. Not like him.'

'You must have been surprised when Mr. Fitzwilliam's men grabbed you,' Fess remarked.

'Fitzwilliam's gorillas. What's a respectable man like that lettin' them outa their cage?'

'Maybe he found out what his son was up to and wanted to put a stop to it.'

'Funny way to do it,' Nifty replied.

'Perhaps he's not as respectable as you think. Perhaps he's the man behind the drug supply, and didn't like Hal getting involved with you, so decided to close you down,' Fess said.

Nifty gave Fess a sardonic grin. 'I heard you had it in for him. Yeah, it's true he knows a lot of crims. Some of the older coves had him defendin' them when he was a barrister and some of the younger coots have tried his Helpin' Hand. No future there, I'd say. No, I'd put me money on Hal goin' it alone.'

'What about the argument you had with Mary?' Jim asked. 'You haven't told us about that? Not jealous that she was going off to see Hal, the ladies' man?'

'I told ya she was pretty and we had some fun together, but I can say that about quite a few sheilas I know. Anyway, if I'd said anythin' like that, she'd have laughed at me. No, she reckoned she was worth more on this job than I was willin' to cut her and we had some argy bargy over it. That's all.'

'You got any more in this fairy story?' Jim asked.

'It ain't no story. It's the dinkum truth. You betta believe me.'

The arrogance was still there, but there was also a pleading tone in his voice. Fess had never seen Nifty pleading before. 'Thank you, Nifty. I hope you'll be willing to assist us further if we need to come back to you,' he said politely.

'Aren't you goin' to let me go now y'can see it wasn't me?' Nifty said, already knowing what the answer would be.'

'No chance,' Jim said and suddenly stood up. He opened the door and called. 'You can take him back now.'

After Nifty left the room, looking no better than when he was brought in, Jim glanced across at Fess and said, 'He hasn't been wasting his time in here. That's quite a story he's cooked up.'

'A story? That's what you think?'

'Bits of it may be true. All good lies have some truth in them. Hal's no angel, I'd bet on that. OK, maybe there were drugs and Mary wanted more of a share than Nifty wanted to give her. When she arrived back to his place they had a fight over that and Nifty killed her.'

'But Nifty would then have the cocaine. Why did he go out to Kew two days later?'

'Maybe Molly and Hal double-crossed him or were planning to. Did you notice how Nifty said that if he showed any jealousy Mary would have laughed at him? But Ferret told you he'd heard her laugh that night. Maybe it was a crime of passion, after all.' Jim smiled at a new thought. 'A few times you've told me the way Mary's body was laid out all neat and tidy doesn't fit a rape. It would if the rapist did actually care for her. Nifty rapes and murders her, goaded by his jealousy, and then shifts her body out of his room into the lane. He doesn't dump her, though: he lays her out respectfully.'

Fess chuckled. 'You can spin a good tale as well. How

about this one? Sanford has been a backer of Squizzy Taylor, using Hal as the link man so Sanford is never at risk. The bad feeling between father and son, which I know has been there for years, reaches the point where Hal decides to go out on his own and recruits Nifty, with the first job being the drugs deal Nifty described, using the source that has been Sanford's until now. Sanford finds out what his son is up to and decides to close him down. He arranges for Mary to be intercepted on her way back to Nifty and the drugs taken from her, but she is raped and murdered as well, maybe as a warning to Nifty not to try and muscle in or maybe to hide the real reason for attacking her. Nifty, the arrogant thug that he is, doesn't know of Sanford's involvement and goes out to Kew to sort out Hal, where he meets Sanford's "gorillas".'

'You really are obsessed by Sanford. Even Nifty knows about it.

Until you can show me some evidence, let him be. All I've seen is that Fitzwilliam's willing to help us.'

'Help himself, you mean.'

'No, help us. He rang me this morning. Said he had an idea that could help with our case and would like to speak with us. Said, if it were not too much trouble, would we mind coming out to Kew again? I told him we were busy early this morning but could fit him in later. We should be on our way. I said twelve o'clock.'

16

As the tram trundled through Fitzroy, it passed along a line of shops, pubs, small factories and warehouses. In Collingwood, some of the shops were replaced by the occasional terrace of workers' cottages, but the pubs remained and Fess was reminded of the Londonderry Hotel, the scene of Leo O'Sullivan's conspiracy. He turned to Jim and said, 'The other day you were complaining to me that the judge sentencing Leo O'Sullivan said nothing about how he'd been allowed to get away with it for so long and you hinted you were doing something to change things. When I asked you what you meant you told me to wait and see. I'm still waiting.'

Jim gave him a thoughtful glance before saying, 'Funny you should ask. Read this.' He reached into his pocket and, instead of producing his tobacco pouch, brought out what looked like some galley proofs that he handed to Fess, who unfolded the sheets, smoothed some creases and began to read the closely-typed text.

History Of Champion "Sugar Bag" Of Victorian Police Force

"HE TEMPTED ME," WAS LEO'S PLEA

—

But It Did Not Tempt The Jury

—

O'Sullivan Gets His Pass for Pentridge — Fowler Was Evidently a Good Judge of What Would Happen in the Court — Brennan's Refusal to Put Leo in the Witness-box Gave Gorman Scope for His Sarcasm — Judge was Responsible for Some Amusing Interludes — Leo's Nervously-delivered Statement from the Dock — His Pitiful Appearance Did Not Move the Jury in a Recommendation for Mercy.

—

Leo asked for a Cottage, and they gave him a Cold, Cold Cell!

The champion "sugar bag" of the Victorian Police Force has been laid by the heels after many years of opulence.

By the conviction of Detective Leo O'Sullivan, Pentridge has received one of the worst blackmailers that has been within its walls, and Melbourne's most profitable and important graft system has been shattered.

O'SULLIVAN departs unwept, unhonoured and unsung, the unregulation copper who "copped" for all he was worth.

UNDOUBTEDLY the C.I.B. is a better place by the going of little Leo from its ranks to pay his debt to society in gaol.

The Callaghan affair was the culmination of five years of "graft", five years of dishonourable service and much money.

Detectives are never popular with a large section of the public, and wild tales are circulated about them.

But no "demon" in the history of the Force ever got the reputation for crookedness that O'Sullivan did, and throughout Victoria he was mentioned as a "grafter" long before Terrence Callaghan's bank balance was reduced by £1000.

When there is smoke there is fire, and the gossip about O'Sullivan was founded on pretty solid ground.

The Beginning

He began life in the railway service, working through the positions of porter, ticket collector and guard to the special inquiry branch, and few railwaymen have a good word to say for him.

His methods were shady, and he worked on the principle that his right-hand should not know what his left-hand was taking. Those who got into trouble soon found out that little Leo's left-hand was particularly sensitive to money, and none but the "mugs" ever went along if they had money.

Played to the Limit

For a dishonest inquiry officer, really a departmental policeman, the railways offer tremendous opportunities for making easy money, and O'Sullivan played the game to the limit. For a consideration he would overlook anything from a breach of regulations to theft, and he kept up his tally of catches by carpeting those who wouldn't pay and the mugs who did not know the ropes.

As a guard on the Gippsland and North-Eastern lines, Little Leo opened up a highly lucrative business, that of "copping" extensively from the cardsharpers and spielers who worked the trains. From this source he got a regular income, and compared with it his departmental salary was small.

O'Sullivan needed it all to satisfy his luxurious tastes, and his many suits and expensive diamond rings were freely commented on.

Had Few Friends

Railway days were happy days for Leo, despite the fact he had few friends in the service. A man who has his former friends carpeted for playing two-up while he allows sharpers to work the trains isn't likely to be popular.

Another cause of Leo's unpopularity was his work checking the ticket collectors, and it is freely maintained that, to get convictions, he resorted to tricks to create cases. Now that he has been exposed for the "sugar-bag" he is, there must be grave doubts about whether justice was done by many of the men he has sent to gaol.

Physically, Leo of the varied sartorial effects, was not of standard policeman size by any means, but that did not deter him from his ambition to get into a more profitable section of the crime detection business. So he pulled the strings, and five or six years ago the late Sir George Stewart, then Chief Commissioner, forgot the police regulations for the time being, and had Leo appointed to the staff of the Criminal Investigation Branch.

Thus Special Inquiry Officer O'Sullivan became Detective O'Sullivan, and the change, so far as Little Leo was concerned, was a beneficial one, though the same cannot be said from the public point of view.

Ostentatious Wealth

Leo prospered, and his prosperity was not hidden modestly. Rather was it made very ostentatious – expensive clothes, jewellery, a Minerva car and a gay life – and Dame Rumour talked openly of O'Sullivan's sources of wealth. The card sharpers still paid their weekly licensing fee, and Leo found the bigger game with the money to pay off exposure.

So obvious did his wealth become that he got a gentle hint that the department would be pleased if he got rid of the Minerva, or at least forbore from flaunting it. The car disappeared from the front of the C.I.B., but Leo continued to be in funds and the owner of a £150 diamond ring, which winked cynically from his little finger.

Success in minor graft egged ambition on to plan bigger coups with an impudence which is amazing, and Terrence Callaghan was picked on as the pigeon to be plucked.

Leo in Danger

Leo, the erstwhile sleuth, will be in danger in gaol if some prisoners get near him. They would not hesitate to kick him to death if they got a chance. Several have sworn to "get him" if the opportunity arises and theirs is no idle boast. He is hated almost fanatically because of his bushranging methods, for some crooks know from bitter experience that O'Sullivan was quite capable of taking a bribe and then doublecrossing the donor. His code of honour has large holes in it.

Menace Removed

His incarceration for three years removes a public menace, a trusted public officer holding powers of life and death almost, who was devoid of all standards.

His exploits rank "Sugar Bag" O'Sullivan with the worst of crooks, for he was simply a devilish blackmailer, whose office gave him immunity.

Of the three "demons" in Stone-haven, O'Sullivan is the worst, and by his going, relief will come to many people — and some crooks will have more money to spend.

'Where did this come from?' Fess asked as he folded the sheets and returned them to Jim.

'Buy *The Truth* on Saturday and you'll see it in there. This is only part of it — the part that interests me. And how did I get a copy?' Jim grinned. 'A mystery really, seeing I have no known connections with the paper. I did go to school with the reporter who wrote this piece, but that was a long time ago and nobody knows about that. He's very good at taking tip-offs and building them into a spicy story. His style suits *The Truth*.'

The tram rattled across Hoddle Street and stopped under the Victoria Park railway bridge where most of the passengers left to join the train to Heidelberg. When the tram was under way again, Fess, who had been silently considering what he had just learnt, said, 'Why did you show me?'

Jim turned to face him directly and asked, 'What did you get out of that piece? What did you think as you read it?'

Fess gave a short laugh. 'One thing I thought was that Sugar-Bag could sue *The Truth*.'

'He won't do that. He won't want any more of his rotten career to come out in a Court. But what about the bosses? What about everyone in the railways talking about his clothes and rings while nothing was done? What about him getting into C.I. against regulations while Chief Commissioner Stewart turned a blind eye? What about him being told to move his flash car so the higher-ups wouldn't be embarrassed? Didn't that make you angry? Haven't I brought it out enough? Is that what you're saying?'

'Whoa. Whoa.' Fess leaned across to pat Jim on the arm. 'So it's them you're really after, not Sugar-Bag?'

'Of course it is. The likes of Sugar-Bag — and there are others trying to do the same as him — they're just low life, like the gangs. I bet there are some in the Carlton Station taking their kick-backs. It's the higher-ups who let them get away with it that I'm after.'

Fess kept his face impassive but immediately thought of the S.P. bookies and the sly grog shops. He'd seen no point in trying to stamp them out and accepted the arrangements Doyle had with them as doing little harm. Jim wouldn't see it that way.

Jim scowled. 'Do you know Herbert Smith? You should; he's the Member for Melbourne in the Upper House. He's calling for an enquiry into police corruption and maladministration. So far he's been concentrating on the Licensing Branch but, when he gets more of this kind of stuff, I know he'll have to widen his scope.' Jim continued in a lower voice, speaking more to himself than Fess. 'This isn't enough, though, is it? You have to read too far into the story to get the point. I need something sensational, a story that'll get their blood running and have everyone demanding a public enquiry.'

The buildings lining the route began to change: the scattering of pubs remained, but the shops were replaced by separate houses, better built than the earlier cottages, and the factories were larger and of more modern design. Fess scratched his ear and grinned at Jim. 'How do you know you can trust me? I might be one of those you're after.'

Jim did not return the grin. 'Earlier on, I gave you a lecture on always protecting yourself, but you caught me at a weak moment. I'd just been sent that article this morning and was desperate to know if it hit the mark. When you started to talk about Sugar Bag, I couldn't resist trying it out on you.' He drew in a breath and became a little brighter. 'Fess Jordan gets another confession. Anyway I can trust you. You know I reckon you're wrong in the way you do your job, the way you treat the low life — you're too soft.'

'You would have enjoyed working with my father,' Fess interjected in a jocular voice.

'But you care about the Force as much as I do. If you put your energy into helping me clean out the corrupt and incompetent bosses, instead of your hopeless obsession with chasing a rich and powerful man who you think might be involved with the gangs, you'd do much better.'

'You reckon my campaign is hopeless. What chance do you think you have — a lowly Senior Constable?'

'More chance than you, I'd say. I'm not stupid like you: I make sure they don't know it's me that's after them.'

They reached the terminus, passing between two imposing buildings of very different design. On the right was the Abbotsford Convent with its steep gabled roof, intricate spire and pebble-dash walls. On the left stood the bulky brick building that housed the Yarra Falls Woollen Mills. Both of them towered over the tram — border castles of strange design. The two policemen stepped down from the tram and walked onto the bridge, which, in the daylight, became even more like the frontier crossing between two different countries — the crowded, industrial grime of Abbotsford, looked down upon by the sylvan lushness of Studley Park. The trees and bushes gleamed invitingly in the sun. No longer were they confronted by the threatening darkness of the previous night.

When they reached the Fitzwilliam house, there was no sign of the red Buick. In its place stood a large black car that Jim identified as a Packard Seven passenger sedan. Within it sat a chauffeur, whose peaked cap and unblinking gaze were enough to dissuade Jim from fondling the bodywork as he had the Buick last night. They were let in by the same maid and had hardly removed their coats when they were greeted by another man just as large as Jenkins, who had met them on their previous visit. This man wore the formal dress of a butler but lacked the usual presence of such men. His tie was slightly askew and his coat strained to fit his bulky frame. He must be Holloway, the man who had helped Jenkins subdue Nifty. He led them down the same passageway to the study where Sanford Fitzwilliam awaited them. Today he wore a fawn tweed suit with a jaunty tie and, to judge by the Zeiss binoculars that sat prominently on his desk, he planned to attend the races after he had dealt with them. He stood and extended a hand to each of them in turn. 'So good of you to come at such short notice,' he said. When they were seated, he began differently from the previous occasion by taking a silver cigarette case from inside his jacket. 'Care for a smoke?'

‘I’m a pipe smoker myself, thank you,’ Jim replied.

‘By all means light up if you wish. And of course you’re a nonsmoker, Senior Constable Jordan.’ He was doing it again: letting Fess know that he was well informed about his personal circumstances and traits. Sanford took a cigarette from the case and lit it while Jim made no attempt to get out his pipe. ‘Tom Blamey was here last night for a spot of cards,’ Sanford said after he had blown a plume of smoke into the air. ‘In between taking his money, we talked about the police. Fine man with great plans. I’d say the Force is in for quite a shake-up when he takes over.’ He regarded them through the faint haze of his cigarette smoke.

‘I didn’t know his appointment had been confirmed,’ Jim said.

‘Absolutely certain. Take it from me. He starts on September the first.’ Sanford looked directly at Jim. ‘You can expect major changes in the C.I.B. He intends to root out the dead wood and give younger men their chance. I told him how impressed I’d been with the way you conduct yourself, Senior Detective.’ Fess was both amused and irritated to see the colour in Jim’s face rise, but then had to contend with Sanford turning his attention to him. ‘Of course, I know you’re not interested in advancement. Happy to follow your father in Carlton, and no one could prise you away. Not that anyone would want to, of course.’

‘Is your son joining us?’ Fess asked as Jim seemed taken up with consideration of his promotion under Blamey.

Fitzwilliam’s face darkened and he shook his head. ‘I’m afraid he is ill.’

Thomas had insisted that he would take the lead but appeared incapable of doing so for the moment. 'I believe you have an idea that will help us with our case,' Fess said.

'Ah, yes.' Fitzwilliam brightened. Although Fess had asked the question, it was to Jim that he responded. 'That scoundrel Naughton has already killed without being brought to justice. This time we must not fail. When he hangs for his crime, the community will be much better off.'

Fess lifted his chin and there was a hint of accusation in his voice when he said, 'Last night you said you didn't know him.'

"That was last night. I've been making enquiries. What I have learnt ...' Fitzwilliam paused to take another drag on his cigarette and turned so that he was again speaking directly to Jim. 'If you will forgive me, I've been looking at this case from the point of view of the defending barrister. Old habits die hard. Whilst I have no doubt Naughton is guilty, your case rests on indirect and circumstantial evidence.'

Fitzwilliam had been making enquiries. Fess would like to have known who had given him such a detailed account of their investigation that he could make this criticism. He was right about the evidence, though, and Fess wondered how he could be so sure Nifty was guilty.

At last Jim entered the conversation. 'To make sure of a conviction we need a witness to the crime.'

'Quite right.' Fitzwilliam beamed at him as though he had just offered a major insight. 'There must have been people in The Narrows who would have seen him. The place is notorious for those who gather there.'

'We've been trying without success to induce someone to come forward,' Jim said defensively.

'I've noted that,' Fitzwilliam reassured him. 'Again, if you'll pardon me, my experience at the bar has taught me a lot about witnesses and the reasons they sometimes hold back. I'm sure you will have made similar observations in your role at the C.I.B.' He leaned forward to stub out his cigarette in a heavy glass ash-tray and cleared his throat. 'Obviously some are reluctant because they, too, have been involved in the crime and are unwilling to incriminate themselves. Others fear retribution from the guilty parties or, more likely, their friends and supporters. Sometimes witnesses are overawed by the processes of the Court and nervous of having to face public exposure. You would be familiar with them, Senior Detective. But have you met that rare witness who has vicariously participated in the crime? He would like to have bashed the victim, raped the poor girl or stolen the money himself and keeps silent because of guilt or sympathy or even envy. One seldom meets such people, but I assure you they exist.' He nodded his head and straightened his shoulders. 'Apart from those in my first category — those fearful of incriminating themselves — reluctance to come forward may be overcome if the witness is brought to realise that he stands to benefit.'

'Yes, the offer of a reward can be very helpful,' Jim agreed. 'When the Government made the funds available in the Gun Alley murder it certainly made a difference, but our resources are very limited in this case.'

Again Fitzwilliam beamed at Jim. 'That's why I've asked you out here. I would like to offer a reward for information leading to a conviction. I am sure we will have a positive response to such an inducement.' His face lost the smile and became the mask that Fess had seen the very first time they met. 'Sometimes, though, it is necessary to make it clear that the consequences of not coming forward outweigh any fears the witness may have.'

The steady way in which Fitzwilliam gazed at Jim, his lids partly hooding his eyes, left Fess in no doubt that he was signalling to him that he would see to it that witnesses did come forward, one way or the other. 'I'm surprised that you should have such an interest in this case,' Fess said.

Fitzwilliam's eyes widened, but then his face relaxed and a small smile appeared. He turned to face Fess as if having just been reminded he was present. 'I have always been interested in the cause of justice, Senior Constable. And when I see the opportunity to help, I try to respond.'

'Most generous of you and most helpful,' Jim replied. He turned to frown at Fess who appeared not to notice, his attention directly on Fitzwilliam.

'What conditions attach to your offer?'

Jim shot Fess another hostile glance but Fitzwilliam was unfazed. He chuckled and said, 'I see you don't trust lawyers, Senior Constable. Very wise.' The smile left his face and he added, 'Apart from insisting that my donation be anonymous, I place no conditions but do have one hope. When we have witnesses come forward, I hope there will be no need for my son to appear in Court. His evidence is at best circumstantial and will not be needed when we have direct witnesses. He has been remarkably foolish to associate with people of this ilk and, as you know, I am always anxious to avoid damage to the family name.'

Jim hastened to get in before Fess. 'I agree there should be no need to call him, provided we do have credible witnesses to the murder.' He put a slight stress on the word 'credible' that was not missed by Fitzwilliam.

'Of course,' he said. 'I'm confident about that. I have already completed the paperwork in the hope you would be willing to accept my help.' He took an envelope from his desk, stood up and handed it to Jim, who had also risen.

Fess remained seated so that he now looked up at Fitzwilliam when he said, 'It's unfortunate your son could not join us. We need to tell him that Naughton is claiming he and your son were engaged in drug dealing, and that, on the night she was murdered, Mary Worthington was acting as a courier between them. He further claims that her attacker's primary motive was theft of the drugs.'

Fitzwilliam sank back into his chair and sighed. 'You do not surprise me.' He passed a hand across his brow and sighed again. 'I see that I must confess I have not been completely frank with you. I should have known that you would eventually drag a full confession from me.' He smiled weakly at Fess. 'That, after all, is what you are renowned for, Senior Constable, is it not?' Jim, who had also resumed his seat, glanced anxiously at Fess, who remained dead still, staring intently at Fitzwilliam as he continued, 'You may recall my telling you some years ago how I could not get my son to settle into a steady career. I told you last night he was leading a dissolute life. What I did not tell you is that he has developed the habit of using cocaine — a filthy drug. To be candid, he has become addicted to the stuff. I have tried to support him and to wean him off it. Sometimes he responds, but then he relapses. His illness today is the result of his overindulgence last night. To obtain his supply he comes into contact with some very unsavoury types, Naughton being but one of them. Although he suffers from severe mood swings, he can at times be quite charming and remains highly attractive to a certain type of woman, who not only forgives his addiction but enjoys participating with him in the habit.

'What he told you last night was all true. I made sure of that after you left. What he did not tell you was that Mary Worthington was such a woman and her interest in him might well have triggered Naughton's violent reaction. I understand he fancies himself when it comes to the ladies and can turn quite nasty if he believes he is being outdone by another. When you were last here you heard Hal say that he was at the Orama Ballroom in Footscray on Saturday night, suggesting he went to try out a new place. He did not tell you that he went there primarily because he sought to avoid meeting Naughton and Mary Worthington at one of the dancehalls he knew they favoured.

'Beyond the fact that Naughton was a supplier to both

Hal and Mary Worthington, there is of course no truth in the claim that my son was in any way in league with him.' He paused and Jim began to stand, but Fitzwilliam had not finished. 'I am most anxious to avoid my son having to face the ordeal of a Court appearance.' Surely you would understand how I feel, Senior Constable Jordan.' Fess stiffened in his chair and Fitzwilliam nodded his head gently as he continued to stare at him. 'I told you that I made enquiries about Naughton this morning. Of course these included enquiries in Carlton where he spends so much of his time. As one does in such circumstances, I was told a number of things that had no bearing on this case.' He gazed earnestly at Fess. 'You know what it is to have a son go astray and you too would wish to avoid him having to appear in Court either as a witness or a defendant, I'm sure.'

Jim jumped to his feet and said, 'Thank you, Mr. Fitzwilliam, for your generous assistance with this case. I will now press ahead with advertising the reward.' Fess remained in his seat. 'Come on, Senior Constable.' Jim turned toward the door, making no attempt at a farewell handshake and, finally, Fess joined him. They walked from the room and were immediately met by Holloway who, like Jenkins the night before, was waiting outside. 'This way, gents,' he said unnecessarily and led them in silence to the hall where they put on their coats and hats.

The car and chauffeur remained in the driveway, but Jim walked past without pausing. As soon as they were in the street he turned to Fess and snapped, 'Do you have to goad Fitzwilliam every time you see him?'

'Me goad him?' he replied indignantly.

'Yeah. He offers to post a reward that will almost certainly get us the evidence to hang Nifty, and all you want to talk about is his son.'

'Are you still blinded by Fitzwilliam dangling a promotion before you?'

'Bollocks!' Jim spat out the word and his face flushed. 'You can never rely on men like him to do you any good. Cross them, though, and, sure as eggs, they'll do you harm. You ought to know that. You've been after him for ages but haven't been able to get near him. He told you why today. He has someone inside your Station who keeps him informed of what you're up to.'

'No, I don't believe that,' Fess responded, his voice carrying more bluster than conviction.

'Come on. There are men in every Station who can be bought for the right price. We're all poorly paid, and you told me the first night we met how badly looked after your single men were. How else would he know how stupid you've been in trying to protect your kid? I warned you that could come back to bite you. He made it plain that, if you keep trying to put the heat on him or his son, he'll get you.'

'So you agree with me? He's a crook — one of the worst kind.'

'Let's say that I do. Let's say Fitzwilliam is bankrolling some of the gangs, maybe even running them behind the scenes. Hal is fed up with his dad's scorn for him and decides to set up on his own, arranging to get the drugs to Nifty via Mary. Sanford finds out what's going on and orders the mugging and even the murder but, you can be sure, was nowhere near at the time. What are our chances of nailing a man like him, with his connections and influence? Nix. Worse still, if we persist in trying to go down that path, Nifty goes free. Fitzwilliam was right. Nifty has got away with murder before and we'd all be better off if we can pin this one on him. With Fitzwilliam's help, we will, too.'

'That's a warped justice.'

Jim turned to Fess as they came toward the bridge. 'You're a dangerous man, Fess. The evidence we have points to Nifty and the evidence we are likely to get will be enough to convict him, a known killer, but you want to put all that at risk by pursuing a hopeless case that will have a powerful man gunning for us. Why can't you see this? Why do you always blunder along, putting yourself at risk?'

'You mean I should see the bigger picture and understand priorities — forego immediate success in the interest of the longer-term.'

'Yeah. You could put it that way.'

'Fitzwilliam put it exactly that way when he was trying to get me to let a couple of thieves in the S.C.F. off, scot-free. He told me my father could see the bigger picture and understood priorities. I said you would have got on well with him.' Suddenly Fess turned away and began to cross the road. 'It's over here,' he said.

'What? What's over where?'

Reaching the other side of the road, Fess entered a

narrow path that immediately divided in two, the right fork leading down the hill and the left curving up and around the ridge through a thick brush of small gums, wattles and tea-trees. 'This is where they would have come,' he said and began to walk up the path.

'We don't need this,' Jim complained but had to hurry to catch up with Fess, who did not pause until, after about a hundred yards, the path widened out on a rocky ledge. At one side a wooden bench stood against the backdrop of the dense bush. On the other side of the path the sheer face of the bluff fell to the Yarra, a hundred feet below. To their right, the river, lined with tall gum trees, bent sharply upstream, and in the elbow they could see the red roof of the boathouse, lit by the rays of the sun, now in the western sky. Immediately across the river were a number of sports ovals, before the bush took over again, encircling the horizon with a heavily wooded ridge that was broken by the solitary towers of the Kew Mental Asylum.

'You can see why it's a favourite spot for young couples in the summer,' Fess said. 'And a good place for a secret exchange of drugs in the winter.'

'You never know when to give up, do you?' Jim shook his head in exasperation. 'When I agreed to have you on this case, I made it clear I was in charge and you accepted that. I'm now ordering you to stop chasing your wild goose. Leave Fitzwilliam alone and let's wrap up the case with Nifty's conviction. Come and catch the tram back to reality.'

They returned to the terminus and stood in silence as a tram approached. When the gripman and the conductor went into the complicated routine Fess had insisted Jim observe on their previous trip, he appeared to take little notice and Jim was happy to puff on his pipe. They boarded the tram and, when the conductor approached them, Fess nodded to him and said, 'G'day. What hours are you working today?'

'On till ten tonight. Same all the week.'

'Were you on this line last Saturday evening?'

'Yeah. We all work the same roster through to Thursday.'

'You don't remember this lass travelling with you last Saturday around eight or nine, do you?' Fess produced the now creased and dog-eared photograph, which he folded so that only Mary was visible.

'Nah.' The conductor rubbed his chin and smiled. 'You could ask Pete, the gripman, but I reckon I'd remember her if she'd been on board.'

He continued on to collect the fares of the other travellers on the dummy, and Jim waited until he reached the other side before exploding. 'That's it. I give you an order and two minutes later you ignore that order. You're more than dangerous. You're suicidal.'

'Everything that Fitzwilliam said to us, including his snide threats to me, makes me positive that Nifty's story is the right one.'

Jim's grin was sarcastic. 'Not everything. You complain to me that Piggott ignores evidence that doesn't suit him. So do you. When the most likely explanation for Mary's rape is a crime of passion, you try to tell me that rape and suffocation isn't the way that Nifty works. Fitzwilliam told you Nifty can turn nasty when he's losing out. Passion changes people and they do things you would have said they weren't capable of. I remember we once had a Quaker, full of the peace of God. His wife had a fling with another member of the Society and, when she remorsefully confessed to her husband, he took to her with a knife. Then it was his turn to be remorseful and he turned it on himself; saved the hangman a job, I s'pose. Nifty was jealous and, when Mary laughed at him — something Ferret told us he'd heard and Nifty tried to deny — he lost it. Whoever said that Hell hath no fury like a woman scorned hadn't met the man who's had the woman he's stuck on give him the push with a laugh of derision.'

'Yeah, you're right,' Fess replied, thoughtfully, surprising Jim. 'I've been so slow to see it. When Fitzwilliam was going on about the various types of reluctant witness, I began to think of him and the things he's let slip. What did Fitzwilliam say? Something about the one who watches in envy?'

'Where are you going now?'

'If Mary did take the tram back about nine it would fit.'

'Stop this.' Jim took a deep breath. 'Senior Constable Jordan, I thank you for the help you've given me in pursuing this case, but I no longer need your assistance. You may return to your fulltime occupation in Carlton, fruitlessly chasing shadows. That is, of course, if you are not suspended for improper behaviour in seeking to protect your son. I will make it clear to all concerned, including Mr. Fitzwilliam and your sergeant, that you are no longer in any way associated with the C.I.'

17

They continued in silence until Fess left the tram at Nicholson Street. Stepping onto the pavement, he looked across to Spy Webb's shop, only a little further along the road. He crossed the street and approached the door of the shop but was disappointed to find a sign behind the glass that told him the shop was shut. Nevertheless, he banged on the door and called out Spy's name. When there was no response, he stepped back to gain a view of the upstairs windows. There was nothing to indicate Spy was at home. Fess leaned his back against the door and settled to wait for his return. After a short time he had a better idea and returned to the tram stop, keeping an eye on the bike shop as he waited for the next tram.

When the tram arrived Fess boarded it and spoke with the conductor and the gripman before alighting at the next stop and returning to await the arrival of the next tram. He continued in this fashion for about an hour before he had any success. When it came, though, he was given more than he expected: Mary's laugh certainly left an impression on people. Now he was even more anxious to speak with Spy, who still had not returned. It was becoming dark and he should report in to the Station. He hadn't been there all day.

When he entered, the Duty Constable greeted him with, 'The sergeant wants to see you.'

'He's still here?'

'Yeah. Been asking for you most of the afternoon.'

As soon as Fess reached the door of Doyle's office he started: 'Where the hell have you been? You don't come in all day. Your wife doesn't know where you are. When I track you down with the C.I., they know where you've been but not where you are. All they can tell me is they've given you the heave-ho. Sick of your so-called help which, I gather, has largely been to waste their time while you chase your own fancies.'

'Why do you want to see me, Sarge?'

Fess' question triggered another angry outburst from the sergeant. 'Yesterday I ordered you to stay out of the investigation of your son's crime, except that we agreed you would lean on him so we could properly nail his accomplice, the Rawson kid. Do you obey my orders? O'course not. First you go straight up to the school for a little chat with the God man, O'Donohue, and tell me nothing about it. It's only when I go up there myself, I find you two have been putting your heads together. I've put a flea in Constable Daley's ear over that. He's been spending too much time in your company and learning too many bad habits.

'Then, first thing this morning, you call on the baker, Manson, and pay him off. When I call on him, he tells me he doesn't want to go on with the charge and gets all coy with me — I have to drag it out of him. You've been butting in where you had no right to be, just to save your son. And then you disappear for the rest of the day, skiving around with the C.I. until they get fed up with you, as well.'

Fess knew it would come out at some stage but was surprised that Doyle had been so active. He hardly ever left the Station, except to collect money due to him for turning a blind eye. It looked like he'd been determined to pursue Kevin and Billy Rawson. It wasn't them he was after, of course; it was Fess. Otherwise, Doyle would have done what he did in all other cases like this: leave it to one of the Senior Constables to bring the boys into the Station and give them a bollocking they wouldn't forget. He wouldn't have worried about the missing money and, as for taking children to Court, he saw it as a waste of time that could be better spent clamping down on the unfortunates who made their living from petty crime. Fess had heard Doyle on this topic often enough. 'Put 'em in Court and they get off with a warning. You have to frighten the tripe out of these kids so they won't do it again.'

'So, what now, Sergeant?' Fess asked quietly.

'Case closed, thanks to your interference. I ought to charge you with obstructing the police.'

Fess relaxed. He had achieved his objective and Jim's fears had come to nothing. To hear Doyle, though, it might have been close.

'Do your job getting the scum off our streets and stop following any other wild ideas or I will put you on a charge.'

Was Doyle Fitzwilliam's man? Jim was sure there was

someone in the Station and this latest threat sounded like a message sent from Fitzwilliam. Or was he seeing Fitzwilliam in every shadow? That's what Jim said: 'Fruitlessly chasing shadows.'

❦ ❧

A light rain was falling, coating the road and giving the lights in Elgin Street a misty glow. Spy Webb was fumbling in his coat pocket for his keys when Fess appeared out of the gloom. 'Spy, I've been waiting for you. Not much of a night for a stroll.'

Spy stepped back in surprise before saying, 'You shouldn't jump out at people like that. Gave me a nasty start, you did.'

'Let's go inside out of the rain.'

Spy unlocked the door, entered the shop and turned to face Fess, who had followed him in. He made no attempt to turn on a light. 'What is it you want, Mr. Jordan?'

'Upstairs, Spy. We'll talk there.'

'That's private up there, Mr. Jordan.'

'That's what I want: a private chat just between you and me. Come on, Spy, you know we should have had this chat a few days ago.'

Reluctantly, Spy walked through to the workshop and climbed the stairs, which led to a small sitting room where he turned on a lamp. The room was sparsely furnished with two padded arm chairs, sitting on either side of a small hearth that was set with crumpled newspaper and kindling wood. Between the chairs was a low table on which stood a pile of magazines and an empty glass. Spy went to sit in one of the chairs, but Fess forestalled him. 'Not yet, Spy. Before we chat I'd like to see your memorial to Mary Worthington. The one you told me about yesterday.'

'No. No. That's for me alone. I show that to no one.' Spy shook with the intensity of his denial.

'Come on now, Spy. I understand why you've been reluctant to face up to things, but you know you must, and the way to start is to show me Mary's memorial.'

Spy did not reply but turned and limped slowly through a door that led to a short passage. At the end of the passage he entered the doorway on the left. The blinds were down and the room would have been in complete darkness were it not for the light from a single candle that stood in a crystal holder on a spindly table set against the far wall. The table, which was the only item of furniture in the room, was covered with a white cloth and also carried a small porcelain vase containing a posy of violets. Leaning against the front of the table was a red umbrella with a twisted amber handle. Newspaper cuttings had been pasted on the wall behind the table. Fess approached close enough to confirm that the cuttings were reports concerning the murder of Mary Worthington. He did not linger in the room but turned back into the corridor and made for the living room, saying over his shoulder. 'Now, Spy, it's time for you to tell me the whole story. You've been wanting that, haven't you? It was just that I was too stupid to get your message.'

❧ ❧

Hal Fitzwilliam had recovered. Looking in the mirror, he could see that his eyes were back to their clear blue and the shave had freshened his skin. His hair needed some attention, but that was next. After applying the hair brush he took one more satisfied look at himself in the mirror and left his room with the intention of driving into town for a spot of lunch and maybe a rubber or two at the club.

'Excuse me, Mr. Fitzwilliam.'

'Yes, Jenkins. What is it? Can't you see I'm on my way out?'

'There's a phone call for you.'

'Did you ask who it was, man?'

'No sir, but she said it was important.'

'Women always say that when they call me,' he replied and walked to the phone, which sat on the polished wood of an occasional table. 'Hal Fitzwilliam here.'

'Oh, Hal. I'm glad I caught you. How are you?'

'Who is this?' he asked impatiently.

'It's Paula. Paula Ryan.' There was an anxious breathiness in her voice, unlike her usual jaunty tone.

'Oh, you. What do you want, Paula?'

'You weren't at Molly's funeral?'

'Afraid not. Busy day.'

'I thought you might say that. We need to talk, Hal. About Molly. About Molly and you.'

Hal leaned across and kicked the door of the room so that it banged shut. 'I don't think we have anything to say to one another about her. Bad business altogether, but rather ends anything you and I might have to chat about.'

'Oh, Hal, don't be difficult. I want your advice.'

'My advice?'

'Yeah. Look Molly told me things – quite a lot of things, actually. I know where she was headin' last Saturday night and what she was goin' there for.'

'No interest to me. I must go, Paula.'

'Hal, wait. You see, they're now offerin' a reward for any information about Molly's death and I'm wonderin' whether I should tell the police what I know.'

'What do you want, Paula?'

'I'd like to talk to you. Get your advice on what I should do. How much I should tell 'em. Can I come out and see you?'

'You can't come here.'

'Well, how about we meet where you used to meet Molly. You could come to the tram and show me the view you showed her.' She seemed to have relaxed and now sounded almost coquettish, more like the Paula Hal knew. 'I'll get there about half past eight tonight. No one should overhear us there.' There was a silence before Paula asked, 'Are you there, Hal?'

'Yes, I'm here. I'll see you tonight.'

When the tram arrived at the terminus, Hal was sitting in his car, having parked a short distance up the road. A small number of people alighted before he saw Paula step from the doorway of the tram and stand uncertainly scanning the road. He left his car and stood beside it, but she did not see him. He began to walk toward her and, although she was looking in his direction, she still did not seem to recognise him. It was only when he came under the light beside the terminal shelter that she smiled and said, 'Ah, there you are.' She remained where she was, apparently expecting him to walk right up to her. She wouldn't know which direction they would take to reach the path.

'This way,' he said gruffly, but still she did not move. The door of the tram opened again and Fess Jordan stepped down to join them. 'What are you doing here?' Hal demanded.

Fess made no response but looked over his shoulder at the conductor. 'Yeah, that's him,' the conductor nodded.

The gripman, who had remained in his place on the dummy, called out. 'The car's parked up the road where it was on Saturday. A little beauty.'

'What the …' Hal got no further.

'Just confirming that you met Mary here last Saturday,' Fess said in a quiet but definite voice. 'Thank you, Paula. You can go back now. Mr. Fitzwilliam and I will go for a walk. The moon is out, so the view should be spectacular. Please join me, sir.'

'Why should I?' Hal demanded.

'I thought it would be better to have a private chat up where you took Mary. That will be less public than taking you to the Station.' Fess took a pace forward and held out a hand as though he was about to grip Hal by the elbow.

'Don't start manhandling me,' he said and turned

so that they walked together over the bridge and along the narrow path to the ledge overlooking the river. The moon, pale through some thin clouds, gave enough light to show the shapes of the surrounding bushes and pick out the white trunks of the gums that lined the river far below.

Fess walked to the edge and looked down at the river before turning to speak to Hal. 'I thought it might be best if I began by telling you what I already know. The crew of an earlier tram confirm that Mary Worthington travelled with them to the terminus last Saturday night. They didn't notice you or your car, but I'm confident you met her and accompanied her to this spot, where you gave her a quantity of cocaine for which she paid you. As you heard, the crew you just met clearly remember that you accompanied her back to the terminus.'

Fess took a deep breath and would have continued, but Hal forestalled him. 'Look, Constable, you have obviously gone to a lot of trouble to establish that I met Molly out here last Saturday night. I don't deny it. But this business about her paying me for drugs; what do you take me for? Yes, we might have shared a bit of snow together. No real harm in that, despite what you coppers might say.'

He smiled at Fess, inviting him to respond as a man-of-the-world, and the policeman nodded with what looked like sympathy. 'You did have a soft spot for Mary Worthington.'

'I was concerned for her. I didn't want her mixed up with that wretched Naughton fellow. I know she didn't care for him. His attraction was that he supplied her with snow. That's why I had some with her on Saturday; it was a way to get her to relax and listen to me. I thought that if I could get her to spend some time with me away from his evil influence I might be able to break his hold on her.'

Again Fess nodded sympathetically. 'It must have been galling to have her reject you so rudely.'

The tension, which had begun to lift from Hal's face, suddenly returned. 'What do you mean?'

'I said the crew clearly remember you returning with Mary. Their recollection is vivid, partly because of Mary Worthington's looks; but what planted you in their memories so firmly was the way in which you two parted. They couldn't miss the passion you put into imploring her to come with you and not board the tram. But she rejected you and, what must have been maddening, laughed in your face. I've been told she had a very distinctive laugh. It certainly impressed the crew, who then watched you return to your car, which was parked a little way up the road as it is tonight.'

'You're right; it is unusual for me to have a lady say no. When I invited her to come with me to the Orama, I had given up trying to persuade her to break with Naughton. After all, I owed her nothing. I thought she might enjoy a night of dancing — she usually did — and it would be my way of seeing her off. But she said she wasn't dressed for going dancing. Implore her, though! Come on, Constable, why would I do that?' The arrogance that Fess had noted at their first meeting now coated every word. 'I don't need to implore any woman.' He sighed and affected regret. 'As things have turned out, I really wish she had come.'

'Yes, the way you pressed her almost suggests you had a premonition.'

'I think your witnesses are being carried away by romantic fancies, Constable. I didn't realise that tram crews were so inclined. When Molly and I parted, we shared a joke — she liked to kid around and she did have a musical laugh. I went back to my car and, as you know, headed off to the Orama, alone. I've told you this already and, given the lengths you have gone to in pursuing me, I'm sure you've checked that I was indeed there.'

'I wouldn't doubt your word on that, sir.'

'So now that you know the whole story, Constable, I hope you will cease hounding me.'

'Ah, but that's the problem. You still haven't told me the whole story.'

'What?'

'After Mary left on the tram you went ahead in your car and parked in Elgin Street to wait for her.'

'This is preposterous.' Hal spoke in explosive puffs that might have been meant to intimidate but came out like air rushing from a balloon that has been ruptured.

Fess continued in the quiet voice he had been using throughout. 'When she got off the tram with the intention of walking up Barkly Street to where Naughton was awaiting her return, you approached her again. Again, she dismissed you with a laugh and you sought to pull her towards your car.'

'You're making this up.' The arrogance in Hal's voice had disappeared and was replaced with the higher pitch of someone trying to bluff their way out of a tight spot.

'It was Mary's laugh that caught the attention of a man watching from the other side of the street. She broke free and ran up the nearby lane, with you in pursuit.'

'And you think I then raped and murdered her? You're told by someone standing on the other side of the street that he saw a man chase Molly up a lane and you jump to the conclusion it must be me, because the tram crew heard her laugh when we parted out at the terminus.' Hal turned away as if he were about to return to the road.

'He followed you up the lane. He is a strange man who spends a lot of time secretly observing the goings on in the lanes of Carlton. He was there when you pushed Mary to the ground. He was there when you began to rape her. He was there when she continued to cry out, despite your efforts to silence her, and he was there when you used your maroon scarf first to stifle and then to suffocate her. You didn't see him, but he saw you at close quarters and has clearly identified you.' Fess paused, but this time Hal said nothing, the only sound coming from his quick shallow breaths. 'I said he was a strange man. He cared for Mary far more than you ever did but he, too, had been laughed at by her, in his case because he was too puny ever to pose a threat to her. So he envied your strength in being able to possess her and took vicarious pleasure in watching you do what he could never do. You left her, a dishevelled corpse, but he honoured her by restoring her clothing and laying her out as if for burial. After it was over, he bore the guilt that has not troubled your conscience. That was what held him back. But now he has confessed and you should, too.'

Hal reached into a pocket of his coat and brought out a small packet, which he opened and, holding it in his right hand, tipped some white powder onto the back of his left hand. He lifted the hand, sniffed the powder into each nostril, shook his head and walked to the edge of the path where he stood looking down into the river. 'I never meant to kill her. I thought of alerting the police as soon as it was over. But after a shot I got to thinking, just as I'm thinking now. I didn't want to hang because some silly skirt led me on and then laughed in my face. So I took back the snow from her pockets — a pity to waste it — and went to the Orama where I would be seen and where no one would be able to say exactly when I arrived.'

For the first time Fess raised his voice. 'And, with the help of your father, you've been covering your tracks ever since — even arranging to send an innocent man to the gallows.'

'My father? He never helps anyone but himself.' Hal turned with his back to the edge and, to Fess' surprise, smiled at him. 'There's a thought. You've been after him for years, haven't you? He's been too fly for you, though, always knowing what you were up to and able to hide behind someone else. He does that with everyone and everything. He's been using me as his go-between. I'm the one who takes the risks and deals with the likes of Squizzy and Nifty, while he just takes the profits. For years he's trampled on me and given me no credit. That's why I got fed up and decided to go out on my own. He's getting past it and should let me take over but he's too vain to admit it.' Hal turned and came closer to Fess with his hands open in front of him, making an offer. 'So here's a bargain for you. I know why you're here by yourself; your mate Thomas got the message from my father and doesn't want to get involved. I'll give you chapter and verse on my father's networks and his dirty dealings with the gangs and the police. You can use it to end his criminal career, probably put him away for a stretch and certainly make him a marked man. In return, you'll forget about the rest of our little chat tonight. That way we both get what we want.' When Fess continued to stare at him without replying, Hal said, 'Come on. I'm giving you your big chance. What do you say?' Still Fess made no response.

There was a movement a short way down the path and Sanford Fitzwilliam emerged from the shadows of the bushes. Quickly, he took the few paces required to bring him in front of his son. In his hand he carried a small revolver, which he waved at Hal. 'How could I have fathered such a son — feckless, addled by drugs, lacking all control, unable to achieve anything except envy of my achievements and now willing to betray me to save his own skin?' He took another step towards Hal and pushed the pistol into his chest. 'You've forfeited any right to my protection, any right to live.'

'Steady on, Dad. I'm just talking this zealot round.'

'Enough. I've put up with your lies but I won't put up

with your betrayal.' As he spoke, Sanford moved even closer and raised his other arm, suddenly shoving Hal with both hands, sending him wheeling down the sheer drop to crash into the trees beside the river.

Fess stepped towards Fitzwilliam, who turned so that he now trained the pistol on him. 'So, what have you to say? Would you have accepted the offer? Is your pursuit of me so ingrained that you would betray your principles to take me down?'

'You mean, would I understand priorities and see the bigger picture, like my father?'

'Ah, your father, that paragon of policing, who died the death of a hero. You are the most stubborn policeman I have known, and I've known many. You deserve to hear the truth.'

'What?'

'My lately departed son told you I have dealings with some members of the Force. Over the years I've found quite a number of them willing to take my money and, in return, grant me certain privileges and favours. Your father was one of the first and the longest serving.'

'I don't believe you.'

'Deny the truth if you will: it's of no account to me. But how could a mere Police Sergeant afford those holidays by the sea? And how could he afford to dress his beautiful wife so well? Can you take your children on such holidays, and does the delightful Bernadette dress like your mother?' Fess scowled at Fitzwilliam, unable to reply. Apparently pleased with the effect his words were having, he continued. 'And most important of all, learn the truth about that hero's death. I was the one who tipped off David Jordan that the gang members were holed up in that house with the proceeds of their bank robbery. He was the one that started the fire to drive them out. He didn't go in to save the family: he went in to grab the cash. He was furious when he found that mother with her children and had to bring them out, but he wasn't a monster, merely dishonest, like many of us. He hadn't been greedy in his dealings with me, but greed was his downfall in the end. Having brought out those poor wretches, he went back against all advice, because he was desperate to get his hands on the money. I was there watching.'

'You're a liar, Fitzwilliam.'

'Yes, I often am. But not on this matter. Anyway, I'm wasting time with you. You know far too much to be allowed to leave here.'

Fess moved into the centre of the path and said, 'You surprised your son but you won't be able to stage a second suicide.'

'No, I'll have to shoot you.'

'That's going to take some explaining when my body is found and the various tram crews, together with Paula Ryan, tell their stories.' Apparently no longer fearful of being pushed over, he returned to stand with his back to the edge, forcing Fitzwilliam to turn to cover him.

'Oh, your body won't be found here. I'll have it moved to one of your Carlton lanes — another gang victim. Goodbye, Senior Constable Jordan.' As Fitzwilliam raised his arm to take aim, there was a cry from behind him and a large black shape flew from the bushes, sending him sprawling to the ground. The shape became recognisable as Constable Tom Daley, who wrestled with Fitzwilliam as he tried to turn the pistol onto his attacker. Fess hovered above them but was unable to intervene, with the two bodies so closely intertwined in the struggle. Eventually Daley was too strong, pinning Fitzwilliam with a knee on his chest and twisting his wrist so that the pistol dropped from his hand. Fess swooped upon it and stood scanning the surrounds while Daley turned Fitzwilliam onto his stomach and secured his arms with handcuffs he had taken from his pocket. He then pulled Fitzwilliam to his feet and stood behind him, gripping his arm.

'I thought he might have brought his men with him,' Fess explained as he turned back from his search of the bushes.

'Oh, no, I would never do that. They alerted me to my son's assignation, so I was able to observe you meet him and bring him up here. But I guessed what might transpire and knew it was family business where I must act alone.' Fitzwilliam was breathing deeply but otherwise retained his usual assured detachment.

Fess ignored him and spoke directly to the constable. 'You had me worried, Daley. I thought you'd left it a bit late.'

'You did say I was only to move if I thought your life was in danger.'

'Did you see him arrive?'

'Yeah, he crept up the path not long after you arrived. I thought you might have seen him, too, but you were both pretty intent on your conversation.'

'What about that? Did you get good notes?'

'Shit. I dropped my notebook when I jumped out. No time to put it in my pocket.'

'Well get cracking. We don't want to lose that.'

Daley scuttled back into the bushes while Fess kept watch on Fitzwilliam, who continued to observe them. 'Here it is.' Daley emerged with a standard issue black notebook which he placed in a pocket of his tunic and buttoned it down. 'Can't see the pencil but I guess that doesn't matter.'

'What matters is that you have a complete record of what happened and what was said,' Fess replied.

'When you first arrived my fingers were stiff from waiting in the cold, but I got all the important stuff, I reckon.'

'Good. Now we have a lot to do. First we must raise the alarm and get some people out searching for Hal. I'll be very surprised if he survived, though. We'll take Mr. Fitzwilliam back to the Station where he can spend the night in one of our cells. As soon as he's secure, you need to convert your notes to a full account of what occurred, I'll top and tail your report and we both will sign it. When that's done, I'll give it to the C.I. and they can take over.'

'You're wasting your time,' Fitzwilliam interjected in a bored tone. 'You've gone to such a lot of trouble, and all you will have achieved is the death of my son. Tomorrow I will be back home and you will be in deep trouble.'

18

The Duty Constable, a young man with ginger hair, was dozing before the drum beat of Fess' boots on the wooden floor brought him awake. 'Yes, sir,' he said as he tried to guess what had brought this unfamiliar figure to Russell Street at such an hour.

'I am Senior Constable Jordan from Carlton Station and want to see the senior man from the C.I. on duty, thank you, Constable.'

The constable sat up and foolishly asked, 'Is it urgent?' Seeing the look in Fess' eyes he quickly added, 'Just a moment, I'll get the Senior.' He turned away from Fess and called to the open door behind him, 'Senior, you're needed out here, please.'

There was a short delay before an older man appeared, buttoning up his tunic. The frown on his face disappeared when he saw Fess, and was replaced by a puzzled smile. 'Fess! What are you doing here at this ungodly hour?'

'Ah, Gordon. I'm glad to see you. I need to speak with the senior man from the C.I. on duty.'

'They're a bit short on at the moment: the flu's hit them badly. Senior Detective Thomas is on call, and I've had to wake him once already this week.'

Now it was Fess who frowned. 'Is no one else available?'

He didn't relish the idea of involving Jim, although he would have to be brought into the picture pretty soon, Mary's murder was his case after all.

'A couple of constables.'

'Well, then, please rouse the Senior Detective.'

Fess paced up and down, trying to decide the line he should take with Jim. He had expected to be dealing with a more senior officer and, after their last encounter, it was hard to predict how Jim would react. Perhaps he should not have rushed down here as soon as they had the report complete. He could hear Jim's grumbling voice before he saw his tousled figure. 'My God, if I'd known it was you, I would have stayed in bed.'

'I'm sorry. I thought this couldn't wait and didn't realise it was you who would be called out.'

'Going behind my back again?'

'Is there somewhere we can talk? I want to report a murder.'

'Not another murder in Carlton? Who is it this time? Or don't you know?'

'It's Hal Fitzwilliam.'

'Shit.' Jim's eyes, previously heavy with interrupted sleep, were now wide open. 'Come along here and tell me about it.' He led Fess to a small room with bare walls and a single window that looked out on a collection of rubbish bins, flicked on the light and waved at the narrow table, which had two straight-backed wooden chairs on either side. After Fess sat on one, Jim took a seat on the opposite side and leaned forward with his elbows on the table and his head propped up by his hands. 'How did it happen?'

'He was murdered by his father.'

'What? Christ! Where? How?' As he spoke, Jim sat up and lifted his head, examining Fess. 'Just a sec. How come you're involved?'

'It's all in our report.' Fess took the report from a small leather satchel he had been carrying and pushed it toward Jim.

'I'll read that later. Take me through what happened.'

'It's quite a long story,' Fess said apologetically.

'Just get on with it.'

As Fess went through what had occurred, the scowl on Jim's face increased and he punctuated the account with snorts and the occasional, 'Bloody hell.' When he reached the point where Hal confessed, Jim broke in with, 'You couldn't have used any of this. You must know that. Having been taken off the case by the officer in charge of the investigation, you persist with your unauthorised enquiries. You lure a man to an isolated location by using a member of the public to misrepresent herself to him. This location is outside your area, but you don't inform the local Station. You accuse him of murder, based on identification by a misfit, the process for that identification being informal and improper.' Jim paused as if just struck by a new thought. 'Who's the other signature on the report?'

'Tom Daley. You met him on the night we found Mary Worthington's body. He was also the one that took care of Basher when we raided the pub. I thought he would give me good protection, and he took very comprehensive notes of what was said and done while he hid in the bushes.'

'You don't care whose future you risk in your chase after Fitzwilliam, do you? Why didn't you come in here when you heard from the tram crews and your mate, Spy, tell us what you've found out and we could have brought Hal in here and had him properly identified.'

'I'll tell you why,' Fess said, exhaustion and irritation combining to break down his usual outward calm. 'First of all, you were so hell-bent on placating Fitzwilliam and hanging Nifty that I had no confidence you would follow up any evidence suggesting it was Hal. I still don't. That's why I hoped not to deal with you when I came in just now. Secondly, if we'd arrested Hal and taken him for interview, Sanford would immediately have been alerted.' Fess paused in his defensive flow and glanced sheepishly at Jim. 'I've thought further about what you said and I reckon you're right. It's probably Sergeant Doyle who's been tipping him off.' Fess straightened himself, returning to his self-justifying tone. 'I reckon Fitzwilliam would soon get at the tram crew and Spy would very likely not testify, anyway, so I needed to go for a confession, and that's what I got. Nifty is innocent.'

'No, you spoke with a man who is now dead, who you say confessed. You have no signed confession.'

'But Daley was there. He heard him.'

'If he continues to stick with you when the heat comes on, he'll be in the same trouble you'll be in. There's no way I'm letting Nifty out on what you've told me. Besides, now the ads have gone out for the reward, I reckon we'll pull in some witnesses.'

'You'd rather hang an innocent man than believe me.'

'I didn't say I didn't believe you. I said you didn't have a case against Hal you could put up in Court. I'm a realist. Why should I go on one of your wild goose chases when I can get a good result by doing what I'm doing? And don't give me that blarney that Nifty is an innocent. He's already killed: we know that.' He yawned before adding, 'Let's get on with your story. Hal hasn't been murdered yet.'

Fess shook his head, unwilling to concede, but eventually sighed and said, 'After Hal confessed, he offered me a deal: he would give me the details of his father's dealings with the gangs and his network of police informers if I didn't arrest him for the murder.'

'He offered you the cops in his pay?' Jim said, suddenly alert. 'That would've been worth having.'

Fess gave a rueful grin. 'I was more interested in his links with the gangs, and I was tempted, but I didn't get to choose. Sanford came out of the darkness where he'd been listening to our conversation, abused Hal for his treachery and then pushed him over the edge. They've recovered the body. His head was smashed in by the impact of his fall.'

'Where's Fitzwilliam now?'

'We put him in a cell at the Station. I've charged him with the murder, but that was just so we could hold him at Carlton until I came down here to report, have the C.I. take over the case and get Fitzwilliam moved to the watch house.' He hadn't yet told Jim what Fitzwilliam had said about his father. Probably no need: it was in the report. Daley had left it out at first, but Fess made him include it.

'How does he seem?'

'As arrogant as ever. Told me he would be out today and I would be in deep trouble.'

Jim looked up sharply and then pressed his lips together in a straight line. 'He's sure to use his contacts, and we know how high up the tree they go. I'll have to pass your report to one of the senior men. Too risky for me to take this one on my own.' He saw the look that Fess gave him and scowled. 'I'm not afraid of Fitzwilliam but I'm not a fool, either. I'll wait until one of the higher-ups gets in. They keep gentlemen's hours, so it won't be for a good while yet.'

'You could give it to your hero, Piggott. He likes to see his name in the papers.'

'I'm sure I could trust him, but I reckon this will go higher than him.' Jim suddenly stood up. 'Why don't you go home and get a few hours' sleep.' For the first time since coming from his bed, his expression softened. 'You look like you could do with it, and you'll need all your wits about you if you're going to stay ahead of Fitzwilliam. Now that I'm up, I don't feel like going back to bed. Plenty of time to read your report.'

When Fess entered the Station, it had gone nine o'clock and he was cross. After he had finally gone to his bed, he hadn't been able sleep but was content to lie there waiting for the dawn and thinking over all that had happened. Then, just at the time he should have been stirring, he drifted into sleep and Bern did not rouse him, believing he needed the rest. By now Jim would have briefed the senior man at the C.I. and the transfer might well be under way. He should have been here for that. 'Morning, Mac.' He gave his usual greeting, but with a new wariness. Could it be possible McKenzie was also in the pay of Fitzwilliam?

The constable made no immediate reply and appeared anxious. Had he realised that Fess was onto him? He had come on duty at six and certainly would know Fitzwilliam was in one of the cells. Eventually he mumbled, 'You have a visitor. Inspector Johnson is waiting to see you. He's in Doyle's office.'

For a time Peter Johnson had been his sergeant at Bendigo. He was a kindly, steady and reliable man, a shrewd judge of character, who always chose the path that would most likely keep him and his Station out of trouble. He was a quiet man and, when he did speak, chose from a range of well-worn phrases to make his point. He prided himself on 'running a tight ship' and was a stickler for 'doing it by the book', often advising his constables to 'keep their noses clean'. Fess respected his integrity and dedication but became impatient with his reluctance to take any risks. Johnson in turn appreciated Fess' enthusiasm and admired his effectiveness but often counselled him not to 'rock the boat'. Nevertheless they had a good working relationship, perhaps because Johnson had been charmed by

Bernadette, whom he designated 'The Belle of Bendigo'. He certainly would not have been pleased to hear Bern's private lampooning of him, when she would order Fess around with commands like, 'Jump to it and keep your feet on the ground'.

Sergeant Johnson's long service and unblemished record were rewarded by promotion to a Headquarters' position that dealt with what were called 'internal matters'. Fess had not been sure of Johnson's actual role, and now wondered whether he was one of those Jim was trying to bring to account for their failure to root out the likes of Leo O'Sullivan. From time to time, Peter would call in to the Station to see him and ask about Bern and the children, but he hadn't done so for quite a while, and Fess was irritated that he should choose the very day he was late to arrive. He was surprised that Doyle's office was so quiet, but when he reached the door he understood. There was no sign of Doyle and, in his place, sat a square-shouldered man with close-clipped grey hair. When Fess entered he rose slowly from his chair. 'Hello, Peter,' Fess said with a lightness he did not feel. 'Sorry I wasn't here to greet you but I've been up most of the night. You may have heard about it.' Was that why he was here — to follow up the arrest of Fitzwilliam? Peter was senior but not part of the C.I.

'Ah, Senior Constable Jordan. Here at last.' Fess noted the formality of Peter's greeting and the absence of any attempt to shake him by the hand. Instead he sat down again and indicated with his arm that Fess should sit across from him. 'No, I haven't. I'm here on a matter that has just come to light and troubles me greatly.' As he spoke Fess could see him watching for a reaction. Puzzlement was all he could manage. 'We have received a report that you have improperly intervened in the investigation of a theft in which your son is alleged to have been involved.'

Had Fitzwilliam moved against him prior to last night? If so, it hadn't done him any good. 'You know we have Sanford Fitzwilliam here in one of our cells.'

'No, I didn't. Quite a celebrity. But I don't see what that has to do with what I've just told you. Have you anything to say about that?'

Just as he had with Jim earlier this morning, Fess let his anger show. 'What I have to say is that the report is false and whoever made the report is acting against me maliciously, in the hope it will interfere with other investigations I've been conducting.'

Johnson jerked back his head and straightened himself, either surprised by the vehemence of Fess' reply or to re-establish his control of the conversation. 'Be that as it may, I have been authorised to conduct a full investigation of the matter and recommend any action that should be taken as a result of the conclusions I reach. You are to take leave immediately. You must not contact anyone who may have a connection with the case that is the subject of my investigation. Everything according to the book. You will attend my office at Russell Street next Monday at 2 p.m., by which time I intend to have completed relevant interviews and will give you the opportunity to be heard. Is there anything you wish to say?'

'Yes, there is. First of all, may I be told the identity of your complainant?' It had to be Doyle. Why wasn't Doyle here? Fess reported to him after all. Was he busy with other things? Dealing with Fitzwilliam? It was a chilling thought.

'No.' Johnson began to get to his feet, anxious to terminate the meeting.

Fess remained sitting. 'I have already told you, I'm involved in an important case involving charges against Mr. Sanford Fitzwilliam. I expect a senior officer from the C.I. will be here shortly and will want to meet with me.'

'Not my concern. I'm sure that officer, when he learns of the situation with respect to yourself, will initiate whatever action he deems fit. Now you must leave the Station.' The poker face, which the inspector had worn throughout, softened a little and he added. 'This is very unpleasant for us all, I'm sure. Better grasp the nettle, though, and get on with it as quickly as we can.'

❧ ❧

On the following Monday afternoon, Fess walked from his home, bound for Russell Street. He was in a far better mood than when he left the Station the previous Friday. It was one of those rare July days when the sun was out and the air was mild, promising that the worst of winter was over. He knew that Melbourne weather often failed to keep its promises, but today, as he walked through Carlton Gardens where a Cootamundra wattle was about to burst into flower, he took the golden buds as an omen that Peter Johnson would tell him he had uncovered nothing seriously wrong with his behaviour. That, after all, was the truth.

In some ways he was grateful for what had occurred; the enforced break from duty had given him the rare opportunity for spending unbroken time with Bern and the kids. It also allowed him to reflect on Fitzwilliam's exposure of his father. A small voice within kept insisting that Fitzwilliam was lying, but this voice was drowned out by a much stronger one that accused him of stupidity. He should have been able to read the signs himself. Hadn't the dislike he took to Fitzwilliam at their first meeting been triggered by his hints about the way his father worked? It was a betrayal – a betrayal of all that David Jordan had professed so strongly to stand for and a betrayal of the standards he insisted his son should follow. When he told Bern about it, he tried to put a good face on it by saying that at least he no longer had to measure himself against his father. She shook her head. 'Much better than that,' she said. 'Now you're free from the need to outdo him.' He had protested, saying she was being silly. She didn't argue with him. She didn't need to.

It was ironic that his enforced leave should have a far more sobering effect on Kevin than anything he had said to him up until then. Kevin was so remorseful, believing that it was his fault and refusing to accept Fess' assurances that he should not blame himself. It was only after he had dutifully done his stint in Mansons' Bakery on Saturday and gone for their picnic at Kew yesterday that he began to cheer up. Sunday was cloudy and cold, nothing like today, and Fess had been keen to avoid the path to Galatea Point, so he had taken them to the Boatshed for their picnic. When he hired one of the squat rowing boats and took the boys out in it, Bern was apprehensive: they hadn't been in a boat before. But when they returned, excitedly telling their mother of their adventure, and she saw the smile on Kevin's face, she gave Fess that quick glance they sometimes exchanged, and he was encouraged to believe they might soon be able to put this whole business behind them. They still had to decide what to do about Kevin's schooling, but there was plenty of time for that.

He was desperate to know what had happened with Fitzwilliam, but no one had been in touch with him and, tempted though he was, he didn't visit the Station or go looking for any of his men. There was nothing in the papers about Sanford or Hal, which was troubling. Probably the C.I. wanted to be absolutely clear on how they were going to proceed against Fitzwilliam before they went public. Peter Johnson surely would know by now. Keen to ensure that he was punctual, he arrived ten minutes early at the same room he had hurried into so early last Friday. The Duty Constable was a different one, still young but taller, with straight dark hair. He rang through to inform Inspector Johnson of Fess' arrival and kept shooting quick glances at him as he sat waiting. Precisely at two o'clock another constable led him along a corridor and up a flight of steps to a door on which he knocked. 'Come,'

Peter Johnson's voice ordered. He might now be an inspector, but his office was hardly bigger than Doyle's. It did boast a filing cabinet in one corner and a faded carpet on the floor but, apart from a much tidier appearance, the desk was no different and the Bentwood chairs no more distinguished.

'Please sit here, Senior Constable Jordan,' Johnson said, maintaining the formality he had adopted at their previous encounter and indicating one of the chairs across the desk from him. He offered no pleasantries and dived straight in. 'I have investigated the allegation that you acted improperly by interfering in an investigation of a theft from Mansons' Bakery, in which your son was involved. I have interviewed Mr. Manson, Brother O'Donohue and several of the men at the Carlton Station, including Sergeant Doyle. As a result of my investigations, I have reached the conclusion that some of your actions, perhaps triggered by concern for your son and under some pressure from the man I have mentioned, were ill-advised. On one account it could be said that you ignored proper procedure to insert yourself into the investigation.' He paused, as if again considering the weight he should place on what he had called 'one account'. 'However, the bulk of the evidence I have gathered, including the testimony of Mr. Manson and Brother O'Donohue, persuade me that you did properly disqualify yourself from investigating the case and that the decision not to charge your son was made on sound grounds. My conclusion is that you acted unwisely but not in contravention of regulations. I will recommend that you be counselled to amend your approach on any similar occasion in the future. Always best to go strictly by the book.' He cleared his throat and asked, 'Is there anything you wish to say?'

Fess had no doubt about the correct reply. 'No, Inspector. There is not.'

'Good.'

Johnson leaned forward and, in a much more conversational tone, said, 'Still diving in where angels fear to tread?'

Fess gave a small smile and nodded his head in a way that he hoped Peter would accept as adequate acknowledgement of his rebuke. 'May I now return to duty?'

Johnson immediately looked most uncomfortable, frowning and avoiding Fess' eye. 'We'll come to that in a minute.' The tip of his tongue flicked across his upper lip and he said, 'Sergeant Doyle? How do you get on with him?'

Fess decided this was no time for playing it safe. 'I cannot prove it but I have come to believe that he is in the pay of Sanford Fitzwilliam, whom I arrested for murder on Friday night. You must have heard of that by now.'

'Ah, yes, we need to talk about him.' Despite his words, the tone of Johnson's voice suggested that he was not at all keen to discuss Sanford Fitzwilliam.

'Are you involved?' Fess asked. 'I expected the C.I. to be dealing with him.'

'I've read your report. Very comprehensive it was, too. This time it wasn't a matter of not going by the book: this time you tore up the book and threw it away. Fess, why did you do it?'

Fess heard Peter use his nickname for the first time since coming to Carlton last Friday, and immediately became anxious. 'What's happened with Fitzwilliam?'

'When Fitzwilliam was brought here he told a very different story from the one contained in your report. You must know there's always another story.'

'What did he say?'

Johnson frowned at Fess. 'Wait. His case went higher in the organisation and I was brought into it because he made some very serious allegations about you and the constable you had with you when you detained him.'

'What did he say?'

'He said you had been harassing his son over the death of a young woman and had come to his house on several occasions to threaten him, although there was abundant evidence that another man, Naughton, had committed the murder.'

'There was no clear evidence.'

Johnson gave Fess a weary frown and continued. 'He admitted his son was a cocaine user and had come into contact with Naughton and the murdered woman, who were supplying him with the drug. He was concerned that his son was vulnerable to the pressure you were putting him under and he became alarmed when he found out that you had succeeded in luring him to a secret rendezvous in an isolated part of Studley Park late at night. He followed his son, and his fears were realised when you falsely accused the young man of murder and asked for money to keep quiet about it. When he refused to bow to your demands, you set upon the young man and Fitzwilliam tried to come to his aid but, in the ensuing scuffle, his son was pushed over the edge and fell to his death. Angry and frustrated, you and the constable you had with you turned on Fitzwilliam, arrested him for the supposed murder of his son and concocted the elaborate report that you presented to the C.I.'

'That's all lies.'

'Can't you see how it looks? Why would a man murder his son?'

'Because he was about to shop his father, who's been involved with the gangs and with bribing police for years. It's all in the report.'

'This man is a pillar of society. Which version do you think is more plausible?'

'But Daley kept good notes of everything that happened. He'll back me to the hilt.'

'Of course he will. According to Fitzwilliam, he's your co-conspirator.' Johnson shook his head sorrowfully. 'And there's more. Over the weekend a couple of witnesses have come forward who say they saw Naughton in the lane arguing with the girl on the night she was murdered. Apparently, there is a reward and that has caused them to come forward.'

'They'll be plants,' Fess growled as he began to see how his case was unravelling.

'They're not the most reliable of witnesses, I would say,'

Johnson acknowledged. 'Upright citizens tend to avoid The Narrows.' He then stared hard at Fess and added, 'The way this case is shaping, I don't think that's going to matter.'

'I guess Jim Thomas is pushing for Naughton to be tried.'

'He's been taken off the case. The C.I. have two more senior men dealing with it now, but you're right. They see it the same way as Thomas.'

Fess had a new thought. 'You said we'd come to my return to duty.'

Again Johnson looked embarrassed. 'You need to know that this whole business has been dealt with at a very senior level. They thought it would come better from me, seeing we know each other from old.' He paused, but Fess said nothing, watching him intently. 'It has been decided that, even if your version of events is correct, there is no prospect of gaining a conviction against Fitzwilliam. Either way, airing the matter will bring great damage to the reputation of the Force. Neither Senior Command nor Mr. Fitzwilliam wish this to occur.'

Fess began to see where Johnson was leading. 'Do you believe me, Peter?'

'I have always known you to be truthful,' he replied, their eyes locked. 'I also know your tendency to rock the boat and I know that this time it would be fatal for you to do so.' He hurried on, apparently anxious to forestall Fess from making any response. 'The official record will show that Mr. Hal Fitzwilliam accidentally fell to his death when walking alone in Studley Park late at night. It will acknowledge that he had been unwell of late and under pressure because of some problems (unspecified) in his personal life. The record will show nothing that might have given rise to criminal charges or disciplinary action. After a distinguished period as a Senior Constable at Carlton, without any adverse comment on your record, you will be promoted to fill the position of Sergeant at Warrnambool, where there is an urgent need for strong leadership.'

'What about Daley?'

'He's already gone to Orbost. A stint in the country will fill out his experience.'

'Hal Fitzwilliam, Tom Daley and me, all quietly buried where we can do no further harm. They had you talk with me because they reckon you're the most likely to persuade me to go quietly.'

'Fess. Fess. Live to fight another day. That's the important thing. You still have your career in front of you. Think of Bernadette and the children.'

19

Fess came slowly awake. Had he heard a sound at the door? There it was again, a light but insistent tapping, nothing like the rap the constables used when calling him out. But just a minute, he's not Senior Constable at Carlton any more. The tapping was repeated, slightly more insistently this time. He rubbed his eyes and began to get out of bed. 'What is it?' Bern asked drowsily.

'Someone at the door, I think. You can go back to sleep.' He wrapped himself in his dressing-gown and walked barefoot to the door. As he reached it, the tapping burst out much louder than before. 'Who is it?' he growled.

'I thought you were never going to wake up.' The words came in a stage whisper that Fess could not immediately recognise. 'It's Jim Thomas. Open up and let me in. I don't want to be seen standing out here.'

Fess opened the door and, for a moment, could not make out Jim, who was huddled in the shadows of the small verandah, with his hat pulled down over his face. When he stepped onto the doormat, Fess stood barring his way. 'What do mean by coming here at this time of night?'

Jim chuckled. 'What's wrong with this time of night? Twice last week you dragged me from my bed around this time.'

'Are you drunk?' The manner in which Jim was bouncing on the balls of his feet and the wide grin on his face caused Fess to wonder.

'No, of course not. We don't want to be seen chatting on your doorstep. Let me in.'

Still uncertain, Fess turned away from the door and Jim hastened in behind him. Bernadette's head appeared around the door to their bedroom and Fess waved her back. 'It's just Jim Thomas, the C.I. bloke I told you about. Don't know what brings him here now, but go back to bed. We have an early start.' He led Jim into their living room where the walls were bare, the grate empty and four tea chests stood beside the couch and armchairs.

'You're packed and ready to go, I see,' Jim said as he removed his hat.

'I don't know about being ready to go, but most of the packing's done. The removals people are s'posed to get here about seven.' They stood facing each another in the space before the fireplace. 'I can't believe you've called round at this hour to bid us farewell.' The sarcastic tone that Fess had used hardened and he said, 'What do you want?'

Jim's face still bore the grin he had entered with and his eyes were mischievous. 'Bit gloomy in here. Do the lights still work?' He walked back to the door and, without asking Fess' permission, switched on the bare light that hung from the centre of the ceiling. 'I've brought you something to read.' He took the folded newspaper that protruded from a pocket of his overcoat, handed it to Fess and made himself comfortable on one of the armchairs.

‘What’s this?’ Fess asked as he unfolded the newspaper and sank into the other chair.

‘It’s this morning’s edition of *The Truth*, hot off the press. I reckoned you’d want to see it before you left. You’ve made the front page.’

Fess looked down at the bold headline, sucked in a breath and began to read.

Truth

THE PEOPLE'S PAPER.

MELBOURNE, SATURDAY JULY, 18, 1925 THREEPENCE

SANFORD FITZWILLIAM ACCUSED OF MURDERING SON

—

Shocking Allegations

—

Hidden Police Report Uncovered

—

Two Deaths Linked

On Saturday July 11, a young woman, Mary Worthington, was brutally raped and murdered in the notorious Carlton laneway known as *The Narrows*. Five days later Henry Fitzwilliam, the son of well-known man-about-town Sanford Fitzwilliam, fell to his death from a ledge above the Yarra in Studley Park. These two apparently unrelated tragedies are brought together in a sensational report, submitted to the C.I.B. by two policemen from Carlton on the very night Fitzwilliam died.

The report alleges that the young blade, Hal, confessed to the rape and murder of Mary Worthington and offered to detail, to the senior of the two policemen, the gangland activities and the secret web of corrupt police that his father funded. He was prevented from spilling the beans, the report says, when his father pushed him to his death.

The Report is Buried

However, it appears that, on orders from on high, that report has been buried deep in the vaults of Russell Street – so deep that its very existence could be denied – and the authors of the report banished to the farthest extremities of the State.

It has only come to light because the unforgiving hand of fate intervened, taking the report on a path that passed through the offices of *The Truth* before reaching its final resting place. Having sighted this explosive report, it is clearly our responsibility not to shirk the issue but to recount the shocking contents, so that all concerned may be subject to public scrutiny.

What Really Happened in Studley Park?

The official police report on the death of Hal Fitzwilliam says that he died while walking alone late at night in Studley Park. It suggests he may have stumbled at a point in the path where a rocky ledge falls sheer to the river far below. It mentions that he was in a delicate state of health at the time and the possibility that he took his own life is left to hang uncertainly in the air.

The buried report tells a very different story. It says that Hal Fitzwilliam was not alone on that rocky ledge. It says that, before falling to his untimely death, he confessed to Senior Constable Jordan, from the Carlton Police Station, that he had raped and murdered Mary Worthington, when she spurned his advances and he was overcome by unbridled and unrequited passion. Terrified of the hangman's noose, he offered to provide Senior Constable Jordan with a detailed list of his father's criminal activities if the policeman would turn a blind eye to his dastardly crime.

It was then that Sanford Fitzwilliam sprang from his hiding place brandishing a pistol, accused his son of betraying him and thrust him over the edge to his death. The report goes on to assert that Fitzwilliam then turned the pistol on Senior Constable Jordan and would have shot him dead had not the other policeman, Constable Daley, who observed all that occurred and recorded all that was said, bravely tackled Fitzwilliam, disarming him and taking him into custody.

Policemen Muzzled

Sanford Fitzwilliam was incarcerated overnight in a cell at the Carlton Station while Senior Constable Jordan and Constable Daley compiled their comprehensive and detailed report. As soon as the report was complete, Senior Constable Jordan took it to Russell Street and handed it to the C.I.B. Next morning Sanford Fitzwilliam was brought, not to the watch house, nor to the C.I.B., but to a select office in Russell Street Headquarters, from which he was soon released and returned to his home.

It appears that the record of Mr. Fitzwilliam's stay in the Carlton cell has been expunged from the record held at the Station. Meanwhile, Senior Constable Jordan was confronted by a senior officer from Headquarters who informed him that it was alleged he had committed an indiscretion in the handling of a case of minor theft in Carlton. Senior Constable Jordan was summarily sent on leave and has not returned to his post although the investigating officer found nothing of substance in the flimsy charge brought against him.

Constable Daley was transferred that day to a posting in distant Orbost and *The Truth* understands that Senior Constable Jordan is to be relocated in Warrnambool with effect from next Monday. It is hard to imagine how these men could be further removed from the scene of the crimes their report describes or separated by a greater distance.

The Rape and Murder in The Narrows

After receipt of the report by Senior Constable Jordan and Constable Daley, handling of the investigation into the rape and murder of Mary Worthington was taken out of the hands of the Detective who had been dealing with the case and located within the office of more senior officers in C.I.B. John (Nifty) Naughton, an infamous rogue from the Carlton area, has subsequently been charged with the crime and has been remanded to appear in the Coroner's Court in two weeks' time.

It is understood that the most telling evidence against him has been provided by two disreputable characters known to frequent The Narrows, who came forward only after the posting of a reward for evidence that would secure a conviction in this case. In yet another curious twist to this tale, *The Truth* has been told that the reward was made possible by a donation from Mr. Sanford Fitzwilliam, who wished his generosity to remain anonymous.

A Man of Influence

Mr. Sanford Fitzwilliam would be well known to many of the people of Melbourne through the frequent press coverage of his presence at many exclusive social and sporting occasions. He also enjoys an enviable reputation as a successful gambler at the race track and in the card room. He first came to prominence as a defence barrister where he showed an uncanny ability to unearth evidence favourable to his client or to undermine the prosecution through the calling of surprise witnesses. He retired from the bar some years ago but continues his association with the criminal classes through his sponsorship of a charity that purports to seek the rehabilitation of offenders.

After retiring from the bar he went into business on his own account and, although little is known of his business ventures, since he keeps the details of them strictly confidential, they are obviously highly profitable as his extravagant lifestyle and his luxurious home in Kew attest. Dame Rumour has from time to time suggested that some of Mr. Fitzwilliam's activities and exploits might be questionable, but nothing has ever come to light. A man of great charm, he has an extensive array of influential friends in high places.

What Now?

It is not for *The Truth* to determine what should happen now, except to say that it is inconceivable the matters raised here not be investigated further. *The Truth* makes no judgment as to who specifically is at fault.

If the detailed and comprehensive report that *The Truth* has seen and which now lies buried in Russell Street, contains any truth, then Mr. Fitzwilliam and the senior officers of the Police Force have much to explain. If the report is fallacious then Senior Constable Jordan, Constable Daley and, again, the senior officers of the Police Force have to account for their actions.

No doubt those responsible for representing Nifty Naughton, as he seeks to defend the charges brought against him, will want to see the report and understand why it has been suppressed.

The Need for a Government Enquiry

It is clear that, whatever the truth of the matter, the command of the Police Force must come under question. For some time now Mr. H. H. Smith, the Member for Melbourne, has been calling for an enquiry into police corruption and maladministration. Whilst he has yet to gain great support from either side of the Parliament, this latest episode surely shows that the need for a full and independent enquiry is urgent. Without a full judicial enquiry, the citizens of Victoria can have no confidence that justice has been served in this matter. It is essential that the real truth emerge and a judicial enquiry is the way to ensure this.

When he reached the end of the article Fess looked up at Jim and said, 'How did they get hold of our report?'

The impish grin returned to Jim's face. 'After this hits the streets, there'll be lots of people asking that question. The nobs in Headquarters for a start.' He became more serious and added, 'I reckon your old sergeant, now Inspector Johnson, will be the prime suspect.'

'He wouldn't have done this.'

'The word is he argued for you, though, when they were deciding what to do. He'll come under pressure from some very scared people, but I reckon he can handle them and they won't be able to prove anything against him. I know that because I know he didn't do it. If they do give him a hard time, it might even persuade him he shouldn't go on covering for them.' Jim gave Fess a questioning smile. 'You haven't worked it out yet, have you?'

'Did you go and see your mate at *The Truth* before handing over the report?'

'Me?' The outrage affected by Jim was too staged to be believed. 'I didn't move from Russell Street that morning until after I'd handed over the report and been taken off the case. The coppers on duty can vouch for that.' Again the grin appeared as he waited for Fess to speak, but he said nothing. Eventually Jim relented. 'After you left me that morning I had a lot of time to kill before my boss would be in, so I read your report very carefully and started thinking about what would happen when he saw it. I pretty much got that spot on. Then it occurred to me that this was the opportunity I'd been looking for to nail those corrupt bludgers. I said I had a lot of time. Maybe someone made a copy of the report and showed it to *The Truth* and they're pretending they've seen the original. I wouldn't know. I've been keeping my ear to the ground over the past week and *The Truth* does seem well informed about what's happened since I handed your report in. I don't know what you mean when you talk about me having a mate at *The Truth*, though.'

'After what I've seen I reckon Fitzwilliam will still find a way to wriggle out of this,' Fess said gloomily.

'He might beat the murder charge. You're right there. I reckon he'll have to go to trial, but he'll claim there was a struggle and Hal tripped. He can be very plausible and a jury might have trouble accepting your account over his, but I don't know. This whole cover-up will put a bloody big hole in his credibility and he mightn't be able to charm those twelve good men and true this time. The man of influence has had his day. None of his toffy friends will want to know him now. Even if he doesn't go down for murder, he's finished. There's sure to be payback. If Nifty gets off his murder charge, he'll be after him and he won't be as careless as he was the first time he went out to Kew. The other gang bosses will know this and stay away from Sanford. He'll be looking over his shoulder for the rest of what might be a short life. You've won.'

'So you reckon Nifty will get off? Aren't you disappointed?'

'I haven't given up hope there. But it was a risk I had to take. Yeah, it'll be a pity if he stays on the street.' Jim shrugged. 'It will be worth it, though, and we'll get him for something else soon — maybe Fitzwilliam's murder.'

Finally Fess managed a smile. 'I see you're still able to see the bigger picture and understand priorities — forego immediate success in the interest of the longer term.'

Rather than respond with a grin, Jim frowned. 'I'm sorry about your father.'

'Thanks, but you needn't be. Bern says that knowing the truth about him has set me free, and I'm beginning to see she's right. And thanks for all your help.'

'Don't thank me. I didn't do this to help you. I did it to get those bastards in Headquarters and make the Force more of an outfit I can respect. Remember me telling you, when I showed you *The Truth* article on Sugar Bag O'Sullivan, that I needed something sensational, a story that would get the public's blood running and have everyone demanding a public enquiry. This is it! I'm glad you're going to Warrnambool. I reckon your approach has a better chance down there and we can bring in the hard man that's needed in Carlton.'

Afterword

My story is fiction, and every character with a speaking role, even though they may occupy a position that existed at the time, has no basis in fact. On the other hand, I have tried to make the references to locations, events and people, which provide the background for the story, as factually based as possible.

For example, the house in Barkly Street where Ma Cutmore lived was subsequently the scene of the gunfight between Snowy Cutmore and Squizzy Taylor on October 27, 1927, when both of them were fatally wounded. To provide this historical detail I drew upon the work of many people, quoting from them at times, and recognise their contribution by listing their publications at the conclusion of this afterword, even though I recently read that Peter Carey wrote, 'A bibliography is as much use to a reader of fiction as a hammer is to a dolphin.' In particular, I acknowledge that the account of the life and crimes of Sugar-Bag O'Sullivan, which my story says Jim Thomas had a hand in writing, is a direct quote from *The Truth* newspaper of Saturday July 18, 1925.

I have been fortunate to gain the assistance of several members of Victoria Police (past and present). My friend Paul Delianis, former Victoria Police Deputy Commissioner, read several drafts and went to a great deal of trouble in trying to ensure I represented the correct police protocols, terms and customs as well as critiquing the plot for me. Through him, I was able to obtain information concerning the Carlton Station in 1925 from Ralph Stavely, a leading member of the Police Historical Unit. Senior Constable Nick Parissis provided me with information on the buildings of the Carlton Station and took me on a comprehensive guided tour of them only a few weeks before the Station closed. I am most grateful to each of these gentlemen.

I am also grateful to Sandy Gillam, the University Archivist at RMIT, who provided me with a copy of the 1925 prospectus for the Working Men's College. Our neighbours, Joy and Basil Frigo, were gracious enough to allow their house to become the residence of the Worthington family in 1925 and also advised me on some of the practices of the Roman Catholic Church. Tess Schwarz conducted me around the Jewish Museum in St. Kilda and told me about the customs of the Sabbath meal. My friend, Judy Biddington, who continues to conduct research into the history of Carlton, read the second draft and suggested sources of further material to authenticate the story.

Noelene Mitchell was kind enough to continue her scrutiny of my writing in an attempt to remove infelicities and straighten out my punctuation, and I thank her. As ever, I thank my two stalwarts, Jo and Bish, who read the drafts and continued to encourage me.

I am most grateful to Ormé Harris, who is a sympathetic, skilled and assiduous editor and thank Barry Dorr and Jo Costello of JoJo Publishing for their support.

Bibliography

Anderson H., Larrikin Crook: *The Rise and Fall of Squizzy Taylor*, Jacaranda, 1971

Barrett B., *The Inner Suburbs: The Evolution of an Industrial Area*, Melbourne University Press, 1971

Bottom R., *The Godfather in Australia: Organised Crime's Australian Connections*, Reed, 1979

Brown G. and Haldane R., *Days of Violence: The 1923 Police Strike in Melbourne*, Hybrid, 1998

Brown-May A., *Melbourne Street Life: The Itinerary of Our Days*, Australian Scholarly Publishing, 1998

Buggy E.H., *The Real John Wren*, Widescope, 1977

Cranston J., *The Melbourne Cable Trams* 1895-1940, Craftsman Publishing, 1988

Davison G., Dunstan D. and McConville C., *The Outcasts of Melbourne: Essays in Social History*, Allen and Unwin, 1985

Dower A., Deadline, Hutchins of Australia, 1979

Fidian M., Clang Clang Clang: *A Study of Melbourne's Tramways*, Packenham Gazette, 1993

Fisher M., Broken Biscuits — *The Changing Face of Carlton*, Yarra-Melbourne Regional Library Corporation, 2005

Haldane R. K., *The People's Force: A History of the Victoria Police*, Melbourne University Press, 1986

Larkins J. and Howard B., *As Time Goes By*, Myer Publications, 1979

Keating J.D., *Mind the Curve! : A History of the Cable Trams*, Transit Australia Publishing, 1996

Logan W.S., *Boom Period and Depression*, Carlton Association, 1973

Logan W.S., *Cosmopolitan Carlton*, Carlton Association, 1973

Morgan K., *Gun Alley: Murder, Lies and Failure of Justice*, Simon and Schuster, 2006

Murray R., *The Confident Years: Australia in the Twenties*, Allen Lane, 1978

Newton R., *Runner*, Penguin Books, 2005

Otto K., Capital: *Melbourne When it was the Capital of Australia 1901 — 1927*, Text, 2009

Prentice B., A *Brief History of the Melbourne*, Brunswick and Coburg Tramways Trust, Tramway Publications, 1999

Potts D., *The Twenties 1919 — 1929*, Cheshire, 1971

Robson L.L., *Australia in the Nineteen Twenties*, Nelson 1980

Rothberg Y., *Thousands of Years Through the Eyes of a Child*, Foundation for Australian Literary Studies, 1980

Warren P., *The Police Strike in Melbourne in 1923*, Self-Published, 1973

Waten J., *Alien Son*, Lloyd O'Neil 1974

Yule P. (Ed.), *Carlton: A History*, Melbourne University Press, 2004

Extract from Report of the Royal Commission on the Victoria Police 1925, Victorian Government Printer

Extract from Police in Victoria 1836-1980, Victoria Police Force

Victorian Newspapers of July, 1925: *The Age*, *The Argus*, *The Herald*, *The Sun News-Pictorial*, *The Truth*

Brian Smith was born and grew up in Melbourne. He studied engineering and worked in industry before joining the Engineering Faculty at RMIT. He was appointed Director of RMIT and subsequently Vice-Chancellor at the University of Western Sydney. After retirement from the University he began writing fiction. *Too Close to Home* is his fourth novel. He lives in the Melbourne suburb of Carlton with his wife, Josephine. They have two daughters and three granddaughters.